PRETEND TO LOVE YOU

JULIA JARRETT

CONTENTS

CHAPTER ONE

Jude

Doc's face is grim as he walks back into the room with a folder in his hands. I know what he's going to say before he opens his mouth. That doesn't stop me from sending a small prayer out into the universe that it isn't as bad as I think it is.

"Well, Jude, I'll be frank with you." He settles down on the rolling stool in front of the bed I'm sitting on with my leg stretched out in front of me. "The damage to your knee is extensive. Given the number of times you've torn the ACL, it's a wonder you're still able to move around at all. Surgery has bought you some time, but that time is running out. My concern is this: one more hit or twist to that joint and you might never walk pain free again, if at all."

I keep my eyes trained forward, my head falling slightly down, letting a piece of brown hair — I'm long overdue for a trim — fall into my face. As prepared as I thought I was, I hadn't let myself think it could be *that bad*. Staring at the brace wrapped around my knee, I let his words sink in. Part of me rebels against them. He's wrong, he has to be. Hockey is who I am; it's all I have. But that fucking brace is impossible to ignore, as are the occasional headaches I still get two weeks after the game that changed everything.

I don't remember much, most of what I know has been pieced together by my teammates, coaches, and my family, who were watching from the team's box that night. Apparently , I was taken down in an ugly trip from one of the opposing team's defensemen. The way he hit me caused my leg to give out underneath me. I twisted, landing on my leg, destroying the ligaments that were already weakened from past injuries. Combine that with the concussion I sustained when I crashed into the boards, and it's been a rough couple of weeks.

"So, you're saying I'm done."

"No, not completely."

My head shoots up to stare at him, my mouth falling open in surprise. Doc holds up a hand, as if he can slow down my racing hope. But my mind is jumping ahead. Hope is a dangerous thing.

"I might not be out for the whole season? Is that what you're saying? I'll do anything, Doc. Extra therapy, hell, I'll pay for a brand new fucking knee if that's what it takes to get me on the ice."

"Jude, stop." His firm voice is the sound of brakes screeching on my runaway thoughts. "Down the line, you will need a knee replacement. That's a given at this point. But not right now. You need to heal from the ligament repair first. Then, with adequate therapy and *time* —" He pauses, letting that one word sink in. "With time, you might skate again. Given your fitness level and what I know is your exceptionally high level of dedication, you're better off than most. But it's extremely doubtful that you'll return to the elite level of play you're used to."

"But there's a chance." I'm being stubborn as hell, I know. But I can't avoid it. Being stubborn is what made me one of the longest running players in the league. It made me a champion. A captain. A leader.

"Jude, there are other ways to be on the ice. Regardless of your rehab potential, the risk of a future life-changing injury is extreme."

That flare of hope starts to flicker out, but my dumb-ass brain holds onto it, tucking it away. I won't give up. Not without one hell of a fight. I rake my fingers through my hair, pushing that annoying piece back again.

"More life-changing than this?" I mumble under my breath, trying to come to grips with the bomb I've had dropped in my lap.

"Yes, Jude. I'm not one to be dramatic; I like to keep it real with my players. I will not be able to sign off on you returning to the team unless you have some sort of miraculous healing. And let's face facts. You're an older player; many guys would have retired by now. Especially with the sheer number of injuries you've had. Hell, it's incredible that you're still playing. I know you don't want to hear this, but it's time to start thinking of what comes next."

My eyes close. I've had my head in the sand for too long, ignoring the fact that I'm one of the oldest guys in the league. Retirement is a dirty word to me, and not the fun kind of dirty. And now I'm paying my dues, being forced to face that very real possibility with absolutely no plans in place.

When Doc speaks again, his voice is gentle, as if he's trying to soften the blow he just dealt me. "You don't have to stay in Billings for rehab. I know your family is up in Canada, and I would be happy to vet any physical therapist of your choosing if you wanted to go up there for a while."

I nod, my eyes still shut. If I don't see the pity that I'm sure is written all over his features, maybe I can convince myself it doesn't exist.

"Let me know what you decide, and we'll go from there."

I nod again. The door opens and closes, and then I'm alone. The arena is empty, with everyone off on an away game series. Doc is joining them, having stayed back just so he and I could meet.

The raw truth is, I've been left behind, while the team I gave everything to for a decade carries on, business as usual. Not that it would be fair to expect anything different, but it brings up a weird sense of abandonment.

The news surrounding my injury immediately after it happened brought a wave of sympathy from my fans. Even as I fought through the pain of injury and surgery, I felt loved. Supported. Like I had people standing behind me, ready to welcome me back with open arms. But that faded over the last ten days or so as the media attention turned, instead, to my replacement as captain and what that meant for the future of the team this season.

I sit there, the silence echoing around me, and the walls start to feel like they're closing in. As much as I want to be left alone to wallow in anger and self-pity, I don't know if I can stay here, in the city that adopted me as one of their own. The same city that celebrated my rise and then forgot about me after my fall.

I climb out of the chauffeured car provided by the team — it's my right knee that's injured, and driving myself is not an option. I hate being dependent on others, especially to this extent, but at the same time, I have to be grateful the team is still taking care of me.

Especially since I'm doing nothing for them in return.

I hobble on my crutches up to the front door of my building, giving a brief nod to Larry, the doorman who's been working here ever since I moved in.

"Hello, Mr. Donnelly," he says in his usual jovial tone. Before my injury, I'd sometimes stay and chat, but I'm not in the mood. I just want to go upstairs, grab the bottle of whiskey that's above my fridge, and sink into my couch and my misery.

"Hey, Larry."

He's good at his job, so he takes my curt greeting in stride, opening the door and closing it behind me with nothing more than a casual nod of his head.

Leaning against the mirrored wall of the elevator, I let my eyes fall closed and scrub my hand over the stubble covering my jaw. I need a haircut and a shave, but I don't give a fuck about either. It's not like maintaining my image is a priority right now.

My knee is aching, of course. I'm past due for my painkillers. Doc would shake his head at me if he knew. I hate those fucking pills. I don't want to dull the pain. That pain reminds me I'm still here, even if my life is crumbling apart around me. Besides, even I'm not fool enough to mix painkillers with alcohol, and right now the emotional numbing the whiskey could bring is more important than the physical numbing of the painkillers.

Making it to my front door, I'm juggling my keys as my phone starts to ring in my back pocket. Whatever. There's no one I want to talk to right now. I push open the door and drop my keys on the table just inside, carefully averting my gaze from the bag of hockey gear that hasn't moved from my front entryway.

I'm becoming an expert in avoidance. And with Doc's crushing words threatening to snuff out the sliver of possibility that I might suit up again, I can't bear to look at that bag.

The emptiness of my apartment feels way too much like the emptiness of the arena. Picking up my phone, I see the missed call is from the girl I've been casually seeing for a few months. Shelley's not the love of my life by a long stretch, but she was fun for a while, and after my injury, she stuck around to help.

Would I feel any better about what Doc said if I wasn't alone tonight? Who the fuck knows. But as soon as I've poured the amber liquor that will hopefully numb things for a while into a glass, my fingers dial her number.

"Hi, Jude."

She sounds off. Detached, somehow. I push my hair back, suddenly questioning my decision to call her back. I'm not exactly good company right now and having her over feels like it's gonna be a lot more work than I want to deal with.

But I'm not a quitter. In anything.

"Hey. You wanna come over tonight? Grab some takeout or something?" God, just saying that feels wrong. Awkward, forced, and not at all what I need right now. For a few seconds, there's silence on the other end. Then I hear her intake of breath.

"No, Jude, I'm not coming over tonight."

"Okay." I mask my relief at her answer. But Shelley keeps going, her next words coming out in a rush.

"I know this is bad timing, but I can't hold it in anymore. I think we need to end things."

I run my hand up and down my face. Part of me expected this, the other part is saying w*hat the fuck*. But Shelley continues before I can say anything.

"The thing is, Jude, this isn't what I signed up for."

There's not a shred of remorse in her tone, but a heavy weight settles over me, pushing me down even further. I don't bother hiding the bite in my voice when I finally reply.

"What, caring for someone when they're injured?"

"Yes! No." She huffs out a sigh. "Come on, think about it from my perspective. I've tried to be patient, but all you do is go to physical therapy, then come home and sit on the couch."

"So, you're missing the parties and dinners out. That's what this is about?" I scoff, picking up my whiskey and draining the glass.

"I miss the life we used to have. The future I thought we could share."

I almost choke as the whiskey burns down my throat. Future? She's making it sound like we had plans for forever, while I figured things were casual. Guess we were on different wavelengths. A month ago, I might have felt bad about the possibility I'd led her on, but right now, I just feel angry. One more person walking away because I can't be who they want me to be.

"You're off the team, so where does that leave us?"

"I'm not off the team, Shelley. I'm on the injured list."

"Come on, Jude, don't make me the bad guy here." She sounds irritated. At what? The fact that I busted my knee playing the game I love? *Jesus Christ.*

"How are you not the bad guy, Shell? You're walking away because I got injured."

"I'm walking away because my life is in Montana and yours most likely isn't anymore."

That statement is like a knife driven straight through my heart, carving away the protective layer I'd built around my deepest fears. My current contract with the Blaze is up next year.

Before this injury, I would have laughed at anyone who dared suggest I might be traded or have to move. There was not a doubt in my mind that I'd be in Montana for the entirety of my NHL career. I just never expected that career to come to a screeching halt so soon.

Suddenly, I'm exhausted. I don't even want to fight her on this anymore, I just want to be done with this conversation and drown my sorrows in whiskey.

"What are you saying? Just spit it out."

"I'm saying I have to focus on what I want and need. And you can't give me that anymore." She pauses, and just when I think she's hung up on me, she speaks again. Only this time, for the first time in the entire conversation, I hear a shred of the compassionate woman I thought she was. "I'm sorry Jude." But then she hangs up.

"Fuck!" I roar into the empty space of my apartment. But the echoing sound of that word bouncing off the walls only reinforces the truth.

I'm alone.

Shelley might not have been anything serious, but I at least thought she cared about me as more than just a professional hockey player who could give her access to a certain lifestyle. I had my doubts; I always do. I'm cynical about women, especially in my line of work. I've seen too many teammates cheat on their wives, or be cheated on, or get divorced and get taken for everything they have. When you're in the limelight like we are, you tend to attract a certain type of woman. I'm not saying every woman out there is like that, but the ones I've experienced only wanted me for two things. Well, maybe three.

My fame. My money. And my dick.

"Fuck them. Fuck all of them," I mutter to myself as I pour another generous shot of whiskey. Fuck my teammates, coaches, trainers, doctors, friends, girlfriends — fuck them all. Fuck them for living the life I should be living. Fuck them for turning their backs on me when I need them most. Fuck them for having everything I've ever wanted, while I'm left empty-handed.

I drain the second glass. Probably too fast, but I don't give a shit right now. Where I used to welcome the pain as a reminder that it could have been worse, now I want oblivion.

I want to forget that the last few weeks ever happened. I want to forget that my life is over. That there's nothing for me but the slimmest thread of hope that I might skate again. A thread that's so tiny, right now it's invisible and might as well be nonexistent.

My thoughts start to feel fuzzy, courtesy of my friend Jameson. Before I let everything go, I manage to type out an email to my agent, telling him to book me a flight to Vancouver and a seaplane over to the island.

I'm going home.

CHAPTER TWO

Jude

My eyes slowly blink open, focusing on the plain beige wall to the side of the unfamiliar bed I'm lying on, taking in the early morning light trickling through the blinds. Beyond those blinds is my hometown, Dogwood Cove. At least here, I don't have to contend with the looks of pity from the team or even from random strangers who recognize me on the street. Of course, the trade off is that eventually, I have to deal with my well-meaning but overbearing family.

Lying on my back, I stare up at the ceiling fan spinning around in a circle. Ceiling fans have it easy. Nothing is expected of them except to keep turning and move the air.

And now I'm thinking of ceiling fans as animate objects. Great.

My phone starts to vibrate, and I reach my arm out to silence it, cringing when I get a whiff of myself. I'm a disgusting mess. I know there's a lot of fucking messages on there. But I need coffee, and probably a shower, before I read them. Most of them came in last night, and I ignored them, setting the *Do Not Disturb* function. I'm betting most of them are from Kasey, my best friend from the Blaze. He's been worried about me, especially after Shelley's dramatic exit. His wife Daphne was the one who took over driving me places, bringing me food, and not letting me wallow in my lonely apartment for the few days before I left to come here. I owe the two of them more than I can say, their friendship kept me sane ever since my injury happened.

Throwing back the covers, I push myself up to sit on the side of the bed, gingerly lowering my leg. The rush of blood flow makes my head spin with the pain. When I can finally blink my eyes open, they immediately go to the small bottle of painkillers sitting on the bedside table. It would probably be wise to take them before my first physical therapy appointment today.

But fuck that. I don't need them.

I grab my crutches, lever myself up, and make my way into the tiny bathroom. This apartment is a far cry from my place in Montana, which is all sleek lines, chrome fixtures, and screams of money. Not that I necessarily like that style, but it's expected. The building is one that several players live in, and it was just easy to settle there. This place is smaller, with nature photos that were clearly shot in the surrounding area adorning the walls, and comfortable-looking furniture. Ethan, the town mayor, and my current landlord, let me know he tried to set up the apartment to be easy on me, removing loose rugs and installing the grab bar and bench seat in the shower that Doc informed him I'd need. There's even an elevator, even though the building is only three stories.

Leaving my crutches leaning against the sink, I slowly spin on one foot and carefully hop over to the shower bench. By the time I get my boxers down to my ankles and sit down, I'm breathing heavily. It's embarrassing, honestly, and I'm glad no one is here to witness this shit. It's shocking how much harder everything is when you've only got one working leg.

A shower might wash away the sweat and travel grime; it might even clear my head from the whiskey. But it can't wash away my reality. Which is what faces me when I eventually turn the water off and look for a towel, only to realize the towel rack is on the other side of the room.

"Fuck."

I manage to get out of the shower using the bench and pull myself up to stand. It's a precarious stretch to reach the towels, but I don't want to try hopping while I'm wet. Even I'm not that much of an idiot; wet feet hopping on a tile floor is a recipe for disaster. Once I'm toweled off, I crutch back into the bedroom completely naked and flop back down on the bed, exhausted.

There's a heaviness that won't leave me alone. I feel as if I'm dragging around a hundred-pound weight on my injured leg all the goddamn time.

I hate that something as simple as taking a shower takes everything out of me.

I hate that I can't sleep without reliving the moments and days after my injury.

I hate that I don't want to see anyone or talk to anyone.

I hate that I have no idea what to do with myself.

I hate that my future has been stolen from me.

A pounding on my door breaks my self-pity spiral. At first, I think it must be Ethan, but then the pounding starts again, and I realize it's way too obnoxious for him. Which means only one thing.

My brothers are here.

"Hold on," I yell out. Reaching down, I grab a pair of boxers out of my suitcase that I left on the floor beside the bed and pull them on before forcing myself up to stand. I make my way slowly to the door and unlock it, opening it and then turning away. I can't make them go away, but I don't have to be welcoming, either.

"Beatle, why the fuck did we have to hear it from your agent that you arrived in town last night?"

That's Sawyer. One of the twins, my youngest brother, and by far the most obnoxious, as evidenced by the goddamn nicknames he gave us all. He means well, but the guy has no filter and no limits.

"What Sawyer means is, if we'd known you were coming so soon, we'd have helped get you set up." There's Beckett, Sawyer's twin, the yin to his yang. They couldn't be more opposite, in every way except appearance.

"How's your leg healing up?" And Max. The oldest of us, and the doctor. Only one missing is our younger sister Kat, but she's probably busy with school.

"Shouldn't you all be at work?" I grunt as way of answering them. Reaching the couch, I sit down and let the crutches fall to the side. "Why are you here?"

The three of them come to stand in front of me. If they weren't my brothers and I didn't have a lifetime of experience dealing with them, I might be intimidated. We're all big dudes, over six feet tall. And right now, they're staring down at me with a mixture of pity, confusion, and frustration.

"We're here so that Mom stops worrying."

My head falls back with a groan. "Remind me to fire Stefan."

The couch sinks beside me. "No. He did the right thing."

I narrow my gaze at Max. "There was a reason I didn't tell anyone I was coming. And it was to avoid this exact situation."

He just stares back at me calmly. As a pediatrician at the local hospital, he's used to dealing with stubborn, grumpy patients. Granted, his are usually a lot younger.

"And if we weren't here, how would you be getting to physical therapy?" he asks pointedly, his eyes going to my leg. "That leg should be elevated."

"I know," I grumble, moving to lift it with my hands to prop it on the coffee table. Sawyer reaches down to help, and I smack his hands away. "I can do it, asshole."

He steps back, lifting his hands up. "Okay, grump, I was just trying to help."

"Max has a point, Jude. How were you going to get to therapy?" Beckett leans against the wall, looking concerned.

I just lift my shoulders in a shrug. Truth be told, I hadn't thought that far ahead. Back in Billings, either the team arranged a car for me or Shelley drove me. After she left, Kasey and Daphne helped out. I guess I never thought about needing rides now that I'm here. Inwardly, I groan, realizing as much as I don't want to depend on anyone, I'll need to.

"Fine. Thanks for coming to take me to therapy. But it doesn't require all three of you."

"Jesus, bro. Did it ever cross your mind we might be worried about you?"

I lift my head at the bark of Sawyer's words. The other two are nodding in agreement, and I feel a trickle of remorse. But it's gone when I remember the last thing I need right now is interfering family members. I just need to be left alone.

"Did it ever cross *your* minds I might want to be left alone?" I bite back.

"That's fair, but right now, you need to get to your appointment," Max points out. I don't bother asking how they know what time I'm due at the clinic; I just add it to the list of things I'll yell at Stefan for later.

"Fine. But I need coffee first."

"Clothes would be a good idea." I catch Sawyer's smirk and glare at him. At least his teasing is better than the hurt I heard in his voice earlier.

I struggle to stand up, but thankfully, my brothers heed my earlier warning and don't try to help. Making my way into the bedroom, I grab the first set of clothes I can, which I'm glad is a pair of sweats and a hoodie. Crutching back into the living room, I catch my brothers standing in a huddle near the door, whispering.

"If you're planning anything involving me, don't." I grab my phone and keys off the counter. "Unless it's to stop at The Nutty Muffin and get coffee."

We make our way outside where I spy Sawyer's truck right out front.

"We figured I'd drive you the next few days. I'm off shift and the truck is probably the easiest for you to get in and out of," he explains, walking over and opening my door. "And yes, we'll get coffee on the way."

I reach the truck and pause. I might be annoyed with them, but I can't help but also feel a little bit grateful.

"Thanks, guys," I say gruffly without meeting their eyes.

Max's hand lands on my shoulder. "Love you, bro. We're here for you."

"Mom's expecting you for dinner on Friday. We're all off for once, so she's moving family dinner from Sunday," Beckett chimes in. "I can come and get you around six." His tone makes it clear there's no getting out of it, so I just nod.

"Okay, let's go." Sawyer claps his hands, and the others say their goodbyes as I climb into his truck.

After stopping for coffee as promised, even though I did make Sawyer go in so I could stay in the truck, we pull into the parking lot for the clinic. My eyes immediately go to a bright yellow Volkswagen parked in one of the spaces. "Jesus that's quite the paint job."

Sawyer glances over after putting his truck in park. "Oh yeah, that's Lily's car. She got it a few years ago. It kinda fits her style, doesn't it?"

"Lily, as in, Kat's friend?"

He looks at me like I'm crazy. "Yeah, dude. Lily, as in, the girl who basically grew up at our house. Remember that time she and Kat glitter bombed Max? She's wild." He chuckles.

Memories of Kat's friend coming over all the time flash through my head, too fast for me to register each of them. But a recent one does stand out. On one of my trips home last season, I ran into Kat and Lily. And let's just say Lily Chapman is not a glitter-bombing little girl anymore. She's a beautiful woman who exudes the kind of upbeat, positive energy most guys would be immediately drawn to.

Most guys. Maybe even me, a couple of months ago.

But right now, the last thing I need is someone spewing rainbows and sunshine all around me.

"She's the receptionist?" I ask, hoping it sounds casual.

Sawyer shakes his head. "Nope, she's a physical therapist. Damn good one, according to my buddy from the station, who went to her after a rotator cuff tear." He gently shoves my shoulder. "Dude, that would be weird if she was *your* therapist."

Weird is one way to put it. Fucking annoying is another.

"Conflict of interest," I grumble. "I'd ask for someone else."

I keep my eyes trained forward, but I can feel the weight of Sawyer's stare. After a minute, he shrugs. "Whatever. I'll be here to pick you up in an hour."

I clumsily maneuver my way out of his truck. "Thanks."

Standing in front of the clinic, I take a second to gather myself. No matter what, I will give physical therapy everything I can.

Doc said I needed a miracle; well, I don't believe in those. But hard work, perseverance, and determination — that, I can do. Especially since it might be my only chance.

CHAPTER THREE

Lily

When Jude Donnelly walks — well, crutches — into the clinic, I just about trip over my feet. I can't remember the last time I saw the second oldest Donnelly brother, and I'm positive Kat never mentioned he was coming to town. Rallying quickly, my mind reaches the obvious conclusion that he's here for his recovery. Makes sense to come home and be surrounded by his family who can help him heal.

His eyes zero in on me immediately, recognition giving a very brief and very faint lift to his scowl.

"Hey, Jude." I give him a giant smile and a wink as I say those two words with a faint musical lilt. He's used to the constant teasing over his name and the fact that his mother openly admits she was in a huge John Lennon phase when she named him.

Thick brows that cover his brown eyes furrow even deeper, which, of course, only makes me smirk. The man is sinfully gorgeous, even with a lot more scruff covering his strong jaw than I'm used to seeing. And his dark hair is long enough to curl

PRETEND TO LOVE YOU

under his ball cap, implying he's overdue for a cut. Heck, even the deep frown covering his features doesn't take away from the fact that Jude Donnelly is one hunky man.

"Lily."

Oh, Lord. One man's voice should not be that powerful.

"You've got an appointment for your knee, I assume?" I ask, forcing even more upbeat energy than normal into my voice. Jude just nods.

"I see all the media training you must have had didn't help expand your vocabulary much. Does the press like your grunts and nods?" I'm teasing and he knows it, judging by the way he cocks his head to the side and stares at me impassively. But I realize too late how it might sound to other people. Me teasing a hockey superstar.

"Lily. Stop bothering our VIP," Gianni, the clinic supervisor, and technically my boss, hisses at me. I hadn't even noticed him approaching. *Crap.*

"It's fine," Jude interjects, to my surprise. "We've known each other for years."

Did Jude Donnelly just come to my rescue?

Gianni *harrumphs*, but Jude's explanation seems to satisfy him. "If you'll come with me, Mr. Donnelly, we'll get started. By the way, I hear the Blaze has a game coming up in Seattle. Are you planning on attending? If you need anyone to accompany you, you know, to help with travel and stuff, I'm available."

My jaw falls open. I cannot believe he seriously just propositioned Jude for tickets within thirty seconds of meeting him.

Judging from the weary expression on Jude's face, this isn't the first time someone has tried it.

"I'm not going."

Gianni's mouth flaps open and shut like a fish, as if he can't believe Jude shot him down like that.

"Can we get started?" Jude starts to crutch past, but he pauses when he's next to me. "Good to see you, Lily."

"Y-you, too," I stutter out, turning to watch him head into the back gym area. My eyes naturally fall to his butt. It should be illegal, the way he fills out those sweatpants.

What I wouldn't give to get my hands on a body like his.

For therapy, of course... Oh, who am I kidding? I'd like my hands on him for other reasons, too.

Jude's at the clinic for just over an hour, working with Gianni. It's kind of embarrassing watching him fawn all over Jude and watching our receptionist try her hardest to flirt with him. Sukhi goes so far as to walk into the gym area no less than three times to offer Jude water. He turns her down each time and seems to ignore Gianni's ridiculous attempts at ingratiating himself.

There's something different about this man from the one I knew when we were younger — or even from the last time I saw him. He's always been a quiet guy, but the permanent frown is new. There's a cloud around him, a dark one. I guess it makes sense; his injury was pretty serious and probably career ending.

Not that I've googled him at length or anything...

It's hard to focus on my own work while Jude is around. As if something in me is magnetized to him, and all my senses are in tune with him. My eyes keep being drawn in his direction, and his deep grumble of a voice hits my ears constantly. Thank goodness I don't have a patient right now.

As he's leaving, Jude brushes off Sukhi's attempts to draw him into conversation, instead crutching over to me. "I'll see you around?"

My head lifts at his question. "Hmm? Oh. Yes, I'm here Tuesday through Saturday, normally." I give him a smile that hopefully hides the fact that I've been watching him out of the corner of my eye the entire time he's been here.

"Okay."

The door to the clinic opens just then, and Sawyer walks in. "Hey, Lil! Don't tell me you're stuck working with Beatle," he says in mock horror. I give him an easy smile.

"No, I'm not his therapist. But he is all done for the day."

"Cool. Let's go, bro." With a wave to me, Sawyer opens the door, holding it for his brother. Jude gives barely a nod in my direction, but it's more than Gianni or Sukhi get.

I stare after him, probably for way too long, before my patient comes in and forces me to get on with my day.

But Jude Donnelly doesn't move far from the front of my thoughts, ever.

Nothing beats Wednesday wing night at Hastings after a full day of clinic. Especially a day like today.

It's such a cliché having a crush on your best friend's older brother. But ever since I was a teenager and first started seeing boys as more than just annoyances, I started to see Jude as something more than one of the annoying Donnelly brothers that teased Kat and me mercilessly. At least Jude wasn't the one who ripped the heads off our Barbie dolls — that was Sawyer, and I still haven't forgiven him completely.

But Jude was different. He was quiet, serious, and broody. He wasn't around much, seeing as hockey consumed his life from an early age. I remember going to watch his games with the Donnellys and marveling at his athleticism as he flew across the ice. I've never told anyone, but it was watching him play that made me decide to go into sports medicine as a focus for my physical therapy career. Working with athletes gives a different set of challenges to my work. Their bodies are well-honed machines, but they break down just the same as anyone else. Helping them recover back to peak strength is so incredibly rewarding.

Of course, working at Dogwood Cove's physical therapy clinic, I don't exactly get the chance to work with many top-tier athletes. Actually, I haven't had any athletes as patients unless you count the rec-league baseball players. Before that, it was in my university days when I landed a clinic spot with the Vancouver professional football team's trainers.

"Hey Dean, can I put the game on?" I call over to the bar owner, who's pulling a pint of something cold and frothy. "And can I get a saison when you get a minute?"

He gives me a quick salute, which in Dean-speak means *yes* and *yes*. I get out of the booth and wander over to the bar, finding the remote for the big screen TVs and switching on the hockey game.

It's not Jude's team playing, but I really don't care. Hockey is hockey, whether it's the NHL or the minors. I love them all.

The speed, power, and gracefulness it takes to play the game is a beautiful thing to watch. Strength, balance, and coordination coming together in perfect harmony. Nothing beats the excitement of watching a hockey game live, and I've been lucky enough to attend more than a few games, courtesy of Jude's family. But I'll take a game at Hastings bar with a plate of wings just as happily.

"Did you already order?"

Kat slides into the booth across from me, her boyfriend Hunter sliding in after.

"Nope, just put on the game and asked Dean for a beer," I say by way of greeting.

"I'll go get our drinks." Hunter kisses Kat's cheek, then stands back up and ambles over to the bar to talk to Dean.

"So." I fold my hands on the table and narrow my eyes at Kat. "Is there a reason I didn't know Jude would be coming to my clinic for therapy until he walked through the doors?" Her face falls and I instantly regret asking the way I did. "Shit, I'm sorry to sound like a bitch. Are you okay?'

Kat nods. "Yeah, I'm glad he's here. But he didn't tell any of us he was coming. He just showed up. I guess he rented an apartment from Ethan, and that was it. We wouldn't have known, except his agent called Mom and Dad to make sure he arrived safely. He hadn't even told Stefan he made it here." Kat takes a paper napkin and starts folding it up, ripping off little pieces as she goes. "I'm worried about him. He's been in such a dark place ever since his injury. The boys went over this morning to take him to the clinic. Beckett called me and said Jude looked awful."

I reach over and cover her hand with mine just as Hunter returns with three beers. He sets them down before sliding back into the booth and wrapping his arm around Kat.

"You okay, Kitty Kat?"

I watch the two of them, Kat melting into his side. I'd be lying if I said I wasn't a little jealous of them. After two years being neighbours, they finally found their way to each other a year ago. Now they live together in Kat's house, and Hunter told me the other week he's going to propose soon. We're going to look at rings for Kat next week.

"Just filling Lily in on the Jude situation," she says.

Just then a server arrives with a tray full of wings I never ordered. They set them down in front of us, and Kat and I both look at Hunter.

"What?" He shrugs. "You think after so many nights spent witnessing you two demolish wings twice a month, I wouldn't know your order?"

"Our hero," Kat says teasingly, dropping her head down onto his shoulder.

I grab a wing and lift it, saluting him in the air. "You're a good man, Hunter Callaghan."

For the next hour we eat wings, drink beer, and watch hockey. It's perfect. Until my phone lights up on the table with a message from my mother.

"Ugh," I groan, flipping the phone over without even reading it. I already know what it says.

"What does she want now?" Kat asks gently.

"Oh, nothing. Just to make sure I tell my wedding date to colour coordinate with the rest of the family. How do guys colour coordinate, anyway? Aren't all suits basically grey, black, or navy? Those go with anything. Of course, I'd need to actually *have* a date, first." I drop my head into my hands. "I wish I didn't have to go."

"Why do you?" Hunter asks. It's a valid question, but one only a person without prior knowledge of my toxic family would ask.

"Don't go there," Kat replies quickly.

I shoot her a grateful smile. I don't really feel like revealing all my damage. I'd rather Hunter not know everything. It makes it easier if I'm just happy, crazy, bold Lily. Not Lily with a family that tries to browbeat her into submission at every chance.

"We could always ask one of the boys to escort you. They'd know how to behave and keep things simple."

"Nah, it's fine. I'll find someone." Plastering on a seductive smile, I scan the bar. "Heck, maybe I'll find someone here tonight. I could use some company, anyway, I'm out of batteries." I waggle my eyebrows and Kat giggles while Hunter looks confused for a second before blushing furiously.

"On that note, we need to head home. I've got an early lecture tomorrow." Kat pushes on Hunter's shoulder, and they both move to get out of the booth. I do the same, and we all put some money down on the table to cover the tab.

"Yeah, I should get to work on my date-finding mission."

Kat gives me a look that says she sees right through my suggestive comment. And I have no doubt that she does. I might have a history of random hookups and short-term relationships, but that doesn't mean it's what I prefer.

And she's the only other person who knows that.

"Be safe, Lily," she whispers as she draws me in for a hug. I squeeze her tightly. Somehow, I hit the jackpot when Kat Donnelly became my best friend, and I never let myself forget that.

"See you kids later. Don't do anything I wouldn't do," I say cheerfully, giving Hunter a brief hug as well. They leave first, and as I slowly put on my coat, I let my eyes wander back to the TV screen that's showing the last few minutes of the hockey game.

"That's a shitty call, ref," I scoff, but there's no one around to hear me.

What I wouldn't give to have a partner to cuddle up to and watch a hockey game with, someone who can handle me yelling when the ref makes a bad call. But I've never had that.

Instead, I'm just the fun one, the life of the party, the good-time girl. It gets lonely when no one wants anything more than a casual hookup with you. When the guys you go home with at the end of the night are in it for sex and nothing else.

It's pretty telling my one relationship that seemed like it might have potential to last more than a month ended in an engagement...

Between him and someone else.

CHAPTER FOUR

Lily

Smoothing my hands down the front of my purple blouse — my favourite because it matches the strands of purple hair I have carefully hidden under a conservative bun — I take a deep breath. It's freezing out here, but at least it isn't raining. Truthfully, the cold November air helps me clear my mind of the negative spiral I always head down when I have to see my family.

Who the heck chooses to have a bridal shower on a Friday afternoon?

The Chapmans, of course.

Heaven forbid they should show consideration for other people. Thankfully, I got the time off approved before today because with the mood Gianni was in this morning after Jude stormed out after his session, I doubt he would have said yes. I didn't overhear exactly what Jude said, but the tension between them was palpable. I give my head a shake to clear thoughts of Jude and work. I need to focus on what I'm about to face.

You are enough. You are enough. You are enough.

I plaster a smile on my face and knock on the ornate door to my aunt's house. Just like everything in my family, it's all for show. Formal and ostentatious. Because appearances are everything to the Chapman empire that exists nowhere except in my mother's and aunt's imaginations.

The door is opened by an older man wearing a suit with actual coattails. Of course, Aunt Dora hired staff for her daughter's bridal shower. *Only the best for Marnie.* I keep my eye roll internal.

We might have been raised together, as closely as if we were sisters and not cousins, but Marnie and I couldn't be more different. She's the Chapman daughter my mother wishes she had. She's elegant, conservative, a brainiac, and a sheep. She did everything asked of her, met every expectation, followed every rule. She went to school, got her engineering degree, and now she's working her way up the ranks of Chapman Consulting, working the jobs my parents expected me to be doing right alongside her.

Doesn't hurt that she even *looks* like Mom and Aunt Dora, with silver blonde hair, blue eyes, and a naturally thin frame. Meanwhile, I got my father's dark looks. Aside from the purple section of my hair, the rest is all brown, which shouldn't come with grey eyes, but does for me. And being as active and athletic as I've always been means I'm more muscular than slender. The fancy-pants clothes my mother wishes I would wear don't work on my frame, something she's always blamed on me, instead of genetics.

And now Marnie is getting married, settling down, and ready to start the next generation of Chapmans.

Walking into the house, I hear the murmur of voices coming from the formal sitting room. Another server wearing black and white hands me a glass of wine, which I take gratefully. Alcohol makes these sorts of events slightly more bearable.

Heads turn when I enter the room, and I suck in a steadying breath. *Here we go.*

"What are you wearing?" My mother's voice hisses in my ear as her fingers dig into my arm. I know if I look over at her, she'll have a serene mask in place, hiding her true feelings.

She taught me that trick. Except where she prefers a cold, indifferent mask, I like a happy, sunshiny one that makes everyone smile.

Well, almost everyone. Present company excluded.

"Clothes, Mother."

I shouldn't bait her but given how long I spent agonizing over which outfit to wear today, I have no patience left.

"Lilian, really. I asked you to dress appropriately and you show up here looking like a circus act. You couldn't do that one thing for me? Must you always seek to embarrass me?"

It never ceases to amaze me how she manages to make all my supposed transgressions a personal attack on her. Still, I glance down, as if expecting myself to be naked or something. "So, a silk blouse and slacks aren't appropriate anymore?"

She waves her hand at my black wide-legged pants and colourful top. "*That* is not..."

I arch a brow, waiting for her to continue. But someone calls her name, and she freezes. I've earned a slight reprieve.

"Lily."

A genuine smile crosses my face at the sound of the one voice I care about hearing at this damn party.

"Hi, Nana." I'm folded into a strong hug that seems like it shouldn't come from a five foot nothing, almost eighty-year-old. But that's Nana. She's strong, smart, and takes shit from no one.

"Alice, be a dear and go fetch me one of those little sandwiches while I catch up with Lily. I want to hear how work is going." Only Nana can get away with commanding my mother like that. I hide my smirk.

"Yes, Mother. Perhaps you can talk some sense into Lilian. She's still wasting her life at that clinic when she could be doing so much more."

My eyes flutter closed at my mother's words. To some, it may sound as if she only wishes me to reach my full potential or some bullcrap like that. But no. To Alice Chapman, the fact that I had the audacity to go into physical therapy as opposed to a more "worthwhile" profession, is a direct insult. I believe her words to me the day I was accepted into the program were *if you insist on this foolish escapade, couldn't you at least have become a doctor?*

Yes, anything other than the top three — lawyer, doctor, engineer — is seen as not good enough by my mom. Never mind the impact I have on people's health and well-being, or the many years of intense schooling I had to undertake to get to where I am. My job means nothing to my mother. Particularly because it doesn't benefit Chapman Consulting in any way.

"I'm glad you came, child."

We sit down on one of Aunt Dora's stiff couches.

"Your blouse is lovely, my dear. Those colours set off your skin tone perfectly." Nana takes my hand, placing it in her lap and squeezing it lovingly.

"Thank you. Can I get you anything to drink?"

Nana snorts delicately. "Oh, Lily. As if your aunt would dare let one of us serve ourselves. No, no. Watch this." Nana lifts her hand, and an instant later the same person who handed me a glass of wine materializes from nowhere.

"Yes, ma'am?"

"My granddaughter and I need a refill on our drinks, if you please."

A slight bow and they disappear. "What the heck was that?"

"That was your aunt wanting to seem far more fancy than she actually is. Who needs waitstaff at a bridal shower? It's over the top."

This is why I adore Nana. She says it like it is and doesn't care who hears. Sure enough, a couple of women in our close vicinity are staring at her, shocked that someone would dare critique my aunt that way.

Nana catches their gaze and narrows her eyes at them. They aren't family, so they must be work colleagues or acquaintances. Heaven forbid the Chapmans have friends.

The server returns with a fresh glass of wine for each of us. I'd barely started the one I had, but it's whisked away before I can say anything.

"I know this isn't easy for you, my dear, but I'm proud of you for being here." Nana's voice is quieter than normal, and I know those words are meant for my ears alone. She's the only reason I did come, and the only reason I'll subject myself to the spectacle that will be Marnie's wedding.

Unfortunately, I can't keep her by my side the entire time. With one last squeeze of my hand, she stands up from the couch. "Excuse me, Lily. I need to pay a visit."

I smile up at her and nod. "I'll be fine."

"Of course, you will be."

I watch her walk off in the direction of the small powder room down the hall from the kitchen. For a brief moment, I relax, sipping my wine. But that moment is over far too soon.

"You actually came."

My cousin's nasally voice sends my eyes rolling into the back of my head. I know I'm meant to be here to celebrate her, but truthfully, I was hoping to avoid her. I never asked to be placed in competition with Marnie, but she embraced that message fully from day one. It's exhausting, really.

"Yes, Marnie. I did." I turn to face my cousin, who sits down primly on a chair across from me, crossing her ankles and folding her hands in her lap. "Are you having a good bridal shower?"

She sniffs, her nose tilted up in the air. If you look up "entitled snob" in the dictionary, I think a picture of Marnie is right there in the definition. "Of course. It's wonderful to be surrounded by everyone that matters in my life, all of them here to celebrate my impending nuptials."

I bite back the retort I want to say. It wouldn't serve any purpose other than to make me feel good. And I've learned over time that with my family, the less I stir the pot, the better the chances of escaping them unscathed.

"Great."

Marnie leans forward slightly. "I realize this is a distasteful subject, but I must ask. The caterer at the hotel needs final numbers and I'm trying to complete the seating plan. You have found a date for the wedding, haven't you?"

My stomach sinks. Briefly, my mind flashes back to Kat's offer to ask one of her brothers, but I just as quickly dismiss it. I can't bring myself to do that. Subject the men that are like brothers to me to my family? Not in a million years.

You don't see Jude as a brother...

I am definitely *not* going there. Nope, no way. I'm not even entertaining that idea. God, I can see it now, if I dared to ask him if he wanted to come. He'd probably laugh at me. Or just look at me like I'm crazy, and I get enough of that from my family.

Marnie reads into my silence correctly and makes a frustrated sound. "Really, Lilian. Don't ruin this for me. If you don't have an escort, I'll be forced to move around the family groupings and place you at a different table. The optics of that would be in extremely poor taste."

I hold back a snort of derision. Poor taste went out the window the day she announced she was dating her now fiancé.

"Oh well, in that case, I'll be sure to bring someone. After all, we wouldn't want the optics to be bad." I spit out the words before I can think of how they'll stoke the fire of antagonism between Marnie and me. Given how her eyes narrow into a glare — but not a frown line to be seen, thanks to her monthly Botox appointments — my sarcasm landed on its mark.

"If you weren't so...*you*, perhaps this wouldn't be such a difficult situation you've put us all in. You're making everyone in the family uncomfortable, Lilian. Truly. Would it kill you to think about someone other than yourself, just once, and cooperate with our plans?

The audacity of what she's just said has my jaw dropping open in shock. I'm used to the gaslighting comments my family loves to sling at me, but this is next-level.

It takes me a second to gather my wits about me to try and formulate a response to Marnie's outrageous comments. And before I have a chance to say anything, there's the sound of silverware clinking against the edge of a glass, and my aunt's voice rises above the conversations, calling Marnie over to her. I watch her flounce off as dread builds in my stomach.

The Chapmans love to make a speech any chance they get. In a normal situation, that wouldn't be cause for concern. But this is anything but normal.

"Thank you all for coming today to celebrate my darling daughter's upcoming wedding. We're so happy for her, and so thrilled to welcome Clay into the Chapman family. Why, I still remember the day Lily brought Clay to the office for some reason or another. The instant he laid eyes on Marnie, sparks started to fly. I knew right then and there that we'd be seeing a lot more of him, and now, here we are."

And there it is. The casual, offhand mention of me, and the role I played in bringing Marnie and Clay together.

I wish I could say there was an awkward silence after Aunt Dora finishes, but there isn't. Because everyone in this room — Nana being the only exception — has drank the Kool-Aid and thinks it's totally fine that Marnie is marrying Clay.

Because yes, it's true that I brought Clay to the office that day to pick something up for my father. And yes, I introduced him to Marnie. However, there's a bit more to it. One important piece that Aunt Dora carefully left out in her speech.

He came with me to the office that day as *my* boyfriend.

Chapter Five

Jude

"He needs to go, Stef."

"Okay. I'll handle it, but don't you think maybe you're over-reacting? You've only had two sessions with the guy, maybe he was starstruck."

I growl into the phone. If my leg wasn't busted, I'd be pacing my living room right now. "If he was any less subtle about wanting me to score him some fucking tickets, he'd have a neon sign around his neck. And how many autographs does one guy need? He's gonna sell them, Stefan. I'm sure of it. Who the fuck asks for ten? Ten!"

"Maybe his family are fans?" Stefan says, but I can hear his doubt coming through.

I grunt instead of replying, and my agent slash somewhat friend lets out a long-suffering sigh. I don't feel bad for him, I pay him more than enough to deal with this shit.

"Get me a different therapist for my next session. Not negotiable." I end the call and toss the phone down on the couch beside me, letting my head fall back on a deep exhale.

As if the shit show with the physical therapist this week wasn't bad enough, tonight I have to go to dinner at my parents' house.

Hence the barrage of text messages flooding the group chat with my siblings, ostensibly to check in on me, but in reality, they just want to remind me of dinner, and that Beckett will be picking me up in a couple of hours. Just the thought of facing all of them makes me want a nap.

Sleep has never come easily to me. I've always been the one to stay up till well after midnight, then toss and turn in bed before dragging my ass to practice at 5 am. I've tried everything from meditation to melatonin. None of it helps.

But the physical demands on my body right now are making it impossible for me to function on the little sleep I'm used to getting. And hell, it's not like I have anything else to do right now. I've already done the home exercises that idiot of a therapist told me to do, and I can only zone out on Sports Zone highlights for so long.

Insomnia is a bitch, but maybe she'll let me have this small reprieve.

I crutch into the bedroom and sink down on the bed, setting an alarm for an hour before closing my eyes in hopes of getting a short break from reality.

That fucking alarm goes off way too soon, and it's echoed by a knock on my door.

"Come in," I shout groggily, assuming it's one of my brothers.

"Why are you in bed?" Max asks, leaning against the doorframe as I slowly swing my legs over the side of the bed.

"It's called a nap," I reply drily. "What are you doing here? I thought Beckett was picking me up."

"He was going to, but I wanted to have a second to check in with you." His eyes move from me to the bottle of whiskey. "See how you're really doing, without the others around."

I grab the crutches and go around him to the bench by the door where my shoes are. "I'm fucking great, Max. Why wouldn't I be?" Sarcasm drips from every word.

"Huh. Okay, cool. So, I'll just ignore the fact that you're going through booze like it's water, clearly not taking your painkillers, oh, and you haven't even told Mom and Dad you're back."

My head whips up. "How the fuck do you know that?"

Max shakes his head at me, making me hate myself even more when I see the disappointment mixed with pity in his eyes. "Bro, there's already an empty bottle on the counter and you've been here what, two days? Three? At least your prescription meds are sitting there untouched. I guess that's the one smart choice you're making by not mixing the two. And Mom called me. She's worried about you. We all are."

I lift a hand to rub at my chest, as if I'm trying to erase the pang of guilt his words spark inside of me. I'm the one suffering, not them. Why should I be so concerned with how they're feeling?

"Obviously, I'm not a dumbass who's going to mix pills and booze. And even more obviously, Mom and Dad know I'm here, just like you and the boys do. They just happen to have the decency to give me some goddamn space."

"I don't think space is what you need, brother."

My eyes narrow in a glare. "Well, you'd be wrong. Can we just go to dinner?"

Max stares at me for a long second before giving a brief nod and walking over. "Yeah. Let's go."

The drive to our childhood home is silent, aside from my asking where Heidi, Max's girlfriend, is tonight. Apparently, she's in Vancouver, visiting her best friend.

Lucky her.

When we pull in the driveway, Mom's already standing outside, her arms wrapped around her middle. I turn to Max accusingly. "Really?"

He just shrugs. "What? All I did was text that we were on our way." I reach for the door handle, and he stops me, his hand gripping my shoulder. "Look Jude, I know you're struggling. If you need to get mad at someone, yell or hit something, call me. I can handle it. Don't take it out on anyone else, okay? That's all I'm gonna ask."

I sit still, not moving at all. I know I'm not easy to be around right now, but it hurts that he thinks I'd intentionally be mean to anyone, especially my family. "Yeah. Fine."

I open the door and unfold my large frame from Max's car. He comes around the back and hands me my crutches silently. Slowly, I make my way up to the front porch where my mother is waiting.

Not a day goes by that I don't know how blessed I am with my family. Claire and Dennis Donnelly created a home full of safety, warmth, love, and respect. And they instilled all of that in each of us kids. We're close, and honestly, being apart from them was the one negative to my career in Montana. I know I've been hurting them with how I'm shutting everyone out right now. But I don't think I fully let myself admit how unfair that was to my parents until just now when I see the tears in Mom's eyes.

"Hey, Mom," I say gruffly.

"Oh, Jude." Her small but strong arms are wrapped around me, and I awkwardly let go of one crutch so I can hug her back. "I'm glad you're here, honey."

She steps back and looks me up and down slowly. "You're thin. You aren't eating properly, are you? And what's this?" Her hand reaches out to touch my cheek, covered in a thick scruff. I fight the urge to pull away. I haven't felt an affectionate touch since right after surgery when they came to visit me in the hospital. Even Shelley wouldn't come too close; I guess she was already on her way out before the anesthetic wore off.

"Well, come on inside. I've cooked all your favourites tonight."

We head inside, and Mom leads me to the living room where Dad's recliner chair is vacant. "Here you go."

I arch my brow at her. "That's Dad's chair. No one sits in Dad's chair."

"You do tonight, son." I turn at the sound of my father's deep voice to see him shuffling into the room, the slight limp from his accident years ago still visible. "Take it."

I know better than to argue with him, so I sit, sinking down and using the lever to lift the footrest gratefully.

"Hey, what the heck? How come Beatle's in Dad's chair?"

"Stop calling me that," I grumble at Sawyer.

"But I've been calling you that since we were kids. I can't stop now." He blinks innocently at me before handing me a beer.

"This," I say, lifting the bottle, "Is the only reason I'm not fighting you on it right now."

"I can accept that." He sinks down on the couch beside my chair just as the door opens and what feels like a crowd of people come in. In reality, it's only Kat, Hunter, Leo, Serena, and Leo's daughter Violet. But after being basically a recluse for several weeks, the increase in bodies and volume is overwhelming. One by one, my family file over to me, say hi, ask how I'm doing, and in Kat's instance, throw their arms around my neck for a strangling hug.

I do my best not to be rude and push anyone away, but it's too fucking much. All of this is too much. I love my family, but I don't want to be here, poisoning them with my negativity.

Somehow, I make it through dinner. Probably only because they all know better than to pester me too much. The conversation flows around me with only the occasional comment or question directed my way. When it's finally time to leave, Mom sends a big bag full of leftovers with Max.

As we're standing on the porch to say goodbye, she hugs me again. This time I return it a little stronger than before.

"Thanks for dinner. I'm sorry I'm not better company."

Her hands lift to cup my cheeks. "Oh honey, we don't need you to be better company. We just need you to let us love you."

"I'm trying."

It's the truth, and the only answer I can give her right now.

Once I'm home and alone again, I finally feel like I can breathe. The full force of the Donnellys, while well-intentioned, was suffocating. All their happiness and excitement for the future — Leo and Serena's wedding, Kat's graduation from grad school — it was too much. Their lives are still moving forward. Their dreams haven't yet come true. They still have hope and happiness to look forward to.

I have none of that.

I have nothing.

CHAPTER SIX

Lily

Butterflies have taken up a home inside of my stomach. They arrived the second I checked my patient list for today and saw Jude's name near the top. I went to Gianni to ask why Jude was transferred to my patient load, and the glare I received made me back away slowly.

Privately, I'm not surprised. I don't know Jude as well as the rest of the Donnellys, given our age gap and the fact that he's gone most of the time, but even I know he values his privacy and doesn't like to be fawned over.

And Gianni was definitely fawning.

I've got about fifteen minutes before Jude's appointment and I'm using it wisely, studying up on ACL rehab post reconstructive surgery. Gianni dumped his patient file onto my work area earlier with a huff of annoyance, so I've had the chance to get up to speed.

As it would turn out, Jude Donnelly has been keeping things from his family. Like the fact that he's had three ACL tears in the last five years and multiple meniscus injuries. His knee has been scoped more times than I can count, and he had a more extensive surgical repair done a few years ago as well. Seeing as I don't remember hearing about *any* of that — from his family or from the media — it would seem the team kept it all tightly under wraps.

Unfortunately, it makes his rehab a hell of a lot more complicated. There's going to be a ton of scar tissue to navigate, not to mention the damage is a lot more than just one ACL tear. I'm starting to understand why the rumours are flying that this could be a career ending injury for him.

When there's just a couple of minutes left until he's due to arrive, I dart into the staff bathroom and splash some cold water on my face. My nerves are ridiculous. I've known Jude my entire life. Okay, fine, I've also had a teeny-tiny crush on him for over a decade, but whatever. He's my patient when he's here. That's all.

I can be professional.

But as I look in the mirror, tugging at the V-neck uniform shirt the clinic mandates we wear, I cringe. Of course, today is the day I had to wear the one that shrunk a little in the dryer. It's not indecent, but it's definitely more formfitting than I prefer at work. Then, I catch sight of the multicoloured beaded earrings that were a gift from an Indigenous friend of mine. I run my hands through my hair that's braided back but has my not-so-secret deep purple section showing prominently.

Damn it. Nothing about me screams professional right now. Will a pro athlete like Jude take me seriously with coloured hair, my too tight uniform, and funky earrings?

But as I move to take the earrings out, I pause.

No.

I'm not going to change who I am. My employer has no problem with my appearance, and I'm a damn good physical therapist. That's all that matters, certainly not something as minor as my earrings or my hair. As long as I show my competence to Jude and help him with his rehab the way I know I can, he'll have to take me seriously.

Riiight. Because that's exactly what always happens to me. Men taking me seriously. Uh-huh, sure.

I shake my head to free my mind of those thoughts. They have no place here. My work is the one place I know I've earned respect. No one bats an eye at my sunny, upbeat attitude or colourful personality here; it's what they expect from me. Along with competence, skill, compassion, and professionalism.

And that's exactly what Jude is going to get.

I stride out of the bathroom, my shoulders back, posture tall. Judging by the moon-eyed expression on Sukhi's face, it's safe to say Jude is here. I head straight toward the only private treatment room we have — the rest of the clinic being an open concept style with equipment in the middle for anyone to use.

Knocking on the door, I wait for a sound of acknowledgment before walking in.

"Lily?"

Shit, he sounds surprised to see me.

"Hi Jude, I'm taking over your physical therapy as of today." I keep my tone crisp and clinical, but the second I meet his deep brown eyes, something inside of me wobbles slightly. I swallow roughly. "I've read your file; I must admit to being somewhat surprised by the number of injuries you've sustained to your knee."

He grunts. Like, literally grunts. "Yeah. That's confidential, right? Anything you learn about me, you can't tell anyone. Not even my sister."

Heat rises at the accusation in his tone. "Yes, Jude. I am a professional and am legally bound not to speak to anyone about our sessions or your progress with the exception of the team physician and your surgeon, without your express permission. You don't need to question my integrity."

"Fuck, I wasn't." He has the decency to sound remorseful. Heaving out a great sigh, his gaze meets mine again. "Sorry. Can we start over?"

Eyeing him, I take in the obvious signs of discomfort, both physical and mental. I'm trained to recognize symptoms of poor pain management, and Jude is showing all of them. Add that to what I imagine is a lot of mental anguish over the possible ramifications of this injury, and I'm willing to cut him some slack.

"Of course." I soften my tone and put on my best comforting smile. "Everything is kept confidential, I promise. Now, if you're ready, I've got the first month of our program mapped out and I want to review it with you."

He gives the barest of nods, but I take it. And over the next ten minutes, I map out my goals to get him walking, focusing on breaking down scar tissue, rebuilding muscle and range of motion, and working on balance and proprioception.

"Any questions?"

He's silent for so long I jump to the assumption he isn't going to answer. "You know, you'll have to actually talk to me occasionally if this is going to work."

His head bounces up from where he's been apparently staring at the sheet of home exercises I gave him. "Excuse me?"

I fold my hands together in my lap and look at him, keeping my smile in place. "You heard me. Conversation makes time go by a lot more enjoyably. I asked if you had any questions."

"You don't want to hear my question." There's a whole lot of emotion laden in those words, enough that I should leave it alone.

I don't. "I do. If I'm going to help you, I need to know everything."

A flash of vulnerability fills his deep brown eyes. "Is this gonna work? Am I going to be able to skate again?"

All my breath escapes me on a *whoosh* as I realize my critical mistake. Every therapeutic relationship should start with a discussion about goals. And I assumed — incorrectly — that Jude knew what reasonable expectations and goals would be for his recovery. Considering my words carefully, I respond.

"I don't make promises, but I will say this. If you listen to me, work hard but within the limits I set, you will heal from your surgery. Anything beyond that is up to your team's doctor."

His face falls for a fraction of a second before settling back into the mask of grumpy indifference. "Got it."

I want so badly to ask him what his plan B is. He had to be nearing retirement anyway, so what were his plans? Knowing those would help shape my therapeutic approach because if he wants to go into management or coaching, that will change how far we need to go with his knee rehab and strengthening. But it doesn't take a genius to realize he's not ready for that conversation.

Instead, I keep our session short for the day, since it becomes quickly apparent that until I break down the scar tissue in his quadriceps, we won't be able to do much else. As we're finishing up, I decide to mention that to him.

"Next time bring some shorts, please."

"Why?"

"Because I'll need to start some manual therapy on your quads and glutes to loosen things up if we're going to hope to activate those muscles at all."

"You mean massage?" He sounds incredulous, and dare I say, nervous?

I nod. "Yes, that was part of the treatment protocol I explained in the beginning."

"Right," he says gruffly. "Fine, shorts."

"Great," I reply as chipper sounding as I can be. "I'll see you in two days. Make sure you do those exercises tomorrow that I gave you."

Another grunt is the only response I get as Jude crutches out of the room. Once he's gone, I sag onto the stool I was sitting on. Holy crap, I expected him to not be in the best mindset, but I was not prepared for Oscar the Grouch combined with Eeyore.

But I'm up for the challenge.

Jude Donnelly and his knee don't stand a chance.

After work, I head home and immediately change into a sports bra and some shorts before unrolling my yoga mat.

I've been flustered all day, thanks to Jude. I seriously under-estimated the potency of, well, him. Being close to him, even in a professional setting, hearing that deep rumbly voice and seeing the muscles bunch and relax as he moved his finely honed body...dang. It got me so wound up and twisted inside, I need a sweaty flow to settle myself.

Especially considering Kat is coming over for a girls night in. And the last thing I need is for Jude's sister to figure out my teenage crush has never gone away.

I finish my practice and take a quick shower, pulling on clothes with minutes to spare before girls night.

"Honey, I'm ho-ome!" Kat sings out as she pushes open my door. I finish braiding my damp hair and go to take some of the bags from her.

"Did you remember my spicy sweet chili Doritos?" I demand, rifling through the bags.

"Of course, I did. And the sour Skittles. I swear, you have the palate of a ten-year-old when it comes to junk food."

I pull out the gummy bears that are her candy of choice and wave them at her. "And these are just so mature?"

"Give me those," she demands, swiping the bag from my hand. "I also grabbed some of those weird sheet masks for our faces. I've been wanting to try one but not around Hunter."

"Listen, if the guy can't handle you looking all creepy with a face mask on, is he even in love with you?"

We both dissolve into giggles. The truth is, Hunter and Kat are what true love is made of. And I'm not jealous. Not even a little.

Okay, maybe a little.

After loading our plates up with the Chinese food that was delivered moments before Kat's arrival, we pour some premade margaritas and head over to the couch.

"Margaritas and mandarin chicken. Perfection," Kat sighs as she takes a bite of food.

"Promise me we'll still be doing this every month, even when you and Hunter have a million kids to chase after," I say before lifting my own chopsticks to my mouth.

My best friend shoves me with her shoulder, making me drop the noodles I had just picked up. "Hey!"

"Hey, yourself. Why would you even ask me something like that? Girls night in is sacred, and no man or child is coming between that."

I drop my head down onto her shoulder. "That's what I hoped you would say."

We finish dinner quickly, clean up the leftover food, and grab our snacks, as well as a refill of margaritas.

"Face mask time," Kat announces, pulling out two packages. It's impossible to contain our laughter as we peel the slimy-feeling masks out of the wrapper and lay them on our faces.

"Oh my God." I almost choke on my margarita when we go into the bathroom and see ourselves in the mirror. "These things are beyond bizarre."

"Definitely no photos allowed tonight." Kat giggles.

We head back to the couch and sit down, sipping our drinks through straws.

"Listen, I know you won't be able to tell me anything because of patient confidentiality, but now that you're treating Jude, I was hoping I could ask you something."

My entire body freezes at Kat's hesitant words. Slowly, I lower my glass down to the table and turn to her, nodding in a gesture for her to continue.

She sits up and faces me. "We're worried about him, Lil. He's not the same. He's so withdrawn and angry all the time. I know he's got a perfectly valid reason to be angry at the world right now, but he's shutting all of us out. I was just hoping since you'll be with him almost every day, you could, I don't know, talk to him. Get him to open up, maybe. Convince him to talk to someone."

"Oh."

"I'm sorry, I know it's a weird thing to ask. You're a physical therapist, not a mental one," Kat rushes on to say. "But he knows you, and maybe he'd trust you enough to just talk. Please, Lily."

I grab her hand and squeeze it tightly.

"I'll be there for him, Kat, however I can."

Chapter Seven

Jude

The second I lift my leg up onto the couch cushion and wrap the towel-covered ice pack around my knee, I groan in relief.

Lily Chapman is a physical therapist taskmaster. She'd fit in well on a professional sports team's roster of trainers with how hard she pushes.

Today was only our second session, and as promised, she started it with what she calls manual therapy — I call it torture. She worked on the scar tissue surrounding my knee, but she didn't stop there. Nope, Lily the sadist continued up my leg, finding every single tense spot along my muscles. After the massage, she put me through my paces, testing my strength, range of motion and balance, and then pushing me to the outer limits of any rehab I've done so far.

It was surprisingly easy to be around her, even having her hands on my body. There's a deep comfort and familiarity with Lily, unexpected, and yet not, all at the same time. I've known the woman most of my life, but there's something different in our dynamic now. She's not my little sister's friend, she's something else.

Adjusting the ice pack slightly, I grab my phone and open the text messages Kasey sent earlier while I was in the shower.

KASEY: Before I show you something, I need to talk to you.

KASEY: I'm guessing you'll never pick up the phone, so text me when you can, bud.

That sounds fucking ominous. Just to prove him wrong, I hit the button to call him.

"Holy shit, Jude Donnelly is making a phone call." His loud voice is almost drowned out by the background noise.

"Where the hell are you?" I ask, pinching the bridge of my nose. I forgot how fucking annoying it is trying to yell just to be heard when you're out on the town.

"Hold on," Kasey says. I can just make out the sound of him telling someone he'll be right back, then the noise fades. "Hey. Sorry, I ducked into the manager's office. We're at The Rose."

At his mention of the bar the team would frequent after practice, the knife that feels permanently lodged in my heart twists. My eyes close as I try to hide my reaction. "Cool. What's so important that I had to call you?"

Kasey doesn't answer right away, which only proves my initial gut instinct. Whatever he's about to say, I'm not gonna like it.

"They announced your permanent replacement for captain today."

My breath leaves me on a heavy exhale. Damn. I knew this day was coming; hell, it's a surprise the team took as long as they did to choose a new captain. I suppose a part of me had hoped it was because they were waiting for me to come back, but obviously, I was wrong.

"It's Pike."

"That fucker?" I sneer, feeling heat rise inside of me. I got along great with everyone on the Blaze. Everyone except Tony Pike. When he was traded to our team two years ago, he brought his arrogance and bad attitude along with him. Unfortunately, he's a damn good hockey player.

"Yeah. Trust me, the guys are not happy. There's a few who even want to go to management and ask them to reconsider."

"That won't work," I retort. "They chose him for a reason, now he's going to have to prove himself to everybody. On the ice and off."

"Well, about that. His off-ice activities are the other reason I needed to talk to you."

Kasey sounds like he swallowed something disgusting.

"Look, man, I'm gonna send you a photo. And you're not gonna like it. But as your best friend, I think it's best you know what's going on and what a bullet you dodged."

Somehow, I already know what I'm about to see. And sure enough, when I open the photo Kasey sends, it's as expected. It's my ex, in the arms of my replacement.

"I hope they're very happy together," I say, sarcasm dripping from every word.

"Dude, it's fucked-up. You've been gone a week and she's jumped beds already. Trust me when I say none of us are impressed with Pike right now. He should know better. Hell, he should —"

"Kasey, it's fine," I interrupt. "Things weren't serious with Shelley, anyway, and as you said, I dodged a bullet. She didn't give a shit about me; she's a puck bunny who wants to be a WAG. Let Pike have her. They deserve each other."

"You're not wrong there. So, you're okay? Like, really okay? I didn't just fuck with your head or anything?"

"Sorry to disappoint, my friend. But no new fuckery going on in my head. Just the same old." I hear Kasey's exhale of relief. I know I'm lucky to have a friend like him. "But you know, if you happened to accidentally body check him into the boards at the next practice, that could be fun to hear about."

Kasey lets out a loud laugh, and I actually feel my own lips turn up in response. It's not a smile, I think I've forgotten how to do that. But I can't deny the sick satisfaction I feel, thinking about Pike eating ice at the hands of my best friend.

After I hang up with Kasey, I let my head fall back against the arm of the couch. I wish I could say I was surprised by what he showed me, but I'm not. It's not the first time I've watched some woman try to go from one player to the next until she finds one who's dumb enough to get sucked in. Puck bunnies, WAGs, most of them — not all, but most — are the same. Only in it for the fame and fortune that comes with being involved with a professional athlete.

I wish I wasn't so cynical, but I've seen it too many times, and now, thanks to Shelley, I've experienced it firsthand.

So, where does that leave me?

The sound of a key turning the lock of my front door makes me lift my head with a frown. No one should have a key to this place except me.

And Sawyer.

I forgot I gave him one, begrudgingly, after he pointed out that for my own safety someone should be able to get in, given my mobility issue at present.

I didn't exactly plan on him using it whenever he damn well wanted to. I push myself up to stand, testing my leg with more of my body weight than I've put on it so far. I know I shouldn't; I know Lily will yell at me that I'm not ready — the way she did earlier today when I tried to take a step without my crutches. But right now, I find it hard to care.

Except that she cares. And *that* is what makes me reach down and grab the goddamn crutches.

I shake my head free of the questions that arise at that realization and make my way to the door as it opens. Not only Sawyer but all three of my brothers and Hunter walk in. They're each holding something, from a six pack of Coke, to a couple of pizza boxes, to a bag with what looks like a tray of poker chips sticking out of it.

I raise my eyebrows at Max who's the last one in. He's carrying a grocery bag that I'm hoping holds a drink stronger than soda. "What the hell is all this?"

He shrugs, giving me a somewhat sheepish smile. "Donnelly style intervention, it seems. They did it to me and Leo. Apparently, it's your turn."

"I don't need an intervention," I grumble under my breath, following them into the kitchen area where the others are sorting food onto plates and pouring drinks. "Is there at least some rye to go in that?" I say to Beckett.

He shakes his head. "No. We kind of thought a night off from the booze might be a good idea." There's more than a hint of reproach in his words, and I don't like what he's implying.

Even if it is the truth.

Sawyer's hand comes down to slap me on the back before he drapes his arm over my shoulder. "Since you don't seem willing to leave this damn apartment, we're forcing a social life on you. You can be a grumpy fucker while you play poker with your bros."

"We've let you wallow here alone for a week, bro. But we can't sit by and watch you suffer all by yourself any longer."

I turn at Beckett's calm voice. "I'm not wallowing."

His direct stare is probing, peeling back the layers of the lie. "Yeah. Sure."

I look away and crutch my way back to the couch. Dropping down, I lift my leg back up to rest it on the table and go to reapply the ice pack, but it's not that cold anymore. A hand reaches over my shoulder and snatches it away.

"I'll get you a fresh one."

I grunt at Max, a half-hearted attempt at a thank you, I realize. When he brings a new one, fresh from the freezer, I take it. This time, I look at my older brother. "Thanks."

He inclines his head before sinking down into the chair next to me and opening the box of poker chips, methodically splitting them between the five of us. "No problem. We just want to help. Any way that you'll let us."

Somehow, his gentle chiding hits me even more squarely than Beckett calling me out on trying to deny the fact that I've been avoiding everyone.

"I'm not in a good place. I don't want to dump that on you," I say quietly so only Max can hear. Out of everyone, he's the one I'm the closest to. He alone knows about my past injuries, the ones we kept out of the press and most certainly away from my family.

"You were here for me when I was at my worst. Let me do the same for you."

All I can do is nod and force back the moisture that threatens to build in my eyes. I'm not a crier but fuck if my brothers aren't making me feel all the damn feelings I don't want right now. Max doesn't even know how those words hit me. He's living a charmed life now, with a career that doesn't have an expiry date looming, and a woman who loves him for who he is — not for what he does. He's happy. And his being here for me won't do shit to give me what he's got. My problems can't be fixed like his were — with some advice and open communication.

My problems need a miracle, according to the experts.

Thankfully, the other guys bring over food and drinks at that moment, sinking into seats around the coffee table, talking about something to do with the winter festival that's coming up in a few months. Max is dealing cards and soon the conversation shifts to poker.

"How long since you last played a hand, Beatle?" Sawyer asks teasingly as I fold for the third time. I shoot him a dirty look and pick up the water glass Beckett brought me a little while ago.

"It's been a while, okay? I was kind of busy playing hockey, not cards."

Everyone falls silent. It takes me a second to realize that's the first time I've even mentioned hockey since I came back.

"Has your surgeon said anything about playing again?" Beckett asks.

I start to shake my head, then stop. I'm not ready to tell them. Not when I haven't fully accepted it myself.

"He said he needs to reassess after a few months of rehab." There, it's not a lie, not entirely.

"How's it going with Lily?"

I turn to Hunter, noticing the protective tone to his voice. I guess he probably knows Lily fairly well, given how close she and Kat are. Still, he doesn't need to worry about me. I've got nothing to offer any woman, much less someone like Lily. She's sunshine and I'm darkness. The two can't exist in the same place.

"It's good. She knows her stuff."

Hunter doesn't press for more, which is a good thing, since I honestly don't know what else to say about that.

Eventually my brothers and Hunter leave. It's late, and as soon as silence falls over the apartment, I realize just how tired I am. Hell, I might even be tired enough to sleep.

Yeah, I don't believe that for a second. But it doesn't stop me from going through the motions of getting ready for bed, even following Lily's instructions, and popping an anti-inflammatory medicine just before sliding beneath the sheets.

I close my eyes and try some of the meditation exercises Kasey's yoga instructor wife Daphne taught me a couple years ago. I feel my mind relax, but it's not enough.

Nothing is ever enough to give me the peace I desperately want.

Chapter Eight

Jude

"You look like shit."

I squint through my sunglasses at my younger brother. "Thanks, jackass."

Sawyer just shrugs. He's driving me again this week thanks to the way his shifts fall and my physical therapy schedule. Don't get me wrong, I appreciate that he's giving up his days off to chauffeur me around, but it grates on me that it's even necessary. Plus, Sawyer's a little too chaotic sometimes. He probably means to be upbeat and positive, but it's just annoying.

Especially right now.

It's my own damn fault. I got sucked into a vortex of self-loathing last night, watching my teammates play our number one rival in the league. Because as painful as it is to admit, Pike is doing a good job leading the team.

Leading *my* team.

Except they aren't my team anymore and might never be again. Hence the vortex of self-loathing that involved a nasty-ass bottle of rotgut I found when I finally unpacked one of the boxes I had shipped up here from Montana. It's been ten days; I might as well stop living out of a suitcase.

As if torturing myself by having the game on wasn't bad enough, as soon as I found that bottle, I was sent back in time to the night after we won the championship game last spring. The party that night lasted until the early morning. The next day, I bought everyone a bottle of gin that was distilled in the city that hosted the final. We agreed we'd all save it and drink it out of the cup the following year, certain that we'd be champions again.

They might get there.

I won't.

So I chugged that shit last night, and I'm paying the price this morning.

"See you in a couple of hours," Sawyer calls out cheerfully as I gingerly climb down from his truck. I lift my hand in acknowledgment, focusing on getting to the front door of the clinic. Goddamn it, why does the sun have to be so bright today?

When I get inside, the receptionist basically trips over her own feet to get around the desk to me. I inwardly groan. I don't need the hero worship from a wannabe puck bunny right now, or ever.

"Hi Jude, how are you today? Can I get you some water? Here, let me take your coat." She reaches out, any excuse to touch me, but I move out of reach.

"I'm fine." I make my way over to a chair closest to the open gym space. It's also conveniently the farthest away from the front desk.

I take off the sunglasses that felt necessary earlier but feel stupid now, thanks to my brother's comment. The pain pill I took earlier had to do double duty this morning, helping with the headache that comes when you're nearing forty and have a hangover, as well as helping with my knee.

Musical laughter hits my ears.

Lily.

I look up to see her dancing with a patient. Yeah, actually dancing. Like some fancy ballroom shit or something. She's smiling and so is the older guy shuffling his feet with her. I almost want to put my sunglasses on again just to dull the brightness that surrounds her. It's too much for me to handle right now.

Yet, I'm so in tune with my body, thanks to years of conditioning, that I can't help but notice my heart rate picks up a little.

Must be from the dread of not knowing what kind of special torture she has in line for me today. I swear, if she expects me to dance, she'll be disappointed.

I watch the two of them out of the corner of my eye. I don't know why, but I can't seem to keep my eyes off Lily. Colourful earrings swing and sway with her movement, and I catch a subtle flash of purple in her hair occasionally.

How did I not notice she has purple hair? My fingers twitch in my lap as a fleeting thought of how soft her hair looks passes through my head. What the fuck is that about?

Lily threads her arm through the crook of the older man's elbow and guides him toward me. Her eyes flare wide for just a second when she sees me, then her attention is back on her other patient.

"Okay, Leonard, I'll see you next week. Don't forget to ask Carmen to help with those exercises."

The old guy salutes her. "Will do, Lily. Thanks again."

She turns to me, popping one hip out and folding her arms across her chest. I get the feeling she's assessing me and somehow finding me lacking.

"Well, let's go, Donnelly." She pivots on her feet and walks swiftly over to the doorway to the private room.

Inwardly, I groan. Great, time for more pain.

When I get inside, I sit down on the edge of the bed and start to toe off my shoes. Lily closes the door and lowers herself on to her stool. "Okay, so, did you remember to take the meds this morning?"

I nod.

"Great. And have you been icing and stretching like I asked?"

Another nod.

"Wonderful." She pauses, and I feel her eyes on me as I lift my legs up onto the table. "Is today a grunt only day or am I going to get some words out of you?"

My eyes lift to meet her clear gaze. Her eyes are a perfect grey, light with a dark rim. They're kind of mesmerizing.

I give my head a shake. Man, I'm starting to lose it if I'm busy describing someone's eyes as mesmerizing.

"Sorry," I rasp. "Tired."

"And hungover, judging by the bloodshot eyes and fumes wafting off your body," Lily notes.

Embarrassment fills me. Somehow, Lily calling me out on the drinking hits way worse than when my brothers do it.

"Sorry," I say again.

Lily drapes a towel over my shorts and picks up the bottle of massage oil. "It's fine. I understand needing to escape for a while, and using alcohol probably feels like the easiest option. But it's not great for rehab. It dulls your senses, slows your reaction time, and adds a layer of discomfort that makes it challenging to determine what is true pain and what's hangover pain. Not to mention the obvious rule of not mixing pain medication with booze, and honestly, the painkillers would do more for you. So in the future, if you could avoid drinking the night before our sessions, that would be helpful."

Well, fuck. Now I want to go home and throw out all the booze. Somehow, this woman's reprimand has me wanting to change the self-destructive habit I've fallen into when nothing else did.

Her warm hands land on my shin and I flinch.

"Oops, that's on me, I should've warned you I was starting. Are you okay with me continuing?"

"Yeah. It's fine."

She starts to move again, keeping her strokes light for now. But I know she'll dig in once she finds the tight spots. For now, I try to force myself to relax.

"It's looser today, that's good," she comments just as her thumb presses in. "Ah wait, there it is."

My teeth grind together as she grabs this wooden thing she calls a scraper and starts to pull down the line of muscle. This isn't even the bad part. That comes when she hits my quads.

"Fuck," I grunt as she digs into the mess around my knee.

"Sorry," she says quietly.

"It's your job."

"I know; I don't like causing pain, though. Even when I know it'll be beneficial in the long run."

I wince again as she pulls the scraper down the side of my thigh. I'm distracted for a second when my phone starts to buzz. But a quick glance shows me it's nothing important, just the family text message thread blowing up.

Sure enough, message after message comes in. I don't even bother reading them, turning my attention back to Lily.

"Let's get you on your side for a bit," she directs. "I need to work your hamstrings and your glutes, if that's okay."

I freeze. My ass? She wants to massage my ass? She senses my unease and quickly clarifies one important thing.

"You'll keep your shorts on. I just want to check some trigger points."

"'kay," I say gruffly and start to roll onto my side. Easier said than done. But Lily's there, helping lift my leg so she can slide a pillow in between. Goddamn it, I hate feeling like a fucking cripple in front of her. She might be my physical therapist, but she's also a beautiful woman and someone who's used to seeing me at my peak. Now she's seeing me as a loser. A nothing. An injured washout.

"Your phone's going nuts. Do you need to answer it?"

I give my head a quick shake. "It's just the family chat."

Her hands still for a second and I hear her suck in a quiet breath. "Must be nice to be home and surrounded by everyone who loves you." There's a hint of wistfulness in her words that makes me pause before grunting out a reply.

"I guess."

Lily switches back to using her hands, pressing in on different tight spots and wiggling her thumb around, alternating that with pinching my fascia and twisting slightly to get it to release. Uncomfortable is an understatement. But that's nothing compared to when she drifts her hand up higher, getting close to the crease where my leg meets my butt.

"Is this okay?" she asks, her tone carefully void of anything but professionalism. I nod and she continues, pressing into various places at the top of my leg and on the side of my glute. My goddamn IT band is tight as hell, and she's finding all the places to work it out.

All the while, my phone is buzzing away. I glance at it, and yeah, it's still just the family chat. It's exhausting trying to keep up with all of it, so I tend to ignore it a lot.

"Are you sure you don't need to check your phone?"

"Yeah. It's fine."

Her hands keep working, keep torturing, and I keep fighting back my grunts of pain. It's pathetic that her thumb digging into a pressure point on my ass is the most action I've had in a while, since before the injury, at least. A depressing thought occurs to me that it's probably the most action I'm gonna have for a long fucking time.

"Your family cares about you, Jude. They're worried."

Her voice is soft, hesitant, as if she knows that comment crosses the line outside of our professional relationship. But Lily is more than just my physical therapist. She's basically an extension of my family. I know that and she knows that. And that's probably the only reason she's saying anything right now.

"I know they are. But it's a lot to adjust to. Being here. Having them all around."

Lily's hands lift off my leg and she takes a step back. I shift so I can look at her, and there's a grin on her face.

"My God, Jude, that's the most words you've ever said to me at one time," she teases. She steps forward again, and her hands return to teasing out the scar tissue in my leg.

A low groan escapes me as she pushes in and around a particularly bad spot. "Yeah, well, if it distracts you from doling out this torture, I'll talk more."

Her laughter is light and easy, and I feel my lips twitch in response. Apparently, the one thing that will almost make me smile is Lily Chapman's laugh.

That's...interesting.

CHAPTER NINE

Lily

"This is fine. Totally fine. Not inappropriate at all," I keep whispering to myself the entire drive from my tiny bungalow to the apartment building Jude is living in. The only problem is, I don't completely believe what I'm saying.

It *is* crossing a line to show up at my patient's house on a day when we don't have therapy. The grey area is that Jude and I have a history. He's more than just a patient, he's a friend — sort of. I'm just hoping he sees it that way and doesn't get too mad at me.

It's been almost two weeks since I started working with Jude and he's made great progress. He can walk without the crutches for short distances, using a cane for stability when he needs it. But his pain control is inconsistent at best. And Kat told me over beers and nachos at Hastings that he isn't leaving his apartment except for our appointments and when his siblings drag him out for family dinners. She's worried; they all are.

The thing is, I don't think Jude is depressed or anything. I think he's just caught up in his own head, trying to process the major change to his life and career he's currently facing. Sure, he's got some unhealthy coping mechanisms, but he hasn't come in hungover since I called him out on it last week. He still hasn't cracked a smile, but Jude was never a smiley kinda guy. He's always been a little grumpy and a lot quiet. This version of him just has an added dark cloud of stress hanging around.

But that's why I'm here today. I love having a weekday off; it lets me get a ton of stuff done during the week instead of having to do it all on Sunday. I should be working today since I'm not working Saturday due to the impending nightmare of Marnie and Clay's wedding. But instead of swapping days, I decided to use a vacation day for Saturday. And having a weekday off is also letting me do this — try to get Jude out of his house and out of his head for a while.

I knock on his door and take a step back, trying not to fidget too much as I wait for him to open up. When he does, my dang heart skips a beat. He's got this rumpled, scruffy, just woke up look going on that is scrumptious. Add in the grey sweatpants that hang low and leave little to the imagination about what's going on underneath, and I suddenly feel overly warm.

"What are you doing here?" he asks, his voice rough. I almost question if he just woke up, but it's after noon already.

"Hi Jude, nice to see you," I say cheerfully, ignoring his question. "It's a beautiful day outside and I felt like going for a walk. And you're going to join me."

He leans against the doorframe, shifting weight off his bad leg, the therapist in me notes. His rich brown eyes are studying me intently, a small frown line furrowing his brow. "We don't have an appointment today, Lily."

Here goes nothing. "I know we don't. But I'm more than just your physical therapist, I'm also your friend. Or, well, sort of. I mean, I'm your sister's friend, so I just thought maybe you'd be open to hanging out. We can call it a free bonus session if you want. But it's not healthy for you to just hole up here all day and not move, so here I am."

I spread my hands wide, trying to hide my nerves as I smile at him. In retrospect, I know it looks crazy, me just showing up here randomly. He has every right to shut the door on my face. But I'm really hoping he doesn't.

I like Jude. I mean, more than just being physically attracted to him, I like him. He's shown me little sneak peeks of the man he used to be, with a dry wit that delivers one-liners like nobody's business. They're few and far between, and often at my expense, whether he's teasing me about dancing with my patients or commenting on my terrible attempts at jokes. Either way, I have a sneaky suspicion he's letting me in more than he's letting anyone else in right now.

And that gives me all sorts of warm fuzzies. And makes me more determined than ever to help this man get back to who he was.

"I'm not holed up here *every* day, I come to see you and I go to family dinner."

His deadpan response snaps me out of my rambling thoughts. My hands find my hips as I arch my brow at him. "Leaving this apartment four times a week to see me and once a week to see your family is not enough. Get your shoes, we're going for a walk."

To my utter shock, Jude doesn't argue. I watch as he turns around and slowly makes his way into the apartment. My clinical eye assesses his movements, noticing where he's stiff and where he's weak.

My not so clinical eye notices how his ass looks when he bends over to pick up his shoes. *God bless hockey butts.* And the way his muscular torso fills out the T-shirt he's wearing before he covers it up with a hoodie. He grabs a baseball hat and pushes it on his head, grabs his keys, and turns back to me.

"Okay. Let's go."

My heart is thumping wildly as Jude follows me into the elevator that suddenly feels way too small. I'm consumed by all my senses registering his presence all at once. The fresh, clean smell of him — not a hint of alcohol anywhere. The sound of his deep breaths. The sight of his large body leaning against the wall, looking a lot more casual and relaxed than I'm feeling.

A few minutes later, we emerge from his building onto the sidewalk, and I blink against the bright sunlight. One of my favourite things about Dogwood Cove is how close we are to the ocean. A fifteen-minute walk or a three-minute drive puts us at the beach where there's a gravel path that winds along the edge of the water. Unfortunately, Jude's leg is not ready for any sort of unstable ground, so we'll just wander around town.

"If you think you can make it all the way to The Nutty Muffin, coffee is on me."

Jude doesn't answer, just inclines his head, and starts walking slowly in the direction of the main square of the town.

"How are you finding the cane? Helpful or a nuisance?" I ask after a couple minutes of silence. I don't exactly want this to feel like a physical therapy session, but at the same time, if he's going to be his usual not talkative self, I'll have to say something.

"It's fine. Wish I didn't need it."

"I understand. Well, I don't, but I can guess. You won't need it for long, you're making great progress."

All I get is a nod.

We turn the corner onto another residential street, and a smile comes to my face. I love these days when the weather is crisp but clear.

Jude is still not talking, so I continue to fill the silence rambling about various things that pop into my head. All I get in reply are random grunts of acknowledgment. I keep an eye on him, making sure he's not fatiguing, but of course, he isn't. The man is a pro athlete, he's got stamina.

We make the final turn onto Main Street, and The Nutty Muffin is just ahead. At that moment, Jude's cane catches on something, and he stumbles. I automatically reach out and grab his arm, supporting him.

"Thanks," he says in a low voice.

"Of course. Wouldn't look good if I let you get hurt when I'm with you, now would it?" I say, feeling a teeny-tiny bit breathless as my body registers the fact that I'm pressed up against his side and he's not pulling away. He might not realize he's leaning on me, but I sure as heck do.

"Lilian?"

"Oh shit," I swear under my breath as the nasally voice of my cousin hits my ears. Jude looks down at me, probably surprised to hear me curse. "Look, Jude, whatever is about to happen, I'm sorry."

I don't know why I say that, but I do. Jude hasn't had the privilege of meeting my family, so he has no idea what he's in for. Sure enough, when I look across the street, there she is. Dressed in one of her uniforms, at least that's what I call the pantsuits Marnie prefers to wear. To be fair, it's what the family business expects of its employees, and Marnie is nothing if not the perfect Chapman employee.

"Hi," I say, hoping she doesn't stick around. But luck is not on my side. She crosses over and stands in front of Jude and I, her beady eyes taking in everything. It's then I realize I'm still clutching his arm.

Shit. I drop it like a hot potato and put some space between us.

"I'm glad I ran into you, actually," Marnie starts, her perfectly manicured hand tucking an invisible strand of hair behind her ear. "You haven't been answering my emails, which is quite inconsiderate of you. After all, I'm sure you can imagine how busy this week is for my family and I, with all the last-minute wedding plans."

Sure. *Her* family. As if they aren't also *my* family. Not that it matters, considering that for the last two months all anyone — my parents included — can seem to talk about is Marnie's wedding.

I might as well not exist.

Oh wait, that's basically my life in a nutshell.

Marnie is still talking, or should I say berating, as usual. "I don't know why you won't show me the dress you're planning on wearing. I truly don't think it's too much to ask that I be able to approve it. After all, Lilian, it's not like your fashion choices are always appropriate. It needs to be suitable, and not a shade of red. The last thing we need is for you to clash with my bridesmaids or look out of place in photos."

If I could mentally roll my eyes, I would. Instead, I keep my gaze steady, refusing to look at Jude and risk seeing his horror at my self-absorbed, superficial bitch of a cousin in all her glory.

"It's not red, Marnie."

She huffs, folding her arms across her chest. "Fine. And your date is aware it's black tie?" Marnie turns her stare to Jude. "That means a tuxedo. Black, no colours."

Oh my God. Oh hell, she thinks Jude is my date?

"Oh, he's not —"

"Yes, of course. My Armani tux is clean and ready to go." Jude's gravelly voice shocks the crap out of me, and my mouth falls open.

Marnie sniffs, her nose up in the air, looking every bit the pretentious snob she is. "Good. Well. I suppose I'll see you at the rehearsal dinner. That will require semiformal apparel, Lilian. I hope you have something appropriate."

"Actually, no, I won't be there," I interject, feeling the tiniest bit of relief that I only have to survive one day of wedding drama. "I have to work, so I'm not coming down until Saturday."

Marnie lets out a sigh that is so laden with judgment and criticism, it's a miracle she can hold herself up under the weight. I'm not sure why, it's not as if she wants me there any more than I want to be there. We're both well aware I'm only going to keep up appearances.

"Fine. Saturday. Don't be late."

She turns and walks back across the street without another word. I'm left standing there frozen, completely floored by what just transpired. I turn, eyes wide, to look at Jude.

"What the heck did you just do?" I whisper.

He pulls his gaze away from where Marnie has walked away, back to me. "I have no idea. But based on what I just experienced, I'm guessing you need a date to that bitch's wedding, and I just volunteered."

I choke back a hysterical laugh. "Um, yeah, that bitch is my cousin. You just claimed to be my date for her circus of a wedding this weekend in Vancouver."

He's silent for a moment, staring at me contemplatively. Meanwhile, my wheels are turning, trying to figure out how I can extricate him from this mess without it coming back to bite me in the ass.

"Don't worry. I'll tell them something came up and you can't go." My hands flap in the air erratically.

"Why?"

Once again, my mouth falls open in shock. "Why?" My voice starts to rise as my stress and panic increases. "*Why?* Because my family is insane and there's not a chance in hell I'd subject you to them for forty-eight hours. No one needs to be tortured but me."

"Your entire family is like that?" he asks, surprise colouring his tone.

"Pretty much." I reply. "It's fine. I can handle them. I appreciate you trying to help or whatever you thought you were doing, but trust me, you don't want to do this."

"What if I do?"

I shake my head emphatically. "Jude, you don't know what you're saying."

"If they're as bad as you say, why should you face them alone? Your cousin seemed set on you having a date, so I'll go."

He makes it sound so simple, but it's anything but. Still, the idea of having someone there with me, someone by my side to help me face the madness, is tempting. But fast on the heels of that comes a new wave of dread.

What's Jude going to think of me after he sees the full force of my family's contempt for me? Worse yet, what's he going to think once he realizes my cousin is marrying my ex-boyfriend?

"You don't have to," I say, but he just starts to walk away, leaving me to chase after him. "Jude, seriously."

He stops again, so abruptly I almost run into his back. "Lily, you said it yourself. We're friends, sort of. You're helping me, so let me help you."

After hesitating a moment longer, I blurt out, "I have a room booked, but I'll get a second one." Holy crap, am I really agreeing to his crazy offer to go to the wedding with me?

Jude just nods, and then continues walking toward the café. When I don't follow right away, he pauses and turns his head over his shoulder. "Are you coming? I was promised coffee."

I hurry after him, fighting back a smile that is finally breaking free.

Jude Donnelly is going to be my date for the wedding from hell, and I'm willing to bet he looks a heck of a lot better in a suit than the groom.

CHAPTER TEN

Lily

Any confidence I felt about having Jude go with me to the wedding has disappeared. If I didn't want to ruin the manicure Kat insisted I get, my nails would be bitten down to the cuticle by now.

I've checked and rechecked my bag, changing things like my choice of pajamas about four times. Why? No idea. It's not as if Jude and I will be sharing a room. He's escorting me to the ceremony and the reception, and I fully intend on letting him disappear as soon as possible. There's no point in both of us suffering through hours of tense drama.

The only amusing part in all of this was witnessing Kat's reaction when I told her Jude was coming with me.

"My Jude? My grumpy older brother who won't do more than grunt at any of us? That Jude offered to go to the bitch's wedding?"

Her jaw fell open and I giggled as I pushed it closed with my finger. "Yeah, I was surprised, too. I gave him every opportunity to bow out, but he insisted on coming."

Kat shook her head. "Wow, I know I asked you to try and get through to him, but I didn't expect this." Her face grew serious. "I think getting out of town for a bit will help. I know it's only been a few weeks since he came back, but I can tell he's feeling kind of smothered by us all."

Her intuition was correct, but I wasn't about to say that. Not when my bestie was obviously hurting over watching her brother suffer. Instead, I just pulled her in for a hug. "He'll be okay."

At the time, I meant it. And I guess I still do. Jude will be okay, it's me I'm worried about. I have to keep my cool, not only around my family, but also around my best friend's older brother, who I may or may not still be crushing on.

When I pull up to his apartment building, Jude's waiting outside just as he said he would be. His cane and a small suitcase sit at his feet, and a suit bag is draped over the suitcase. I indulge myself for a minute while his head is down, focused on something on his phone.

His dark brown hair is that perfect blend of messy yet stylish, and it looks freshly trimmed. The fact that he went to the effort of getting a haircut before this weekend seems insignificant yet says a lot to me about Jude. He's taking this seriously — helping me, that is. He might think all he's doing is attending a wedding, but the truth is, he's saving me from facing my demons alone. The combination of pity on some people's faces and smug condescension on others that I'm sure I'll experience this weekend has had my stomach in knots for weeks. But the knot loosened just a tiny bit that day on the sidewalk when Jude offered to come with me.

Several hours later, we reach the hotel in downtown Vancouver where Marnie and Clay are holding the ceremony and reception. It's swanky, that's for damn sure. But every Devereaux hotel is. I vaguely remember Kat's boss Mila telling a story about how Cole Devereaux, the CEO, tried to buy Oceanside Resort to convert it into some fancy beachfront complex. But her best friend and sister-in-law Summer, who had inherited the place from her dad, refused. Now Oceanside is a chill, fun place that is always packed with families all summer.

We reach the front desk, and I give my name.

"I called earlier this week to add a second room to the reservation, were you able to get them on the same floor?" I ask politely. Not that it really matters where our rooms are, but for convenience, I'm hoping we're close by.

The clerk stares at their computer screen for what seems like too long, then looks at me apologetically. "I'm so sorry, Miss Chapman, but it seems there was an error in processing that request. I don't see a second room added to your reservation."

"Oh, okay," I say. "Well, can you just add one now?"

The clerk's frown deepens. "Unfortunately, no. We're fully booked tonight. Not only do we have the Chapman wedding, but we also have a convention in town that booked the rest of our rooms. I do apologize for the inconvenience, but we only have your original booking available."

My original booking was for a single queen room. The cheapest option since I'm footing the bill for myself. I feel the heat start to rise from my chest. "You're sure you have nothing else?" My voice is sounding shrill even to my ears. Just then, a warm hand lands on my upper back.

"It's fine. Thank you." He takes the key from the clerk and guides us toward the elevator.

"Jude, I'm so sorry. I honestly did call and try to get a second room. This is embarrassing. I can find somewhere else to stay. Maybe with my parents or something."

I'm babbling and panicking but honestly, this couldn't get any worse. How the heck are we meant to share a room with only one bed?

The elevator doors close on us, and Jude turns to me, placing his hands on my shoulders. He looks so calm, so at ease. I have no clue how or why.

"Lily, it's fine. Breathe for me, okay?"

I nod rapidly.

His lips start to almost turn up but then they stop. "I mean it. Deep breaths."

I force air out of my lungs and drag in a deep breath.

"That's better. Now. We're both adults here, we can figure this out. Right?"

"How are you so calm?" I blurt out. He lifts his shoulders and lets them fall again.

"In the grand scheme of things, a hotel room doesn't seem worth freaking out over."

I arch a brow at him. "Are you still going to think that when I tell you I booked a room with only one bed?"

I don't intend to insinuate anything with my words, but holy hell. Jude's eyes darken and his voice goes impossibly deep.

"Like I said, we're adults. We can figure it out."

A shiver runs down my spine as an image of Jude stretched out next to me in bed — or better yet, tangled in the sheets with me in bed — runs through my mind.

The elevator chooses that second to open on our floor and the crackling tension is broken. We make our way down the hall in silence, and Jude slides the key card in and opens the door.

I step inside and gulp. The room is small. There's only one bed. And as Jude steps up behind me, the very feeling of him fills the space completely.

"Right, so, I'll just, uh, go into the bathroom to get ready. Unless you need to use it."

Good grief, my voice sounds shrill even to my own ears. Granted, I sort of feel that way right now as well. Completely unhinged and like I have zero control over anything right now. I don't like it.

I dash into the bathroom, which is, thankfully, a decent size. Leaning against the counter, I force three slow breaths in and out, willing my heart to slow down and my mind to settle.

"You can do this, Lily Chapman," I whisper to my reflection. With one final nod, I turn and unzip my suitcase, removing my dress, makeup bag, and hair products. Everything gets laid out, and then it's go time.

Less than an hour later, and with just thirty minutes before the ceremony is due to start, I open the bathroom door cautiously.

"Jude? Is it okay for me to come out?"

"Yep."

I step out, my heels dangling from my hand. No sense in putting them on until I have to. "You can use the bathroom now." My words die out as I take in the sight of Jude stretched out on the bed. He's every woman's fantasy come to life, in perfectly pressed black pants and a crisp white shirt with a bow tie hanging untied around his neck.

He glances up from his phone and it falls from his hand. "Lily. Wow."

A smile spreads across my face at his reaction. Slowly, I approach him and turn around. "Could you help me with the zipper?"

I hear his sharp intake of breath and my small smile grows. It's empowering, his obviously appreciative reaction. I'm not fool enough to think it means anything, but what woman doesn't enjoy making a handsome man drool with nothing more than some eyeliner and a sexy dress?

I hear him slowly stand up, and then his warm hands are on my back, lightly grazing over me as he pulls the zipper up.

"Thanks," I murmur, stepping forward and looking over my shoulder at him. "We should go. Do you need your cane?"

He shakes his head slowly, and although the therapist in me wants to object, I can see by the firm set to his face that he's determined not to show weakness tonight. I'll just keep an eye on him and make sure he doesn't push himself too much.

We slowly make our way downstairs to the room that is set for the ceremony. I do my best to ignore the curious looks that get thrown my way, my eyes searching out the one person I want to see today.

"Come on, I see my grandmother," I say, taking Jude's hand and leading him over to Nana, who's sitting in the second row fanning herself lightly with the gold embossed program for the wedding.

"Hi, Nana," I say, leaning down to press a kiss to her cheek.

"My darling. You're here."

She looks up at us with a big smile that grows even bigger when she takes in Jude. It's at that moment I realize I'm still holding his hand. But strangely, when I loosen my grip, he doesn't do the same.

"And who's this fine young man with you, Lily?" Nana looks from me to Jude and back again, her eyes twinkling.

"Hello, ma'am, I'm Jude Donnelly, a friend of your granddaughter. It's a pleasure to meet you." Jude holds out his free hand and shakes Nana's in return. I'm too busy staring at him, shocked by the fact that he did more than just grunt out a single word to a complete stranger, to realize the room is filling up around us. That is, until my mother taps me on the shoulder with her sharp fingernails. Her eyes rake up and down my body, those lips thinning with disapproval. But for once, Marnie comes to my rescue, in a way, because I'm saved from

Mom's criticism by someone announcing that the ceremony is starting.

"Take your seat, Lilian," She bites out.

I drop Jude's hand and this time he lets go as we slowly lower ourselves into the seats next to my grandmother, Jude being on the outside, so he can stretch his knee. The imprint of his knee brace presses against the fabric of his pants, making the therapist in me happy that he's at least got that support. A string quartet starts up, but I still hear Nana when she leans over and whispers in my ear.

"He's a good one, my darling, I can tell."

Before I can say anything in return and clarify my relationship status with Jude, or heck, ask her how she knows that after just meeting him, the music dies down, then starts up with the unmistakable sound of the wedding march.

Here we go.

My ex-boyfriend is now officially my cousin-in-law. There's a weird statement.

I tell Jude to stay seated as I escort Nana and follow the bridal party and my immediate family over to where Marnie and Clay want to do photos. The bridesmaids are less than subtle with their open stares and whispers behind their bouquets. I know they're talking about me.

But there's nothing I can do about it except try to keep my head held high. As soon as I can escape, I make my way back to Jude as Marnie, Clay, and the wedding party head outside for some more photos.

"Do you need to go with them?" Jude asks when I reach his chair.

I just wave my hand in dismissal. As if Marnie would want me anywhere near her wedding photos. "I did the obligatory family pose. I won't be needed for anymore."

"But you're her cousin. Doesn't that matter?"

I let out a light huff of derisive laughter. "Barely."

His eyes are inscrutable as he stares at me. "Then let's find a drink." Jude offers me his elbow and I take it gratefully.

"That's a genius idea."

We make our way slowly into the ballroom where guests are milling around high-top tables, sipping champagne. Waitstaff are walking around with silver trays that probably hold some disgustingly fancy hors d'oeuvres. Even though my stomach is growling, you won't find me eating caviar.

"I'd kill for a burger and a beer right now. What are the chances of finding one here?" Jude mutters under his breath.

"Slim to none, I'm afraid. But if you like champagne and caviar, you're in luck."

The look of horror Jude gives me brings some much needed relief to the tension building inside of me ever since we first set foot in the hotel.

"Don't worry. If you can manage to last through cocktail hour, you can leave after that. I'll tell them your leg was starting to bother you." I pat his arm comfortingly, but Jude just shakes his head.

"I'm good." He looks over to the bar. "But how about I get our drinks."

I nod in agreement and reluctantly remove my arm from his. It might have been for show, and a way for him to get out of using a cane, but it felt good to be close to him like that.

Really good.

As Jude joins the line up, my eyes can't seem to leave him. Somehow, his presence has made this day bearable — far more bearable than I expected it to be. Even the judgmental comments and open stares that make me feel like a ticking time bomb everyone is waiting to witness explode haven't hit as hard as they normally do.

"I have to admit, Lilian, I'm impressed."

I flinch at Clay's snide voice. Apparently, photos didn't take very long.

I honestly don't remember him being such a jerk when we were together. Slowly, I turn to see his condescending stare boring into me.

"Marnie and I honestly thought you'd either make a scene or simply not show up. You had her very stressed out if you must know."

I try not to show how uncomfortable I am around him. For the life of me, I cannot see what I ever was attracted to in Clay.

Or maybe, he's just changed that much since being snared by Marnie.

"I wouldn't do that, Clay. Contrary to what you might have been told about me, I don't intentionally set out to upset my family," I say stiffly. I hate that I feel the need to defend myself to this man.

"I'm not so sure about that."

My mouth falls open at his caustic reply. "What did I ever do to you, Clay? Why do you feel you have the right to hurt me more than you already have?" I fold my arms around myself, fighting back tears. He's not worth my tears anymore.

"Oh stop it, Lilian. See? Here you are, starting a scene. Just get over it. Get over me. You were fun, but you were never the girl I was going to end up with."

After all this time, you'd think those words wouldn't hurt. But maybe it's the fact that I'm stuck here at his wedding to my cousin, or maybe it's the fact that my own family has clearly poisoned him against me, or maybe it's the fact that he's echoing a sentiment I've felt from many men.

I'm the good-time girl, not the long-term girl.

Chapter Eleven

Jude

This has been a shit show from start to finish. How did I never realize Lily's family were pretentious monsters? I get that there's an eight-year age gap between us, but still. I've watched her brightness slowly dull over the last couple of hours with every snide comment or critical look.

At least now it makes sense that she was always at our house growing up and Kat never seemed to go over to hers. My protective older brother instinct rears up at the thought of Kat being around these people. Interestingly enough, there's a similar instinct inside of me that is desperate to defend Lily. But it's definitely not brotherly in nature.

Her own mother didn't even have a nice thing to say about how beautiful she looks. Instead, after the long drawn out ceremony, she turned to Lily and hissed, legit hissed like a snake, and tugged at the dark purple section of Lily's hair that was just barely visible underneath the half up hairdo she'd managed to achieve. I thought the subtle pop of colour was unique and perfectly Lily, but apparently, her mom disagrees.

These people who claim to be her family seem determined to crush her spirit. And it's really starting to piss me off.

It's not only her family, either. I don't think I'm imagining the weird curious looks Lily keeps getting thrown her way. She doesn't seem to notice them, but I sure as hell do.

"I'm just surprised she even came. I don't think I could've done it."

"Oh, me either. Going to an ex-boyfriend's wedding would be bad enough, but when your ex is marrying your cousin? Talk about embarrassing."

Wait. Who the fuck are they talking about?

My head whips around to find the source of those horrifying words. Dread mixes with rage in my stomach. If they're saying what I think they're saying, Lily's a better person than I thought. And has faced more bullshit than I realized.

Someone bumps into me, and I wince as it throws me off-balance, making me put too much weight on my bad leg. Damn it, I should've brought the fucking cane.

"Oops, sorry." The woman, who I recognize as a bridesmaid, giggles. She's the one who said the ex-boyfriend thing. Her eyes rake up and down my body in a way I've come to recognize as a clear indicator that she knows who I am. But there's not a chance in hell I'm letting her near me.

I take a step back just in time for the bartender to deposit my drinks in front of me. I slide a tip into the glass jar, pick them up with a nod of thanks, then limp straight back to where I left Lily. Only she isn't alone anymore.

Fuck. Her cousin, and the douchebag who I now know is Lily's ex, are standing in front of her. And beautiful, bright, happy Lily has almost folded in on herself.

I set the drinks down on the table next to her, and without thinking twice about it, slide my arm around her waist and tug her into my side, shifting my weight mostly onto my good leg. My head tips down and my lips find the top of her head.

"Hey, sunshine."

I feel her tense up, but then relax underneath my arm. Turning my head slightly, so I'm facing away from the others, I whisper in her ear. "Breathe."

Then, I school my expression to one of complete indifference. A useful tactic I honed over years of facing down annoying interviewers, puck bunnies, and ruthless sportscasters. It's a face that says *I don't give a flying fuck who you are or what you're saying, but I'm not gonna be rude about it.*

"Hi. Jude Donnelly." I hold out my hand and accept the limp and pathetic handshake Lily's ex gives in return.

"Clay Townsend."

Turning to Lily's cousin without giving the douchebag a second more of my time, I incline my head. "Marnie. Nice wedding."

Her face looks pinched. I'm guessing she's used to people piling on the praise, but that's not my style. Unfortunately, this bitch has her claws out and ready to sink into the woman at my side.

"I have to admit, I'm surprised to see you here. I wasn't entirely certain you were serious the other day when you said you were coming. Still, it was nice of you to come and help poor Lilian save face tonight. We try not to mention her brief connection to my husband, but people love to gossip." She lays her hand on Clay's chest possessively but without any affection. There's clearly not a lot of love between those two. Not genuine love, at least, not if the fact that his eyes are scanning the crowd, his attention more on the drink in his hand than his new bride.

But Marnie's cruel words hit their intended target dead-on. I feel Lily push back against my hand as if trying to escape.

Fuck that.

I look her evil cousin straight in the eye. "Any chance to be with Lily is an honour. I consider myself one lucky man that she chooses to be with me. How any guy could ever let her go is beyond my comprehension. I mean, I've never met anyone as beautiful, kind, intelligent, or just damn good-hearted as Lily. She outshines anyone around her, no matter the occasion."

Am I being blunt and yet obtuse at the same time? Damn straight. Do I care that what I'm saying is a thinly veiled insult to the fucking bride? Hell no.

Because the instant I feel Lily's arm wrap around my torso and her fingers squeeze my side, I know I've done the right thing.

"C'mon sunshine, let's dance."

I gently guide Lily away, abandoning our drinks and the horrible people she has to call family. It's hard to mask my limp, but I push away the pain and do it anyway. Leading her out onto the dance floor, I turn her in my arms and lift hers up to wrap around my neck. "I can't do more than sway, but dance with me."

Her big grey eyes look up at mine, and I hate that I see tears shining in them. "Thank you."

I pull her in close, tucking her head under my chin. "I've got you," I say gruffly.

We stand there swaying for a few minutes until the song ends. My knee is throbbing, but the pain is worth it right now. But eventually, despite every part of me not wanting to, I make myself step back, not thinking about *why* exactly I don't want to.

"Let's get outta here," I say in a low voice. "I don't have an appetite for pretentious bullshit anymore; we can order room service instead. Unless they're gonna miss you at dinner?" I give her the option, knowing if she chooses to stay, I'll stay with her. Not a chance in hell I'm leaving her alone with these wolves.

Lily shakes her head vehemently. "I'm done. If my leaving gives them more to talk about, who the heck cares anymore."

I take her hand. "Yeah, you're gonna have to fill in some details for me, because *what the fuck*."

I watch her shoulders lift and drop as Lily takes in a big sigh. "That requires booze."

I give a crisp nod and lead her over to the end of the bar. Flagging down a bartender, I lean over, whisper my request, and slide a couple of bills across to him. His eyebrows raise, but I see the second he realizes who I am, and thankfully, that's enough to get me what I want.

Moments later, an unopened bottle of tequila in hand, Lily and I make our way to the elevators. As soon as the doors slide closed, she reaches down and pulls off her shoes with a sigh of relief.

"Let me know what I owe you for the booze."

I frown at her. "Excuse me?"

Her eyes open and she stares at me. "I saw you pass the bartender cash to get that bottle from the open bar. I'm all for making Marnie and Clay pay for it, but you can at least let me split the tip you gave him to score an unopened bottle."

I scoff. "Not a chance."

The elevator opens and I take off down the hall as fast as my bum leg will let me go, which admittedly, isn't very fast at all. Thankfully, our room isn't far, and pretty soon I've unlocked the door and can finally sit down.

Unfortunately, I can't hold back the grunt of pain when I do so. Lily's face is wreathed in worry as she hurries over to me.

"Crap, you spent way too long standing and walking, and not in supportive shoes. I'm so sorry, Jude." She starts to fuss with my leg, but I bat her away.

"Go. Change out of that sexy dress and put something comfortable on. I'm gonna get room service to bring up some ice and food. My leg will be fine."

Her eyes flare when I call her dress sexy. I crossed a line tonight, pretending we were something we're not. But it got her out of a bad situation, and hopefully, helped her feel less alone, so I don't regret it for a second. The problem is, crossing that line has opened my eyes to the truth.

It's not just Lily's dress that's sexy.

It's her.

I loosen and remove my tie, tossing it and my suit jacket over the chair in the corner of the room. My shirt follows, leaving me in just a white T-shirt and my pants. I could get up and grab some sweats from my suitcase, but that requires standing, and despite what I told Lily, my leg is definitely not fine right now. If I wasn't such a stubborn idiot, I would have brought some painkillers with me, but of course, I didn't.

Hopefully tequila numbs it a bit.

I pick up the phone and place an order with room service, hanging up just as the bathroom door opens and Lily walks out, wearing what I assume are her pajamas. Except she's obviously not wearing a bra under the tank top, and the sliver of skin where her tank top doesn't quite meet the top of her pants is teasing me, begging to be touched.

Shit. No. The line might have been crossed when I kissed her head earlier, but that doesn't mean I have any right to her. Or that she'd have any interest in me.

Still, my eyes follow her as she pads over to the other side of the bed and gingerly sits down on the edge. She tosses me a bottle of pills, and when I realize she brought me some painkillers, the wall around my heart cracks just a little.

"Thanks," I say gruffly, then hold out the bottle. "Ice isn't here yet, but want to get started?"

She takes it but doesn't open it right away. "It's not a nice story, Jude."

I exhale slowly. "I kind of assumed that. Okay, new plan. We eat, we drink, we fall asleep, and then we get the hell away from here in the morning."

Lily doesn't answer right away. Then, I watch her open the tequila, lift the bottle to her lips, and take a long sip. Damn if that isn't a sexy sight.

She lowers the bottle and wipes her hand across her lips daintily before looking me in the eye.

"Clay was my boyfriend, I introduced him to Marnie, he chose her over me, now they're married. Oh, and my entire family thinks I'm a useless fuckup. End of story. Now, drink up."

I'm not a man of many words at the best of times, but right now I'm at a complete loss for them. I suspected what she just told me was the case, but hearing her lay it out like that, hearing her try to remain emotionless but with pain running through her words, nonetheless — I'm speechless.

A knock on the door has Lily springing off the bed as if she needs to get away from the baggage she just unloaded. I let her usher in the hotel staff who is delivering our food, and I still say nothing when Lily reaches into her wallet for a tip. I'll deal with that later.

After locking the door behind the server, I watch her walk swiftly back over to the other side of the bed.

"What was that plan? Eat, drink, sleep, then go home?" Lily lifts one of the silver domes off the plates of food. "I'm good with that idea."

She lifts a burger up to her mouth and takes a big bite. Even after she sets the food down and starts putting ice into the plastic bag I requested from room service for my knee, she still won't look at me, her eyes going everywhere around the room but in my direction.

"Lily."

Slowly, her gaze shifts toward me.

"Lily, he's a dumbass who didn't deserve you, and your family is wrong. Dead wrong."

I hand her the tequila, taking the makeshift ice pack from her in return. But when I try to get it to lay on my leg, it keeps sliding off.

A quiet huff of laughter has me glancing up at Lily, who to my relief has a tiny smile on her face. She goes to the bathroom, returning with a large bath towel.

Gesturing to my leg, she asks, "May I?"

I lift my hands off. "By all means, you're the expert."

She quickly wraps the ice pack in the towel, then wraps the entire thing around my leg, using the ends of the towel to secure it.

"Thanks," I say as she finally sits back down beside me.

"I feel like I should be thanking you." She starts to pick at the label of the bottle. "What you said down there and just now. Thank you." When her eyes meet mine, the pain and tension is almost gone, even though her usual sparkle hasn't returned. "You made this day a lot easier to get through."

I shift slightly so I can look at her. I'm starting to wonder if Lily's cheerful, outgoing personality is truly her, or if it's a front she uses to hide all of this mess.

And on the heels of that thought comes another. Does she have anyone in her life who's on her side? Who knows just how bad it is with her family and is willing to be there for her and remind her they're wrong?

I need to talk to my sister when we get home. She's the one person I can think of who might be able to shed some light on things. And I need to know, I need to understand.

For the first time since my injury, I'm focused on something other than hockey and the likely end of my career.

Because Lily Chapman is everything I said she was when we were in front of her cousin and more. But she's also vulnerable. And while I might not have the first clue what to do about it, I can't deny the truth that's settled in me.

I want to protect her. I want to show her she's not alone.

CHAPTER TWELVE

Jude

The sound of very light snoring is the first thing that registers as I blink my eyes open. The second thing is the warm weight of a body draped over top of me.

It takes a second for me to remember *why* I'm not alone in bed. And then, since apparently this morning is the morning for all the surprises, I realize I don't remember being awake most of the night.

I slept.

For the first time in God knows how long, I actually slept soundly through the night. And the only difference between last night and countless others is the woman in bed with me.

Slowly, I lift my hand up to stroke back her hair. She's tucked into my side, her head on my shoulder, her leg draped over my good one, and a curtain of dark hair is tickling my bare chest.

I'm not surprised to wake up shirtless, but a quick check reassures me I didn't also take off my sweats. That's a relief, seeing as most nights I end up naked, thanks to a tendency to overheat. It's going to be weird enough for Lily to wake up and realize she cuddled me all night like a koala bear, I can't imagine how she would handle it if I was in the buff.

I like this. Waking up with Lily. Feeling her in my arms. And it's not just because she's a woman, or that any warm body would do — it's her.

I'm drawn to her warmth and light, like a moth to a flame. There's a familiarity there, sure. I've known her most of my life. But it's different, too. That protective feeling stirring inside of me has nothing to do with her being Kat's best friend, and everything to do with her being an incredible woman who makes me feel better, simply by being nearby.

For the first time since my accident, I feel calm. At peace. Dare I say content.

My lips brush over the top of her head, the floral scent of her shampoo filling my senses. It's no more than what I did last night, kissing her hair in front of her cousin. But in the morning quiet, with our limbs tangled together, it feels far more intimate.

She lets out a soft sigh and rubs against me, stirring my already half-mast dick. Morning wood hasn't been an issue for a while, but it sure as shit is today. I try to shift away, but koala-Lily just pulls in closer.

I'll blame it on not being fully awake. That's the only reason why I kiss her again, this time on her forehead. And when her head tips up, inviting me to explore, I do. My lips trail across her skin, covering every inch of her face except her rosebud mouth, her small sounds of arousal and her hands moving over my bare torso are all the permission my semiconscious brain needs.

A part of me knows I probably shouldn't be doing this. *We* shouldn't be doing this. But I don't want to listen to reason right now.

"Jude," she murmurs, raking her fingers through my hair, then down my arms. "Kiss me."

Our lips come together instantly. I'm awake now, all parts of me, completely. There's no denying what's happening.

I'm kissing Lily Chapman.

It feels as if every single nerve ending is suddenly waking up after being asleep for months. Our lips fit together perfectly, and when her tongue traces the seam of my mouth, I open instantly, dancing with her. Normally, I'd take control of a kiss, but I'm surprisingly content to let this be balanced between us. To just explore her and let her explore me.

Sure, there's a small part of me that wonders if we should be doing this, but that voice is easy to silence.

Her eyes blink open to meet mine, and we pause ever so briefly. Then she presses back into me, shifting her body until she's straddling me. My hands find her firm ass, squeezing the flesh, pushing her down so my hard cock is trapped between us. When her hips move, grinding ever so slowly into me, I groan into our kiss, and the little minx does it again.

When she starts to rub her body up and down my length, even separated by our clothes, I feel it like a bolt of electricity straight to my core. Our kisses turn messy, desperate, even. We're on borrowed time and we know it.

Sure enough, just as my hands start to gently pull up her tank top, the hotel room phone rings, jarring us out of the lust-fueled haze. At the same time, my phone starts to dance on the bedside table, vibrating with an incoming call.

We break apart, breathing heavily. Lily's skin is flushed and I can see the pink disappearing down behind her top. I want so badly to finish what I started and pull it up to free her tits just to see how far the colour spreads.

But Lily springs out of bed, even though she could easily reach the phone from where she is. With her back to me, I hear her breathless "hello."

I pick up my cell to see a missed call from Stefan. I hit the call button since it's obvious the moment is lost between Lily and me.

Probably for the best.

"Are you still in Vancouver?" Stef says by way of greeting.

"Yeah."

"Good. We need to meet."

We make plans to meet up at a restaurant nearby for lunch. I don't particularly want to since the only time Stef insists on meeting in person is when he's got bad news. But I also don't have a good reason not to. Besides, judging by the tension radiating off Lily, she might appreciate not having to drive me home.

"That was the front desk confirming our check out time." Lily's fidgeting, twisting her fingers together, not meeting my gaze.

I gesture to my phone. "That was my agent asking if I can meet him today."

Awkward silence falls over us. I hate the idea that she might regret what happened, or feel embarrassed, but I'll be damned if I know what to do about it.

"I'm gonna stay in town and meet Stefan, you okay to head home without me? I'll catch a float plane later."

She doesn't deserve me sounding gruff and distant, but then again, maybe that's exactly what we need. My grumpy ass putting some space between us. Because if I'm mixed up over what just happened, I can only imagine she is, too.

We get ready quickly, without talking, Lily disappearing into the bathroom and coming back with her hair braided and clothes on. The cute pink blush is gone from her skin. Any trace of what happened earlier is gone. When the door to our room closes behind us, it's clear the metaphorical door that had cracked open between us is closed as well.

The elevator opens up into the lobby for me and I take a step out, using the goddamn cane, thanks to my leg still throbbing from yesterday. Pausing, I turn back. I can't just walk away and say nothing.

"I'll see you at therapy tomorrow?"

It's part statement, part question. Because I need to know that we can go back to what we had. Not just because she's a damn good physical therapist, but because she was becoming a friend. Someone I could relax around and not worry about offending with my piss-poor attitude. Out of everyone, Lily's the one who lets my grumpiness roll off her. Or maybe, it's that when I'm around her, I don't feel so down.

Either way, I don't want to lose her just because we let our baser instincts take over. A few minutes of making out can't be what pushes her away.

"Yeah. See you tomorrow." The elevator door starts to close, but her hand shoots out, stopping it. "And I know I said it yesterday, but I need to say it again. Thank you. For coming, for putting up with my family, for being there." Her tongue darts out and moistens those pillowy soft lips I can still feel under mine. "And I'm sorry. For earlier. You know, um, sitting on you and stuff."

My mouth falls open and I know I need to say something, but her hand drops and the door closes before I get a chance. Then I'm staring at the metal wall of the elevator that is carrying her down to the parking garage, wondering why her apology stings so badly. And why I already miss her.

My meeting with Stefan is exactly what I anticipated with no small amount of dread, with him presenting me with a contract buyout offer from the Blaze.

The team I dedicated my life to doesn't want me back.

My hockey career is officially over.

I hobble into my apartment in Dogwood Cove that evening, at a loss as to what comes next. I didn't sign the offer, but the papers are burning a hole through the side of my suitcase.

Now, in the dim light coming in from outside, I sit down on the couch and stare at the bottle and glass I set on the table. I could get drunk and try to forget this entire day ever happened. From the obliteration of any boundaries between Lily and I this morning, to the conversation with Stefan, to now. My knee hurts, my heart hurts, and I've never felt more alone.

A knock on my door snaps me out of the downward spiral. No one knows I didn't come back with Lily, so it could be any one of my family members who all expected me to be home earlier today. I don't really have the energy for any of them right now, but I'm fully aware they won't leave. That's the thing with us Donnellys. We don't back down and we don't walk away when someone needs us.

"It's open," I yell out from my spot on the couch.

The door opens behind me and I hear the sound of someone setting something down, then more stuff, then finally, the door closes. I look over my shoulder, curiosity getting the better of me.

My eyes land on a pet carrier. "What the hell is that?" I ask Kat, who's setting a box down on my kitchen counter. She opens the box and lifts out a bag of pet food and some other shit.

"*That* is a kitten who needs a home. She's the last one left from her litter and a shelter is no place for a little thing like her. I volunteered you to be her foster dad."

My eyebrows furrow even as my scowl deepens. "Excuse me?"

"You heard me," my sister says airily. I watch in disbelief as she opens the door to the carrier, and sure as shit, lifts out a tiny grey ball of fluff. She rounds the end of the couch and sits down next to me before placing the thing in my lap. "There you go. Now you won't be so lonely when you're brooding."

My eyes flick down to the kitten, who's standing up and arching its back, and then to Kat, then back to the kitten. "What the fuck, Kat. I don't need a kitten."

"Well, too bad, the kitten needs you. Now, how was the wedding?"

My head shoots up at her question. "What do you mean?"

Her eyes narrow at the weird sound of my voice. "What do I mean? I mean, how was the wedding? How awful was Lily's family? Did something happen?"

"Have you talked to Lily?" I say cautiously, tempering my tone.

"No, I came here straight from the shelter. I was going to call her later. What's going on, Jude? Is she okay?"

Now that I'm fairly certain Kat has no clue about this morning, I relax slightly. But not a lot, thanks to the fluff ball that has started kneading my leg with sharp as knives claws. "Ow. Stop it." I lift the kitten off my lap and set her on the floor where she starts to wander around. "She's fine. I think." Turning to face Kat, I remember my resolve to ask her more about Lily's fucked-up situation. "But a little warning about her shitty family would've been nice. Did you know her cousin married Lily's ex-boyfriend?"

Kat frowns. "Yeah. It's messed up. I forget that you weren't around as much when we were growing up. The short version is her parents are insane; her mother and aunt have pitted Lily and Marnie against each other since day one. But where Lily hated it and had zero desire to compete with Marnie, Marnie took it the opposite direction. Her life goal has been to put Lily down and make her feel like the loser of the family. And Marnie's mom, and Lily's, never stopped her."

"From what I saw, her parents were just as guilty of putting her down as Marnie," I grumble. Nothing that Kat said surprises me, based on what I experienced over the last forty-eight hours. But damn, it's depressing to hear my sister confirm it. "That's fucked-up. Has she ever had anyone on her side?"

"Her Nana." Kat smiles. "She's awesome. Doesn't take shit from anyone. Unfortunately, the rest of the family doesn't seem willing to change. Lily's had to deal with her parents, her cousin, and her aunt and uncle basically shunning her for years. When she told them she wanted to go into physical therapy, they took away the education fund that she and Marnie both had. They said the money was meant to be used for something worthwhile, but what they meant was, anything that didn't toe the family line was unworthy."

"Damn." I whistle under my breath.

Kat stands up from the couch. "She's my best friend, Jude. She deserves everything, but she doesn't see it. Because no one has ever made her *feel* it."

I stay seated, lost in thought as Kat gathers up her things and heads to the door.

"I'm glad you were with her this weekend. She needs someone who can stand up to her toxic family."

There's meaning layered into what she's saying, meaning that I'm worried is Kat making assumptions that she really shouldn't be making. But when I push up to stand and make my way over to her, intent on clearing things up, she just wraps her arms around my waist.

"I love you, big brother. Take care of the kitten, and yourself, okay?"

"Love you," I reply gruffly. The door closes behind her, and tiny claws dig into my pants. I look down to see the damn kitten trying valiantly to climb my leg. I detach it from me and make my way back to the couch, sitting down and swinging my legs up. Despite actually sleeping last night, I'm exhausted.

But when I wake up an hour later from dreams that involved Lily, a bed, and a lot less clothes than there were this morning, it's not her weight I feel on my chest.

It's the goddamn kitten curled up, purring.

CHAPTER THIRTEEN

Lily

Sleep did not happen for me last night. Nope. Not even after I pulled out my box of toys and tried to orgasm myself into oblivion.

The orgasms happened, that's for damn sure. All I had to do was remember the feel of Jude's hard body underneath me, his hands gripping my ass, his lips covering mine, and I was going off like a rocket.

All day yesterday I had to pinch myself to be reminded that it really happened. We might have been half asleep, emotionally hung over from the day before and the disaster of my family, but we were both fully aware of what was happening. I trust Jude to know he would have never crossed the line if he thought I wasn't on board.

And oh boy, was I on board.

If the damn room phone hadn't interrupted us, I honestly don't know if I would have stopped him from stripping me bare and doing God knows what.

But last night when I was all alone, unable to sleep, I couldn't stop obsessing over how much of a disaster that would have been.

I'm not averse to casual sex. Not by a long shot. One-night stand? Sure, no problem. But not when the guy is my best friend's older brother *and* a patient of mine. That has *bad idea* written all over it.

I recognize Jude's question at the elevator for what it was. He needed reassurance that we'd go back to Jude and Lily, physical therapist and patient, casual friends, and what happened yesterday morning wouldn't rock the boat.

"Morning, Sukhi," I say as I push open the door to the clinic. She looks up at me from behind the desk. I see we're going full-on red with the lipstick today. I'm not a fool, I've noticed — just like I'm sure everyone has — that she piles on the makeup the days Jude has an appointment.

Something roils in my gut. It can't be jealousy. I've got no hold on him, he's free to do whatever with whoever. Whatever the feeling is, it's not pleasant.

I go through my appointments for the day. Jude's up second, which means I have just over an hour to prepare myself for seeing him again. I practiced what I'll say. Something along the lines of, we're adults, it happens, it doesn't mean anything.

But when he shows up early and I'm still finishing up with Hattie Henderson's arthritic elbow pain, my greedy eyes drink him in deeply. I know what lies beneath the tight-fitting T-shirt and shorts he's wearing. I've felt him, all eight or nine inches of him, pressed against me.

"It's so nice having Jude back in town, isn't it?" Hattie comments, a devious lilt to her voice. I jolt back to her, just in time to realize I've had my hand on her forearm for probably an awkward amount of time.

"Yeah. I mean, yes. I'm sure his family is happy to have him here, even if it is under not great circumstances."

Hattie just gives me a weird smile. Damn it, she's way too perceptive. Kat and I always laugh about how she sits at The Nutty Muffin, writing letters to her sister. We're positive they're full of town gossip. Somehow, this woman knows more than anyone about whatever is going on around town.

"Okay, you're all done for this week. Don't forget the stretches, and you can book your next appointment with Sukhi." I give Hattie a wide smile, pointedly not looking at Jude as I make my way to the front with the older woman. But my ability to avoid him doesn't last long.

"Hi Jude, come on back."

I turn on my heel and walk to the room we usually use without pausing. I don't need to. I know he's following me; I can feel him.

He closes the door behind him and lifts his body up on to the table. "Hey, Lily."

His usual grumpy tone is softer. That alone makes me look at him at last.

"How was your ferry ride?" He's settling on his back, used to the way we start things with a deep tissue massage to stretch out the muscles and break down scar tissue. But is he…is he making small talk?

"Fine," I say, that one word coming out way too shrill. I clear my throat and try again. "It was fine. Smooth sailing. How was your float plane ride?" I go through the motions, laying down a sheet to protect his clothing and getting the oil I use to help my hands glide more easily.

"Fine," he parrots back my response.

I get to work, the usual silence falling between us. At least this is the same and familiar. Jude rarely talks during our sessions unless he's asked a question. His grunts of discomfort when I hit tight spots serve to ease the weird tension I'm feeling even more. This is fine. We can just act as if nothing happened.

"I want to apologize for letting things get out of hand yesterday."

Or maybe not.

Thank God his eyes are closed, so he can't see the flush of embarrassment I feel rising in me at his apology. I've fooled around a decent amount, and I've never had a guy apologize before. Not for that. I gotta say, I don't like it. It feels icky, like we did something wrong, like I was some dirty mistake he made.

Oh, heck no.

"There's nothing to apologize for," I say brightly. "We're two adults who got caught up in some sort of early morning madness. It's fine. It meant nothing."

Jude doesn't reply. I finish the hands-on portion of our session and step back.

"Okay, take your time getting up, I'll meet you out in the gym and we'll go through some new exercises."

There. Back to normal.

So why does it feel so weird?

We finish out our session, and just as I do with every patient, I walk Jude to the front. Sukhi immediately leans over the desk, batting her lashes at him.

"Hi Jude, I can get you booked for your next time if you want."

I bet she'd like to book him for more than just an appointment. I fight back an eye roll and turn to go prep for my next patient, but his hand on my arm stops me in my tracks.

"Thanks, Lily. I don't know if I've said this, but you're good at what you do. I'm grateful for all your help."

I stare at him, examining his facial expressions, but I don't see even a hint that he's lying or just placating me.

"Thank you," is my quiet reply. "But you're doing the work. I'm just helping."

"You do a hell of a lot more than that. Don't sell yourself short."

Stunned, all I can do is nod. Jude turns and walks out the door without even acknowledging Sukhi. I watch through the glass as he climbs into his brother's car and drives off.

"He didn't rebook." The petulant whine to Sukhi's voice makes me turn around. And even though I know I shouldn't, I can't help but dig at her.

"That's fine, I have his number. I'll text him later to rebook."

I walk into the back of the clinic without letting her say anything about the smile creeping across my face.

Jude Donnelly thinks I'm a good physical therapist.

The next morning before work, I head to The Nutty Muffin to meet Kat like I promised. I know she wants to ask about the wedding, and I already know I'll tell her absolutely nothing about what happened after the ceremony.

It's not like I want to keep a secret from my best friend. It's more that I don't know how she'll react.

But all bets are off when she walks through the door and beelines over to the table I'm already seated at. She drops her bag and jacket down, sits down, and leans forward. There's a strange expression on her face, a mixture of excitement and disbelief.

"Care to explain why, when I was grabbing some things at a grocery store in Westport, I overheard some woman talking about Marnie Chapman's cousin and the hot guy she was seen leaving with, hand in hand, before the reception was even over? She was scandalized that you dared leave the wedding early, but I'm more curious about the hand holding."

My mouth falls open. Oh, shit. How did I not think about what kind of rumours might be passed around by all of Marnie's cronies?

"I...I don't know..."

Chapter Fourteen

Jude

When Kat demanded I meet her at The Nutty Muffin today, I didn't stop to think about why.

But walking up to her and Lily just in time to catch that last sentence, I'm rethinking my easy acceptance of the invitation.

"Hey Kat, Lily, what's going on?"

My sister turns in her seat and folds her arms across her chest. "That's what I want to know. Sit."

I do so, sparing a quick glance to Lily, who looks like a deer caught in the headlights of a semitruck.

"I was just telling Lily that yesterday, when I was in Westport after class grabbing some things, I overheard a woman talking about the Chapman wedding. But it wasn't Marnie's dress or the flowers she was talking about. Nope, apparently, the story of the hour is about Marnie's cousin —" Kat shoots her eyes at Lily "— leaving early with some man." Her laser beam eyes turn their focus on me. "And I'd like to know exactly *why* that was newsworthy."

"Listen, Kat, it's not what you're thinking."

"So, you didn't dance with her, then disappear somewhere holding hands?"

"Well, we did, but..." I hesitate, because that much is true and seems innocent enough. But Kat's eyes light up, and my slow brain can't quite catch up to why.

"Oh my God, this is amazing." She pushes her chair back with a clamour and pulls Lily up into a hug. "This is seriously just the best."

"Wait, what?" Lily fumbles, her eyes finding mine over Kat's shoulders. I shrug at her *what the fuck* expression because honestly, I'm just as lost.

"I want to be mad that you never said anything, but I can't because I'm just so happy!" Kat pulls back, and sure enough, her eyes are shining. What the goddamn hell is going on?

"You dating one of my brothers was literally what I used to wish for when we were younger. I didn't even care which one." She laughs and sniffs away a tear, and that's when I catch on.

Ah, shit. But before I can say anything and rescue Lily, who's frozen with shock, Kat continues.

"Then again, I should've known it would be Jude. You guys have so much in common. Ooh, Lil! We could be sisters for *real* one day!"

"Seriously, Kat?" I croak out as I manage to find my voice at last.

But that was a mistake. Because my sister is never more fired up than when she's defending someone she loves. And right now, that love is directed at Lily. Which means the defending part is directed at me.

"If you hurt her, so help me, I'll kill you. I've got three other brothers; I can afford to lose one. But there's only one Lily, and she's everything to me. You need to treat her like gold. No more grumpy Jude, okay?"

She spins back to Lily and pulls her in for another hug. The poor woman is still too stunned to do or say anything, and I don't blame her. I'm feeling pretty floored myself.

"Okay. I have to go, thank you both for meeting me here and making my dreams come true. Love you guys!"

Kat grabs her things and disappears out the door of the café and then it's just Lily and I, staring at each other.

"What..." Lily clears her throat and turns panic-filled eyes to mine. "What was that?"

"*That* was hurricane Kat jumping to some wild conclusions." I exhale loudly, raking my hand through my hair. "Shit, I can't believe she just went crazy like that."

Lily slowly lowers herself into her chair. "What are we going to do about her?"

"I honestly don't know."

Her tongue darts out to moisten her lips and my eyes follow the movement greedily. Fuck, that mouth of hers. My only regret from the other morning is that I didn't get to experience more of her.

Which is entirely the problem. I can't be having those feelings about her. She deserves way more than a grumpy, washed-up hockey player. Kat's not the only one who would kill me if I ever hurt Lily. Guaranteed, my entire family would. And there's nothing that I can offer her. Which means, eventually, she'd be disappointed by me.

"I'll talk to her, set her straight. It's okay."

Lily sags back against her chair and picks up the coffee cup in front of her.

"Yeah, I should talk to her as well. I can't believe she actually thought you and I..." Lily gestures between us.

"Right," I say. But inside, a small voice is asking, why is that so unbelievable?

And why do I wish it wasn't?

The conversation with Kat and Lily leaves me unsettled all morning. So, when Stefan calls to ask if I've signed the buyout paperwork, I snap at him. He doesn't deserve my wrath, but there's no one else around, so he gets it.

After that call, I mope around the apartment for a while. When my phone vibrates with a text message, I glance at it out of habit. But seeing my dad's name on the display actually makes me pause. Dad's like me — quiet and happier staying out of the chaos. He's the one who would take me to practice every morning, I suspect to escape the noisy madness that was our house each day. It's not unheard of for him to text me, but it's also not very common.

DAD: Hey son, got time for your old man later today?

I have no idea why he wants to meet up, but suddenly, that sounds like exactly what I need.

JUDE: Yeah. 2 pm?

DAD: That works, your mom will be out with Violet so the house will be quiet.

A slight frown crosses my face. I barely know my cousin Leo's daughter, but she's become a close member of our family, thanks to my mom babysitting her. I realize I've isolated myself since being back, and my family has done their best to give me that space. But maybe it's time I stopped being such a loner.

I confirm plans with Dad, then decide to take a shower. It's a lot easier now that I can stand and bear weight on my leg. I have to admit, a lot of that is thanks to Lily. She's got great instincts for knowing just how far to push my body and my recovery without taking it past a safe limit. Combined with the stretching and exercises I'm doing at home, the hot-cold therapy she's introduced recently, and that goddamn massage she starts every session with, and my leg is feeling stronger and steadier every day.

I'm determined to ditch the cane this week, and Lily's agreed to up the strengthening aspect of my rehab so we can progress my conditioning. I miss being on the ice. Even if I never get back to my former level, I miss skating.

While I'm in the shower, letting the hot water pound down on my back, I see my phone light up on the bathroom counter.

Damn it, I need to talk to Kat before she starts blabbing to everyone that Lily and I are together.

Although, would that be so bad?

Fuck. Yes. Lily has made it clear she wants to forget anything happened and keep things purely platonic and professional. I promised her I would talk to Kat, and I have to follow through.

No matter how good it felt waking up with her in my arms.

After drying off, I wrap a towel around my waist and grab my phone to see how much damage my sister has caused. But to my surprise, it's not the family chat. It's a missed call from a number listed as the Westport Ravens.

Weird. The name triggers some sort of recognition in me, but I'll be damned if I know what. A Google search reveals that the Ravens are the new Western Hockey League team in the province. I send off a text to Stefan, asking if he knows why they're calling me and what the deal is with the team. Instead of texting me back, my phone starts ringing. I accept the call, turning on speakerphone so I can get dressed.

"That was fast. I didn't think they'd call today or I would've prepped you."

"So, it's legit?" I ask, sitting on the bed to pull on some sweats.

"Oh, fuck yeah. You know who launched the team, right?" Stef sounds weirdly excited. "That's Gilles LaRoy's baby. He and his third wife wanted to relocate to the island, but rumour has it he was already in talks with Hockey Canada about starting up a team. They gave him full control over location, and he chose Westport. I'm telling you, man, it's serendipity. Have you talked to them yet?"

"Jesus. No. They called while I was in the shower." I pull on a hoodie, my voice muffled. "What the hell do they want with me?"

Stefan barks out a laugh. "They want you to coach! Jude. My man. This is your chance. They want you to be the head coach."

I sink down onto the edge of my bed, stunned. "I don't know the first thing about coaching."

"You think they care? You're a star player, a former captain, a cup winner. That's the important shit." His voice sobers. "Call them back, Jude. Seriously."

My mouth dries up. Because while I can see this is potentially a fantastic opportunity, it's also one more slam of the door on my professional career. And just like signing those fucking papers, I don't know if I'm ready for it.

"I gotta finish getting ready. I'll talk to you soon." I hang up on Stefan before he can push any further. Falling back, I lay down on the bed and stare at the ceiling.

Do I want to coach? Do I want to watch other guys live my dream?

A plaintive meow makes me shift upright. Looking down, I see the grey fuzz ball Kat dropped off yesterday sitting at my feet, staring at me.

"What?"

The kitten just meows again, then lifts up and tries to climb my leg. I bend over and pick her up, dumping her on the bed.

"You gotta stop using me as a tree, little lady. It hurts. And your future owners won't like it. Trust me."

Of course, the kitten ignores me, pouncing on an invisible piece of something on the bed.

"You're cute, I have to admit." I reach a hand out and stroke its back, and the immediate start of a very loud purr has me almost smiling.

"Okay, I gotta go. Don't destroy my place."

It takes a while for me to walk to my parents' house. But it's a decent day, and Lily did say I was ready to start walking every day.

When I reach their house, however, my leg is protesting. Dad lets me in without comment, but I feel his eyes on me as I go straight to the couch, sit down, and elevate my leg.

He heads into the kitchen and returns a couple minutes later carrying a tray, walking slowly. I move to get up, but he fixes me with a look.

When he sets the tray down, I see two cups of coffee, an ice pack, and some pain relievers. He hands me the ice pack first, which I dutifully strap onto my knee, then the coffee.

"Thanks, Dad."

"Do you need those?" he asks, inclining his head to the medication, but I shake my head.

"Nah. Just the ice is good."

"How is your rehab progressing?"

"Good. Fine. I mean, I think fine. Lily's a great therapist, and I honestly didn't think I'd be walking without a crutch or a cane so soon, not after the surgery I had, but she said I'm ready."

Dad nods slowly. For some reason, I talk more with him than I do anyone else in my family. Maybe because he's quiet, like me, so I don't feel the need to use my words sparingly.

"I'm glad to hear it. I'm glad you came today, also."

We sip coffee in silence for a minute. I know he has a reason for asking me to come over, just as I know he'll get to that reason when he's ready. Sure enough, my mug is half empty when Dad decides to speak again.

"After my accident, there were several months when I honestly didn't know how I'd ever get by. Everything changed. I couldn't kick a soccer ball in the yard with you boys, I couldn't take the dog for a walk, I was in constant pain, and I couldn't do my job. I couldn't provide for my family anymore."

His dark eyes, the mirror to my own, stare at me with compassion. How did it not dawn on me until now that out of anyone, Dad would understand the best what I'm going through. A drunk driver almost took him from us nine years ago. Thankfully, he survived, but the damage to his body remains. It's why all of us Donnellys take extra precautions when we go out, always ensuring a sober driver for everyone.

"I loved my work with the forest service. But there was no chance in hell of me traipsing through the woods, surveying trails and the like. I had to face facts; my career was over well before I was ready for it to be."

I open my mouth, but he holds up his hand to stop me.

"You're going to say I was nearing retirement age, so it can't have been that big of a deal, but it was. Not only did we need the money from my income, but I enjoyed my work. And when it was gone, because of some idiot and not because I chose to retire, I grieved that loss. Your mother knew how I was struggling, but we tried hard to keep it from you kids. It was bad enough you had to go through watching me heal in the hospital and at home, you didn't need to know your old man was depressed, as well."

"Dad," I murmur, but he keeps going.

"I'm not telling you this now for any reason of my own. I'm telling you this, so that you know, it's okay to grieve. It's okay to be sad or angry that your career was taken from you. But learn from my experience. It's a hell of a lot easier to get through that grief if you let the people who love you stand beside you. If it hadn't been for your mother holding my hand, and you kids carrying on with your lives, showing me how much I still had to be thankful for, I don't know how I would've made it through those first few months."

He lifts his coffee mug to his lips but pauses before taking a sip. "Your family loves you, Jude, whether you play in the NHL or become a garbage collector. Your worth is not tied up in hockey. It might take you some time to see that, but I hope you do, sooner rather than later."

Those words stick with me long after I leave my parents' house after promising Dad I'd come by for dinner tomorrow.

It's not like he said anything new or earth-shattering. Of course, I'm grieving the loss of my career. Isn't it obvious? But something about hearing him own up to his struggles, which I truly had no clue he ever experienced, makes it feel that much more real.

I just don't know if I can let everyone in, let everyone see how lost I feel. How untethered I feel without hockey.

And why, when I *do* think of letting someone in, showing them how much I'm struggling, is Lily's face the one I see?

Chapter Fifteen

Lily

After that insane coffee date with Kat, where she blew my mind with how easily she jumped to conclusions, I'm in a bit of a fog. So much so that I don't notice how Sukhi is not her usual helpful self until she huffs at my perfectly reasonable request for her to fax a list of equipment recommendations to our usual vendor.

"Did I do something?" I ask, baffled at why she's being snippy.

Instead of an answer, I get an eye roll. "I'll send it when I have time." She snatches the paper and storms off, leaving me standing at the front desk completely confused.

"Lily, if you have a moment, we need to discuss something." Gianni's voice has me turning around. There's an inscrutable look on his face, but his posture tells me he's also perturbed.

"I've got a break between patients right now," I say, and he turns on his heel and walks to the private treatment room I usually use with Jude.

He doesn't close the door, but I still get the distinct feeling I've been pulled into the principal's office. But why am I in trouble?

"It would not be appropriate for me to pass any judgment on your personal choices. However, I do feel I should remind you that any relationships with patients outside of the clinic, while not forbidden, need to have no impact on the services you provide. It would be outside of your professional code of ethics to provide physical therapy in an unlicensed setting or to provide preferential treatment based solely on personal relationships."

My mouth falls open in shock. "I'm sorry, what now?" I give my head a shake, certain I'm misunderstanding. Is he implying...

Oh. Shit.

"It's not what you think," I start, but Gianni holds both hands up to stop me.

"As I said, I cannot pass judgment on your choices. It's not my place. Not to mention the NDA we all signed regarding a certain patient. You're an excellent therapist and I trust you can remain professional. Should the need arise pass on a client to a team member, please notify me immediately."

He steps out of the room, and for the *third* time in as many hours, I am left stunned by the assumptions people make.

Dread pools in my stomach. Just how many people are talking about me and Jude at the wedding? And it's not as if we were all over each other. He kissed my head, we danced, we left holding hands. That's it! How is it spreading like wildfire that we're somehow romantically involved?

But there's no time to dwell on this insanity. The rest of my day flies by, and soon I'm driving home, intent on opening a beer — or maybe something stronger — and calling Kat to set her straight. I'm reasonably confident she isn't the one telling everyone Jude and I are together. No, my suspicion is it's Marnie's sorority friends who were her bridesmaids. I saw the way they were eyeing Jude at the wedding. It's a wonder none of them pounced on him. If I'm correct, then they're the ones blabbing about whatever they *think* they saw. Considering that a couple of them live in nearby Westport, it's easy to see how word would spread from them.

My plan is derailed when my phone rings and it's my grandmother calling.

"Hi, Nana," I say, balancing the phone between my shoulder and my ear as I unlock my front door.

"Hello, darling. How is your week going?"

A slightly hysterical laugh escapes me, but I cover it up quickly "Oh good, nothing special. You?"

"Just fine, dear. Now, I was hoping you could find some time to visit this weekend? Perhaps take your nana for lunch at Camille's?"

A warm smile stretches across my face. "Of course. I would love that."

I hear the satisfaction in her voice at my reply. "Wonderful. I do love when we have time together. And please do bring that lovely young man you were with at the wedding. You two are just so marvelous together."

It's a good thing I hadn't yet taken a sip of the local craft beer I just poured or I would have spit it back out. Is *everyone* in this town convinced Jude and I are a thing?

"Nana," I start, but apparently, she's not done.

"I'm not getting any younger and seeing you so happy with such a handsome man made my heart feel full. You deserve love and happiness, Lily, and I'm just thrilled you've found it. It would mean everything to me if I could get to know the man who stood by your side and made you smile."

Well, shit.

You know those moments when you're faced with an impossible choice? Neither one is great, but you're forced to choose, anyway?

This feels like that moment.

It was bad enough that my best friend and my coworkers somehow thought Jude and I were an item. I could handle that, clear up the misconceptions and move on. But my grandmother? She sounds so hopeful, so relieved, even. I know she worries about me being alone and never settling down. She knows I haven't had anything serious with a man in years — not since Clay dumped me for Marnie, and even *that* wasn't really a serious relationship.

I don't want to lie to her, but I also really don't want to disappoint her. She's the only person in my family who has ever been happy for me, even proud of me. And yet, every time we go for lunch, or have tea at her apartment, she asks if I'm seeing anyone, and I have to watch her face fall when I say *no*. She tries to hide it, but I see it.

Which is exactly why there's really only one choice.

"Okay, I'll bring Jude."

After the call with Nana, I quickly change out of my work clothes and grab my keys again. On the way to my car, I send Jude a text asking if he's home. Without waiting for a reply, I drive over there.

Thankfully, he is, so I take the stairs to his apartment two at a time, a crazy idea forming in my head.

He opens the door, looking deliciously rumpled, as if he just took a nap or something. I push past him without waiting for an invitation, then freeze when a grey blur flies around the corner of the couch and bounces off my leg.

"You got a cat?" I blurt out, my reason for coming over momentarily forgotten.

Jude limps past me and sits down on the couch. "No, Kat dropped off a fucking kitten and apparently, I'm stuck with it for now."

Despite the chaos brewing in my head, I grin. "That's adorable. What's its name?"

Jude scowls. "She doesn't have one. Her actual owners can name her."

My smile stays in place as I sink down on a chair next to his couch. "So, what, you just call it kitten? Why Jude, that's awfully flirtatious." I give him a wink, so he knows I'm teasing, but I'm in no way prepared for the way his expression morphs from one full of frustration to pure molten heat.

"What are you doing here, Lily?" he asks, the words sounding rumbly in the best possible way. Does he know he's sexy even when he's being a grump? Probably not.

"Right. So, we have a problem." I get straight to the point, because if I don't get this all out, I'll probably lose my nerve. "It's more than just your sister who thinks we're involved somehow. I got pulled in by my boss today —"

"Shit, I'll talk to him. This should in no way affect your job," Jude interrupts, but I'm already shaking my head in denial.

"No, it's fine, it's not a problem. He can't do anything to me. But what I'm saying is, somehow word is getting around that you and I are a thing." I bite my lip, fighting back the blush that is rapidly rising. "My grandmother called me tonight, asking if I would bring you to have lunch with her."

His face is impassive, impossible to read.

"She's the only person in my family who's ever been on my side," I continue, quieter now. "And ever since Clay and Marnie got together, she's worried about me ending up single forever." My eyes fall to the rug in front of me. Because depending on his reaction to what I'm about to propose, I might not want to see his face. "When she said she wanted to get to know you better, there was such hope and relief in her voice. I know it's silly; I don't need a relationship to be happy, but she's old-fashioned. And she just really wants to know that I'm not going to be alone the rest of my life. So..." I take a deep breath. Here goes. "I was thinking maybe we let everyone believe the lie for a little bit."

There. I said it. It's out in the open, and now all I can do is wait and see if Jude thinks I've gone certifiably insane, or if the idea makes sense. My hands twist together as I force myself to just wait it out until he replies.

"My sister was really excited about the idea of you and I being together. Why is that?"

My head lifts slowly. Whatever reaction I was expecting, this isn't it. There isn't any condescension or judgment in his face, just curiosity and...something else.

"I have no idea," I say. His brows lift, questioning, and I can't stop myself from smirking slightly. "Okay, fine, I had a crush on you when I was younger. You're a hot hockey player. It's only natural."

To my shock, the light dims in his eyes.

"I'm not a hockey player anymore."

The raw pain in those words pulses between us. I want to reassure him that it doesn't matter to me, especially not since whatever we do would purely be fake. Yet, I get the distinct impression that he doesn't want my platitudes right now.

He tilts his head to the side, still studying me. "My family might stop worrying so much about me if they thought I was involved with someone. But you're close to all of them. How do we handle this ending eventually?"

There's a steady acceptance in his voice, no trace of the earlier grief. I latch onto his response, relieved that he isn't automatically pushing me out the door and telling me to never come back.

"We'll just pretend for a couple of months or so, then part ways amicably. No one expects me to have a serious relationship, anyway, so it'll be easy."

I say that last bit airily, hoping he doesn't see my own pain the way I saw his. Judging from the serious way he's studying me, I failed. Guess I have to hope he doesn't call me out on it.

"Fine. We'll let everyone think we're together for a while. What exactly did you have in mind?"

"We can keep it simple. A date here and there, just to be seen in public. You'll come with me to lunch with my nana. Most importantly, we won't bother correcting anyone's assumptions."

"You think that'll be enough?"

"I...I mean..." I sputter, unsure how to respond.

"You'll have to come with me to family dinner, and probably more than a date here and there. We'll need to be affectionate. Hold hands. Maybe even kiss."

"I can handle that if you can."

Brown eyes twinkle back at me; he's close enough I can see the flecks of gold in them, but his features remain impassive.

"You'll have to smile, Jude. At least once or twice."

His lips quirk up ever so slightly. "Don't push it."

Good enough for now. But I think I have a new mission in life. Make Jude smile.

CHAPTER SIXTEEN

Lily

Turns out, Jude being the quiet one out of the two of us is a good thing. At least, it is when he isn't being a grouch. His steady, serious silence is oddly centering for me. Which is very much needed, since today is the day we go live with our ruse. It's our lunch date with Nana at Camille's. It accomplishes two things — spending time with Nana, and the two of us being together in a public space to confirm the rumours.

I'm nervous, but Jude is calm. I can see why he was such a natural leader for his team. Nothing rattles him, not even my incessant rambling as we drive from his apartment back to my house to pick up a book that I promised to lend my grandmother.

"I'll just be a minute; did you want to come in or wait here?" I say, turning off my car and staring straight ahead at my house.

"I'll come in."

I don't bother questioning why, after all, I really am going to be fast. Well, hopefully, assuming I can find the book.

When I push open my front door, I step aside nervously to let Jude in. Part of me wonders what he'll think. He's probably used to fancier homes, despite the basic apartment he's renting right now. After all, Dogwood Cove isn't exactly a hotbed for swanky condos. But my place is the exact opposite of swanky. I grew up surrounded by formality, with expensive artwork and furniture that was definitely not comfortable. Which is why, when I bought this bungalow, I went wild with colour and textures. Soft fluffy pillows and blankets cover the couch, photographs adorn the walls, most of them of Kat and I or the natural beauty surrounding Dogwood Cove. Plants are tucked into every nook and cranny; anywhere the sun reaches, I put some greenery.

And of course, the focal point is my bookshelves. They cover an entire wall and are filled with books, more plants, and little mementos I've collected over the years.

That's where I head, scanning the shelves for the book Nana wants to borrow. She and I both love literature. She's the one who started my collection of early editions of many of the classics, and most of our lunch dates end up in discussions about the latest book. A few of the women in town, including Paige Millstone who owns a bookstore in Dogwood Cove appropriately named Pages, have a monthly book club that Kat and I were invited to. But according to Kat, whose cousin is engaged to Serena, one of the members, they prefer spicy romance novels. I've got nothing against a good smutty book, but I also love science fiction, mysteries, and just like Nana, the classics.

"This is impressive," Jude comments, his hands in his pockets, eyes scanning the shelves.

"Thanks." Abandoning my search for the Margaret Atwood book Nana wanted, I wander over to stand beside him. "That's the sci-fi section. I love to read about different worlds and civilizations. There's something about escaping into the pages of a book and letting my imagination run free with nothing but the words to guide me."

I pull out one of my favourites and hand it to him. "Here, if you're set on avoiding people, maybe aliens will be better company."

He makes a sound that is suspiciously close to laughter. I narrow my eyes, popping my hands on my hips. "My God. Did you just...laugh?"

There's that tiny uptick of his lips again. "Don't get your hopes up."

"You keep challenging me like that and you're going to be surprised by what happens," I fire back.

Tilting his head to the side, he arches one brow at me. "Challenging you?"

I nod. "Yup. You said I was pushing it, asking for you to smile the other day, and now I'm getting my hopes up wanting you to laugh. I know you're committed to this Oscar the Grouch routine, but you should know that I'm just as committed to breaking you out of it."

For a moment, I worry I've gone too far. That once again I've been too much. But then his frown almost completely disappears.

"I was going for more of a Squidward vibe, not Oscar, but whatever."

My giggle comes out as more of a very unattractive snort, but any embarrassment is forgotten when I see it. It's small, but it's there.

"You just smiled. Oh my God, you smiled. And you made a joke. Jude! I'm so proud!"

I throw my arms around his neck without thinking about it. Until, that is, I realize his arms are still hanging by his side. Dropping mine quickly, I take a step back and whirl away from him. Spying the book Nana wants, I grab it and make to head for the door, only to be stopped by his hand running down my arm. The simple caress gives me goosebumps.

"You make it hard to stay grumpy."

His hand falls away and I instantly miss his touch. And when he brushes past me, limping to the door, I know better than to say anything. But his confession hits me in all the feels. I'm not going to read too much into it, but I definitely kind of like the fact that I'm the reason he's almost smiling.

We get back in my car and make the short drive to Camille's in silence. We could have walked here, but I happen to know firsthand how hard Jude worked at physical therapy yesterday and don't want him to overdo it.

When we find parking and get out of my car, I spy Nana through the window, already sitting at a table with what I'm guessing is a cup of decaf coffee. Doesn't matter the time of day, Nana loves coffee. Coffee flavoured anything, in fact.

Jude holds open the door to the café, and his hand settles on my lower back as I walk through, making me jump.

"Easy there. Remember? We have to touch each other?" he whispers, his mouth close enough to my ears that I feel his warm breath.

I nod jerkily. His hand stays in place as we make our way over to Nana, who lifts her head up with a smile.

"There you are, my darling girl."

I bend down and kiss her cheek, letting her squeeze my hand in her strong grip. "Hi Nana, sorry we're late, but I had to pop home and get that book for you."

I place it on the table in front of her, but her attention is solely focused on Jude. "I'm so glad you were able to join us, Jude. It makes this old girl's heart happy to see her favourite granddaughter with someone who obviously cares deeply for her. Aside from the unmentionable one, I've never met a man Lily has been involved with."

That's because the men I'm usually involved with don't mean anything to me.

Just like I don't mean anything to them. I never have, not to any of the men from my past.

None of them were worthy of meeting my grandmother. Which makes this a brand-new experience for me, and the fact that it's all a lie makes my stomach turn. I hate lying to Nana. Especially when she really does seem thrilled to see us together.

"I appreciate that, ma'am. Lily is a wonderful woman and I know you're very important to her. I'm honoured to have the chance to get to know you."

If I didn't know better, I would swear this is real. That's how convincing Jude is with just one simple statement layered with more emotion than I expected.

Nana waves her hand in dismissal. "Enough of that 'ma'am' business. I refuse to be that stuffy, call me Margaret or call me Nana. Your choice."

Jude inclines his head in acknowledgment, stretching his arm over the back of my chair at the same time. His fingertips drift over my shoulder, lighting every place he touches on fire. It's simply not fair that my body responds like this when I can't do anything about it.

But there's no denying the physical chemistry between Jude and me. That's probably the biggest reason why I believe we can pull this off. You can't fake attraction, and that's the one true thing we've got. But I've learned my lesson; chemistry and attraction only take you so far.

The pattern in all of my relationships is clear. I'm the fuck buddy, the one they have some fun with before settling down. The guy I lost my virginity to in high school messed around with me a few times before asking someone else to prom and ended up dating her for years. My college experiences were much the same — short-lived and barely existing outside of a bed. The one man I dated when I first went to Vancouver for my degree lasted a month before dumping me. Last I heard, the woman he went out with next has been his wife for five years and counting.

I've done okay at ignoring how much it hurts being cast aside so many times, and for the most part, I embrace my inner sex goddess. But the pain is there. And despite her having the best of intentions, Nana always brings it to the surface with her unending desire to see me settle down.

And that right there is why Jude is sitting next to me, pretending to be interested in me when I know darn well he isn't.

He couldn't be.

All of the women I've seen him with in the news and online have been gorgeous, modelesque, perfectly dressed, with flawless hair and makeup. They certainly aren't the black sheep of their family, more comfortable in leggings than dresses, with an obsession for colourful earrings. They probably sip chardonnay, not shoot tequila or chug beer the way I prefer.

No, there's not a chance of anything real ever happening between me and Jude. Whatever that was the morning after the wedding, it meant nothing.

Nothing.

Pushing my chair back, I stand up, needing a little bit of space from the overwhelming swell of confusion rising in me. Because I see right through my own lie. It wasn't *nothing*, waking up in Jude's arms.

It was wonderful.

"I'm going to order food," I say brightly. "The usual, Nana?"

"Yes dear, thank you."

I turn to Jude. "Sandwich? Wrap? Soup?"

His eyes are penetrating me, like he sees that I'm out of sorts right now. I give a tiny shake of my head, hoping he lets it go. To my relief, he does, simply replying, "Club sandwich, thanks."

I dart over to the counter and place our order. Thank God Kat isn't working here today or this would be even harder. Nana's scrutiny combined with my own turmoil is enough.

Once I've ordered and paid, I make my way back to the table. Nana is smiling, and Jude is, well, not smiling. But he looks okay.

"What did I miss?" I say breezily, dropping back down into my chair. Jude's hand instantly lands back on my shoulder, and to my surprise, the weight of it grounds me. It's a reminder that I'm not in this madness alone. He gets something out of us pretending, as well. He gets his family off his back, so he can have space to breathe and heal from the anger and grief bubbling inside of him.

And if I can help him heal, physically and maybe even emotionally, then maybe I'll feel like it's a fair trade.

I just have to remember it's all pretend...

CHAPTER SEVENTEEN

Jude

I don't know what I expected when I agreed to pretend to date Lily. But it doesn't feel like much has changed. Aside from the lunch with her grandmother, we've gone out for dinner twice, and she's dragged me out for a walk on her days off. Nothing has happened beyond holding hands or the limited touches in public. At the clinic, we have to be extra careful, walking a fine line between wanting to be convincing but not inappropriate, given she's still my therapist.

The problem is, the more time I spend with her, the more time I *want* to spend with her. And the more I touch her, the more I *want* to touch her. She's a beautiful woman, but more than that, she's the most warm, genuine, authentically good person I know outside of my own family. And to top it off, I can't forget how fucking good it felt waking up with her in my arms and kissing her.

I really want to kiss her again.

But I can't tell if she wants that or if she wants to steer clear of anything physical. Which is giving me some fucking blue as hell balls.

The only silver lining is that the worried expressions on my mom's and sister's faces have faded when they look at me. Of course, the flip side is having to deal with their not so subtle attempts at interrogating me on how and when things started with Lily. I've deflected so far, but Mom is insisting Lily come to a family dinner, and soon. That should be interesting.

Tonight I let my brothers drag me out for drinks at Hastings. When Max mentioned Heidi was going to stop by as well, I sent a quick message to Lily.

JUDE: Drinks at Hastings with my siblings? Could be a good chance to put on a show.

LILY: That makes me feel like a Vegas showgirl. I'm not busting out the go-go boots for you, sir.

JUDE: Part of me really wants to know if you actually have go-go boots.

LILY: Only part of you?

JUDE: Well the other part of me is worried that if you do, that means my sister does. And that's an image I don't need.

LILY: Prude.

JUDE: Older brother.

LILY: My, my, Jude. Look at you, being borderline flirty with the banter. We're bantering. I'm impressed. Wait. Are you smiling?

Damn it, my lips are turned up. It feels weird, like the muscles haven't been used in a long time.

JUDE: Of course not. I don't smile.

LILY: Uh-huh.

JUDE: Listen. Are you coming to the bar or not?

LILY: Kat and I were already planning on it. She's been texting with Heidi.

When Beckett, my chauffeur for the night, and I arrive at the bar, Sawyer, Max, and Heidi are already there, a pitcher of beer and a stack of glasses on the table. They're in the middle of a conversation but abruptly stop when we walk up.

"Well, if that isn't a sign you were talking about one of us, I don't know what is," I comment drily, sliding into a chair.

"We were discussing Beck's collection of glasses. Did you know he has a pair for each day of the week?" Sawyer says, poking fun at his twin.

To his credit, Beckett doesn't rise to the bait. He pours a beer and slides it across to me, then without missing a beat, he crumples up a napkin and chucks it at Sawyer's head.

I lift my glass in acknowledgment of his impeccable aim, then turn my attention to Heidi. I don't know Max's girlfriend very well. They only really figured their shit out right before my accident. But she seems nice, and she gave the oldest Donnelly another chance when he almost screwed their entire relationship up earlier this year. They might have had an unconventional start to their relationship, what with Max hating her guts for reasons I still don't fully understand, but now they're in that disgustingly corny honeymoon phase where they can't keep their hands off each other.

Watching Max and the way he can't seem to keep his eyes off her, the little smiles that cross his face without warning, the way they're always touching somehow, makes me wonder if Lily and I are doing enough to sell our relationship. I'm sure no one expects us to be like these two, but are we affectionate enough?

Fuck knows, I'm not averse to more affection. The woman is crawling beneath my skin without even trying, and I just want more. If I thought there was a chance in hell of her wanting the same, I'd pursue it. But what the hell do I have to offer as a washed-up hockey player with a busted leg and sour attitude.

"How do you like working at the hospital as a full-fledged doctor? I'm guessing you don't miss Max bossing you around."

Heidi's eyes glint at my question. "I prefer him bossing me around in other places, so yeah, it's good."

I shake my head with a slight grimace. "Things I didn't need to know about my brother."

Heidi just laughs as Max glares at me. "Your time is coming, brother. Lily's on her way, isn't she?"

Of course, the stink eye I give him rolls off him, unfazed. Brothers never pass up an opportunity to give each other a hard time, so I know to take him at his word. It's our first time acting as a couple in front of my family. And given Lily's history with us, this could get challenging.

"A table full of Donnellys. This looks like trouble. Handsome trouble, but trouble, nonetheless."

My head whips around at Lily's flirtatious voice. There's no reason for my heart to speed up. But it does.

"Dude, what's wrong with your face?" Sawyer grabs my chin and forces my head to swing around. "Guys. Jude's almost smiling. Holy shit, the world is ending."

I wrench my head out of his hand and glower at him. "Fuck off."

An arm drapes across my shoulder and the light floral scent that I know is Lily wafts over me. "Be nice, Sawyer. I'm making him work more than just the muscles in his leg, if you know what I mean."

The table erupts in laughter at her innuendo, but their comments stick with me. I know I've always been the more serious brother. Less likely to crack a joke or goof off. But have I really become that much of a grumpy asshole?

All the times that Lily has teased me about smiling and laughing start to add up in my head, and with a sinking feeling in my gut, I realize that yeah, I have.

"Relax, Jude." Fingers toy with the hair at the nape of my neck. I know that if I turn my head just slightly, my lips will brush against Lily's.

That's tempting. Very tempting.

But I resist.

"Oh, come on, what kind of shit call was that?" Lily's hand falls away as she throws both up in the air. I follow her gaze to the big screen television that's streaming a hockey game.

"Seriously? Icing? Jesus. This must be the ref that's out to get them." She shakes her head as she grumbles. It's fucking adorable — and surprising. I had no clue she was a hockey fan.

Lily pours herself a beer, glancing over at me briefly. "Are you okay with having the game on? We could ask Dean to change it."

Her consideration is touching but totally unnecessary. Just because I can't play doesn't mean I don't love the game. The only ones I have a hard time watching are when my former team is playing.

"And deprive myself of the fascinating experience of watching you watch hockey? Never." I respond and a grin covers Lily's face. Amusement dances in her eyes.

"You need to realize something, Jude Donnelly. I've loved hockey since long before you became a big deal."

"It's true," Kat pipes in. "She was the only girl trading hockey cards in elementary school."

I turn back to Lily, studying her with this new information taking root in my head. Her love of hockey only makes her all the more appealing. And only adds to the increasing confusion brewing in my brain.

She's Lily, Kat's best friend. And she's Lily, my physical therapist. And she's Lily, the woman I'm pretending to date. *And* she's quickly becoming Lily, the woman I'm insanely attracted to. No, more than that. The woman I'm *attached* to. The woman who brings me out of the darkness just enough that I can feel her warmth.

"I would never have expected that from you."

Lily's smile falters. It's slight, but I see it and it makes my eyebrows draw together in concern. But then she's back to yelling at the television, and the moment has passed.

I let myself be drawn into conversation with my brothers, and to my surprise, the evening passes quickly. I expected a lot more harassing about me and Lily, but for some reason, we get off easy.

Max and Heidi are the first ones to leave. Max has a shift tomorrow at the hospital, and they live in Westport.

After they're gone, Kat drags Hunter out onto the tiny corner of the bar designated as a pseudo-dance floor.

"I think I want nachos. Anyone else want nachos?" Lily announces with a smack of her hands on the table. She pushes back without waiting for anyone to answer and sashays up to the bar. My eyes follow her, unbidden. It's as if she has a tracking beacon only I can see, drawing me to her everywhere she goes.

"Dude, I almost didn't believe it when Kat told us you two had hooked up. But look at you." Beckett leans over quietly. "You really like her."

I turn to him sharply. "Yeah. I do." The lie falls off my tongue easily. *Maybe because it's not much of a lie.*

"That's good. Lily's awesome. And she deserves someone good. I'm just surprised, I guess. Never knew you had a thing for her."

"Neither did I, until recently," I reply, and yet again, it's the goddamn truth.

"She's basically like another sister to us. I honestly can't see her any other way, but if you can, more power to you, bro," Sawyer chimes in.

"Thanks?" I say, sarcasm clear in my tone.

"Whoa, hold up, who the fuck is that?" The change in Sawyer's tone has me instantly on alert. Sweeping my gaze around the bar, I naturally land back on Lily. She's still up at the main counter, only now there's some asswipe leaning way too close into her space, judging by how far she's leaning *back* trying to get away.

I stand up quickly, wincing as my knee protests. But I push the pain aside and make my way over to her as quickly as I can. And when I reach her, I don't think, I just act.

Seems to be a pattern when it comes to my behaviour around Lily. Especially when there's another man involved.

I use my broad upper body to shove in between the two of them, effectively forcing the other guy away. Not stopping there, my head leans down, my lips finding hers, instantly reigniting the fire that's been smouldering away inside of me ever since the morning after that shitshow of a wedding.

She's frozen, but only for a split second before I feel her melt into me, making a growl of satisfaction escape from my mouth. My hands tangle in her hair as I take the kiss even deeper, and her hands wrap around my waist and tuck into the back pockets of my jeans.

Goddamn, that feels good. *She* feels good.

"If you guys don't mind toning it down a notch or two, I'd rather not have a health code violation."

The dry voice of Dean Hastings, the owner of the bar, breaks through the lust-filled haze surrounding us.

"Sorry," Lily squeaks out, her eyes glued to mine. She tugs her lower lip between her teeth, but I shake my head slightly and lift my thumb up to free it. When she gasps, I ignore what Dean just said.

I have to kiss her again.

"Okay, lovebirds. Take your nachos and go."

Reluctantly, I pull back. It does something to me to see the dazed, but definitely satisfied, look on Lily's face. Turning to Dean, I take the plate of nachos from him, grab Lily's hand with my other, and lead her back to the table.

Sawyer's grin is annoyingly big when we sit down. "I'm not sure what's hotter. The jalapeños on these nachos or that lip-lock."

I glare at Sawyer, even as some primal part inside of me crows with pride.

"Did I seriously just see you two making out by the bar? That was hot! And weird. But definitely hot!"

Kat drops into a chair across from us, her excitement barely contained. She reaches across the table, grabs Lily's hand, and squeals. Legit squeals.

"Aren't you meant to be all grown-up and professional and shit?" I say to her, but she just rolls her eyes.

"Shut up, Jude. My best friend and my big brother are falling in love. I'm allowed to be giddy. This is like, every little girl's dream come true."

My brain stutters on those three words. Falling in love? Hell, no. Nope. No way. I *like* Lily, sure. I can't deny that. But it's nothing more than physical attraction and friendship.

Right?

Chapter Eighteen

Lily

The Donnellys were always the family I wished I had. Warm, inviting, loving, loud, and full of fun. I was at their house as much as possible. They had an open-door policy for me, no questions asked. And even in the years that have passed since my dysfunctional childhood, I've been over here for dinner countless times.

And every time, I've always just walked right on in.

So, why this time, do I feel frozen in place? Why am I stuck here, in my car, in their driveway, unable to make myself just walk in the house?

The answer is obvious. Because I kissed Jude last night. And it was...wow.

I've never felt consumed like that. Overwhelmed in the best possible way.

For a moment, I lost myself in the kiss. Forgot that we were pretending and let myself believe it was real. That Jude wanted me.

Except that's not reality. Reality is that guys only want me for one thing. And I'm getting really tired of that.

My phone chimes with a text message. When I dig it out of my purse and see Jude's name on the screen, I bite my lip.

JUDE: If you don't come inside my family is going to think something's wrong.

I look up but can't see through the windows, thanks to the reflection of the setting sun.

JUDE: Get in here before my mom comes out and drags you in.

That's enough to spur me into action. Claire Donnelly is the second to last woman on earth I would ever want to disappoint, falling only behind Nana on that list.

I grab my bag and climb out of my car. As I reach the stairs leading up to the front porch, the door opens and the woman herself steps out.

"Hi, sweetheart," Claire greets me warmly, her arms opening for a hug. I walk straight into them and let her wrap me up in her embrace.

"Hi." My words are muffled with my head tucked into her shoulder. "Thanks for having me."

"Honey, you know you're always welcome."

I follow her inside, where the volume increases exponentially. The sound brings a smile to my face. This is what a home should sound like, full of life and laughter. I head into the living room, where just as I expected, I find Jude sitting in the chair by the window.

"Did you enjoy creeping on me?" I tease, walking over to him. But I stop as I reach him, suddenly unsure how to greet him. Do we hug? Kiss? There's no one in the room right now that we need to pretend in front of.

Jude answers the question for me, unfolding his tall body and standing up before pulling me into his side. "Yup."

His arm rests across my shoulders as he guides me into the kitchen where the rest of the family has gathered. His gait is slow, but steady and smooth, and the therapist side of me preens at the progress he's making.

"Great, Lily can settle this," Kat announces. She grasps my shoulders and stares me straight in the eye. "Do you remember that summer when we recreated the Olympics with all the different events and stuff? Who won the handstand contest? Sawyer here is claiming he did and saying I stole the gymnastics medal from him, but I distinctly remember otherwise."

"Of course, I do. You won, hands down." I pause, tilting my head thoughtfully. "No pun intended."

The room erupts in laughter, but Sawyer's groan rises above it. "Come on, no way, you're both wrong. I totally won!"

I arch a look at Sawyer. "Really? Because I'm pretty sure you saw a bug or something in the grass in front of your face and fell over after two seconds. Maybe three."

Sawyer pouts. "Why you gotta hurt me like that, Lilypad? I thought we were friends."

Jude's lips find the side of my head, and I lean into him, giving Sawyer a saucy smirk. "We are. But that doesn't mean my loyalties have shifted. Team Kat all the way."

"I would've guessed it would be Team Jude now," he fires back.

A blush fills my face with heat as I stammer out a retort. "I mean, yeah, I can be on two teams. Go team!" I raise my hand in a feeble fist pump just as Jude comes to my rescue.

"You're looking a little green with envy, Sawyer. Why don't you back off my girl and pass over one of those beers instead. Besides, why are we talking about something that happened over a decade ago?"

Goosebumps erupt over my skin when he calls me *his girl*. I know he doesn't mean it the way my body — and okay, my heart — want to take it. But still, it feels good.

"Because Sawyer's a poor sport and accused me of stealing the win," Kat says, her arms crossed in front of her. "And I don't cheat."

"Children of mine, if you need to argue, take it outside," Claire announces breezily as she walks past us all, carrying a platter of something that smells delicious. "Or better yet, channel that energy into something useful and set the table for dinner."

Everyone disperses to meet her request. That's the difference between Claire and my mother. Claire earns respect with clear expectations and a warm heart. My mother demands it and punishes with her cruel words when she doesn't receive it.

As usual, dinner with the Donnellys is loud and filled with laughter and delicious food. This time, however, there's an added element — the electric charge I feel with Jude sitting next to me, his legs spread so his thigh is pressed against mine. He's not shy about casually touching me, whether it's sweeping my hair back or resting his arm across my shoulder. Maybe I should wonder why he's so committed to this ruse, why he's so dang good at pretending to be my boyfriend, but my inner goddess is too busy basking in the physical affection.

What can I say, it's been a long time — for me — since I was with a man. And I'm a woman who thrives on intimacy and touch. Probably because I was starved for it growing up, but that's a conversation for a therapist.

After dinner, we congregate in the living room. Jude settles down in the corner of the sectional, lifting his bad leg up. I gingerly lower myself next to him because that's what a girlfriend would do, sit next to her guy, right?

I wish I could get over how weird I feel. It's not like me to blush or hesitate. Especially not when it comes to men, and definitely not around the Donnellys. They're the people I have always felt the most comfortable and confident around. Safe to be myself and not worry about criticism or judgment.

Somehow, pretending in front of them is just as much of a challenge as it was with Nana. Probably because my deepest fear is that when this thing we're doing ends, when Jude is no longer playing the role of my boyfriend, it will change my relationship with his family.

Jude doesn't seem to have the same reservations. Not from the way he grabs me and hauls me in close to his side. After holding myself stiff for a second, my body relaxes. It's not a conscious choice, I just melt into him. Because it's Jude.

He makes me feel safe.

As the night goes on, my eyelids grow heavy. At some point, my head falls to rest on Jude's chest. I didn't think I'd actually fall asleep, but the next thing I remember is Jude's hand rubbing up and down my arm gently and his murmur in my ear.

"Wake up, sunshine. Unless you want me in physical therapy for a lot longer, I probably shouldn't drive us home."

I bolt upright, blinking my eyes. To my surprise, the living room is empty and dark, save for one table lamp.

"Where is everyone?"

"They left. You were passed out, so I figured I'd let you sleep a bit, but I need to get home."

Standing up, I lift my hands overhead for a big stretch. When my eyes glance down, to my surprise, Jude's staring at me intently with no small amount of heat. My entire body shivers in response.

"Sorry I was such a sleepyhead." I lick my lips and swallow. There's something about the intimate feel of the dimly lit room and the two of us alone that triggers the memory of waking up with him after the wedding.

I take a step back and then another. Those memories will do me no good.

We head out to my car in silence. And for once, I'm not itching to fill it. The drive back to Jude's apartment is the same. When we arrive, whatever exhaustion I was experiencing before has disappeared.

I feel restless. Unsettled.

In the past, this feeling would lead to one of two things. Either I'd go for a long walk along the waterfront or I would find a guy to hook up with. I'd call someone I'd recently met; once I even drove to Westport to find a bar and a willing one-night stand. I'm not proud of it, and it never felt good afterward, seeing as all it did was cement the belief that I'm not worthy of anything serious with a man. But losing myself in sex was sometimes the only way to shut off that part of my brain that was constantly overthinking and criticizing every decision, every action, every minute detail of my life.

Since option two is not possible, I decide option one is necessary. I'll drop Jude off, then head home and grab my runners.

Except, I guess I'm more transparent than I thought. Because when we pull up outside of his building, Jude doesn't get out of the car. He shifts in his seat and faces me.

"Your mouth might have been silent for a change, but your thoughts were loud enough to make up for it. What's going on?"

I take the keys out of the ignition. "Sorry. My mind is just —" I let out a huff "— going a little crazy, I guess. But it's fine. I'm fine."

"You're not fine. C'mon." Jude opens the car door and slowly gets out. When he realizes I'm not moving, he leans back down into the open door. "Lily, come on. Inside."

The gruff command in his voice makes my limbs move before my brain can catch up. I get out and trail after him up to the door to his building and into the elevator. We ride in silence up to his floor and all the way down the hall to his apartment. Inside, Jude's on a mission, heading straight to the kitchen and filling a kettle with water.

A quiet meow draws my gaze down to the floor. "You still have the kitten," I say, a smile crossing my face at last. Jude's grunt of acknowledgment is exactly what I expected from him. "Did you name her?" I look up to see him watching me intently. He shakes his head.

"Jude, she needs a name."

"No, she doesn't. She isn't staying."

I make a point of turning slowly, taking in the cat toys that are all over the floor and the bag of treats sitting on the counter. "Uh-huh, sure, she isn't."

He turns back to the stove and the kettle that is now whistling. Methodically, he takes two mugs down, puts in a teabag, and covers it with water before turning back to me. "Sit down. I'll bring over the tea. Chamomile is okay, I hope, it's all I have."

"It's fine," I say quietly, making my way to the couch. When he sets the mug down in front of me, I pick it up and blow across the steam. "I have to admit, and this sounds bad, but I'm surprised a guy like you has chamomile tea."

The way he shifts on the couch next to me makes me wonder if he's embarrassed. Suddenly, I feel bad for commenting on it at all.

"But I'm glad you do," I hurry to say.

"I don't sleep very well."

My heart stutters at his quiet confession. "Oh."

"Insomnia. It's been that way for as long as I can remember." He sucks in a breath, his eyes dropping down before lifting back to me, raw vulnerability shining out of their brown depths. "The night we spent together after the wedding was the first night in years I actually slept."

I stare at him, my mind whirling as it tries to unpack the significance behind that. But there's no chance for me to respond before Jude shifts on the couch and changes the subject.

"What has you all up in your head tonight?"

The switch from talking about tea and Jude's sleep habits to talking about me is jarring, but not unexpected. He's not a guy who likes to show weakness. Still, it takes me a minute to figure out what, exactly, I want to say. How, exactly, I feel.

"I guess it just hit me that when we end this thing, everything changes."

"In what way?"

I grip the tea mug tightly, letting the heat from it get borderline painful before I release my hold. "I know we said we could walk away and make sure everyone knew it was amicable and easy. But the reality is, you're in town for the near future. Which means you'll be with your family. Which means I probably should *not* be with your family. Except, for most of my life, your parents and siblings have been my safe place. I've spent more time with them than my own family, especially since I moved out of my parents' house. But it would be weird if I kept hanging out with all of you after we've supposedly broken up. And my brain is spiraling with the idea of not being around you or your family anymore."

The quiet that follows my verbal vomit makes me want to stand up and run. Then Jude takes my hand in his and starts tracing a circle on my palm.

"What — what are you doing?" I stutter. There's no need for him to hold my hand right now. No one's here. No one's watching.

"It's a grounding technique I learned years ago. The sensation of a rhythmic motion can help you slow your mind if you focus on it and breathe."

He does it for a few more seconds, then stops, lifting his eyes to meet mine. "Now. Listen. What you have with my family is important. I know that now, having met your shitty relatives, more than ever. Which is why I promise I'll do everything possible to make sure nothing is awkward and weird, and you never lose that connection. The last thing I want to do is hurt you, sunshine."

It's the second time tonight he's called me by that nickname. And the first time — in my entire life — that a man has truly made me believe that he cares about me. Even if it is just as a friend.

"Thank you," I say quietly. My head does, in fact, feel calmer, and I'm not spinning quite as badly with worry about how things will change after this is all over. I stand up, abandoning the tea with a small pang of guilt, but I need to go before I fall any deeper. "I think I should get home."

Jude follows me to the door. "Text me when you get home." He's leaning against the door frame, close enough for me to see his chest rise and fall.

I nod. And for a long second, we just stand there, staring at each other. The intimacy of our conversation hums around us, as if it's a sentient energy in the air. On impulse, I place my hand on his shoulder and lift up on my toes to kiss his cheek. My lips linger there a beat longer than they should before I lower back down.

"Thank you for tonight, I'll see you tomo—"

Jude's lips cover mine before I can even finish talking. He swallows my gasp as his large hands grip my hips, pulling me in close. My hands are trapped between our bodies, but I manage to get a grip on his shirt.

Our tongues start to tangle, fighting for dominance. I'm used to being the more forward one in any intimate encounter, but something tells me Jude is not exactly submissive. His hands travel to my ass, squeezing until I want to climb him like a tree.

In fact, I probably would if it weren't for his injury. No sooner does that thought cross my mind does Jude grunt, this time in pain, not pleasure.

"Fuck. Sorry. My knee." He's breathing heavily and leans his forehead down to meet mine.

"I should go, anyway." I'm equally breathless. Neither one of us makes any move to separate. Until I feel him shift his stance. I let go of his shirt, smoothing my hands over the wrinkles caused by my death grip. Taking a step back and a deep breath in and out, I tilt my head up to smile at him. "Goodnight, Jude."

He takes my hands, wrapping them up in his much larger ones. Then, to my surprise, he lifts them to his mouth and kisses them lightly. "Goodnight, Lily."

When I get home, I no longer feel the need to go for a long walk. My mind is quiet. Calm. Content.

Happy.

Chapter Nineteen

Jude

"How much longer until I can drive?" I try to not let the question sound too whiny, but it's hard. I'm so goddamn tired of having to rely on people to take me everywhere. I miss my independence.

Lily just smirks, keeping her eyes on the road ahead of us. "Like I said at your appointment, maybe another week or two. I need to see you have a lot more control and less pain spasms before I sign off on it."

"Hard-ass," I grumble, but it's good-natured. I trust Lily, professionally and personally.

Lily flashes me a cheeky smile. I want to kiss her. But I always seem to want to kiss her, as the other night at my apartment proved. We shared something that night, and when she was going to leave, I needed to taste her lips again.

She brings a lightness everywhere she goes that I'm becoming addicted to.

Her hand lands on my thigh, where she pats my leg in a teasing gesture. "You're welcome."

A short while later, we pull up at our destination — the university campus down in Victoria where Kat is graduating with a master's degree in nursing. I'm so insanely proud of my baby sister. And I have to grudgingly admit, I wouldn't be here today to watch her walk across that stage if I was still playing hockey.

It's a thin silver lining, but it is one.

I climb out of Lily's car with a groan. "Why do you have to own such a small car?"

She runs her hand over the yellow paint lovingly. "Because she's cute."

It's such a Lily response, I just shake my head.

"Careful, Jude, you're almost smiling."

I look down at her as she threads her hand in mine. She's been a lot more relaxed with giving and receiving affection with me. It hit me yesterday that I had expected her to be far more bold and forward based on what I'd heard from my brothers about her being a massive flirt when it comes to men. But she's been the opposite with me. It makes me wonder who her true self is. The quieter version I'm seeing, or the bold, flirtatious version. Either way, she's loosened up lately. And my traitor of a dick notices every time she initiates touching me.

"One of these days, I'll show you a smile, and you'll run in fear."

Lily comes to a stop. "Don't tease."

I tug on her hand to keep us moving. "C'mon. Let's find everyone else."

The ceremony is thankfully short since it's only the nursing program graduating today. I'm extra grateful for this, since the rows of seating don't allow me to extend my knee very far, and the ache that is my constant companion is growing worse.

I can tell Lily notices me shifting around, trying to get comfortable, but when she gives me a questioning glance, I answer with a shake of my head. There's nothing I can do, and I don't want my family feeling bad for me. Today is about Kat.

After the ceremony, Mom and Dad insist on taking us all out for dinner. On the drive over, Lily wordlessly hands me a bottle of anti-inflammatories from her purse, and I swallow two.

"Thanks."

"Just tell me you'll let me know if it gets to be too much."

I make a noncommittal sound, but thankfully, she doesn't push. The medicine does its job and we enjoy dinner. Then Hunter and Kat tell everyone to meet back at Hastings for another drink. My sister's tipsy, and I don't blame her for wanting to celebrate. But it's the last damn thing I want to do. Max, Heidi, Leo, and Serena all bow out, but the twins agree.

And when Lily turns to me with her big beautiful smile, I know I'll suffer through an hour or two at the bar if it keeps her happy.

The bar is packed, which makes sense for a Saturday night. For a while, there's nowhere to sit and I'm forced to stand.

"I'm sorry. We can go," Lily says for the second time, her hands wringing in front of her. "You're already in pain and now this."

"Lily, it's fine. I'll get Dean to find me a chair if I have to." *Like hell I will.* The only thing worse than being injured is the looks of pity I get sometimes.

"Let's dance!" Kat cries out, grabbing Lily's hands. With one final worried glance over her shoulder at me, Lily lets herself be dragged out onto the dance floor. I watch the two of them — well, Lily, mostly. I can tell the second she lets go and loses herself in the music. Her body starts to sway and it's the sexiest thing I've ever seen. Mostly because I can tell she isn't even trying to be seductive. She's just Lily.

"Goddamn." Hunter whistles, passing me a beer. His eyes are glued on Kat the way they should be, but I can't resist a dig.

"Careful, Callaghan, that's my baby sister you're drooling over."

He just turns to me with a big dopey smile. "Yeah."

"Guys, a table just opened up."

I turn at Beckett's words, grateful as fuck to follow him over to where Sawyer's already setting out glasses and a pitcher. I sit down, stifling my groan of discomfort. Instead of joining Hunter and the twins' conversation, I find myself searching out Lily again. She and Kat are still dancing, and she's still stirring up all kinds of needs and wants in me.

The song ends and the girls make their way over to us. Kat sinks down in Hunter's lap, since there's only four chairs. Even though she'll feel the result of me watching her dance, I pat my good leg and pull Lily down to sit.

She does so gingerly until I wrap my arms around her middle and tug her more firmly onto me. The second her ass brushes my dick, she gasps, her hair brushing across my face as she whips her head around.

"I can't help what you do to me," I whisper. "But if it makes you uncomfortable, I'll find another chair for you."

Her mouth falls open ever so slightly as she slowly shakes her head. Our gazes are locked on each other and the rest of the bar fades away. I lift my beer and take a sip before inclining the glass in her direction. She takes it and drinks, and I swear I feel my dick leak in my pants just from her lips landing where mine had just been.

Something clicks inside my head at that moment. Someday, I may look back and wonder why the simple act of sharing a drink tipped me over the edge, but right now, I don't give a fuck. All I know is I need to have her. *All of her.*

She brings out a long-buried want in me. A want for a life here in Dogwood Cove, surrounded by my family and friends. A life where there's more than just hockey consuming my mind and body.

A life where I let myself love someone and be loved.

Her hand drifts up to stroke down my cheek, and I don't know who moves first, but then we're kissing. And everything feels perfect. I kiss the hell out of her, sucking on her perfect pliant lips. I have no idea how long we sit there lost in each other. But when her hips start to grind down on me, all bets are off.

"It's time to go, sunshine," I growl. Her sharp inhale tells me everything I need to know.

She's on the same page about what's happening tonight.

We say our goodbyes and I make a point of ignoring the smirks my brothers are giving me. Out at her car, I pull Lily in for another kiss. I can't help it. Those lips drive me wild.

Thank God for small towns because it's not long before we pull up in front of my building and Lily cuts the engine. I'm done pretending that I don't want her. Even if the feelings aren't real, the attraction is. She might never want me for anything more than sex, but since that's about all I can offer, I'll take what I can get.

"Upstairs. I need you naked."

Her tongue darts out to moisten her lips as she turns hooded eyes on me and nods slowly. We get out and make our way to the door. I have to use the cane, since my knee is hating how much standing and walking I did today. Inwardly, I curse because what I want to do is lift Lily up, feel those long legs wrap around my waist, and carry her inside. Fuck, I'd settle for getting to my apartment faster than this.

But if she's feeling that same frustration, she doesn't let it show. When we get inside, Lily's the one who spins around, and pushes me against the door before running her hands underneath my shirt and pressing her lips to mine desperately.

"Sunshine, I appreciate the enthusiasm, but we need to be horizontal until my physical therapist clears me."

Her giggle is perfection. Then she pivots and starts to walk away from me, kicking her shoes off as she goes. Another step toward my bedroom and she lifts her sweater off over her head and drops it on the couch with a saucy wink back over her shoulder.

"I think I'll need to perform a thorough assessment of your stamina." Her bra comes off next, landing on top of her sweater.

I break free of the trance I'm in just from seeing her bare skin and move after her. By the time I reach the bedroom, my shirt is gone and I'm making quick work of my pants. But the sight that greets me makes me freeze.

Lily is stretched out on my bed, wearing nothing but a tiny scrap of red lace between her legs.

"God fucking damn, sunshine," I say hoarsely. "You're gorgeous."

She gives me a seductive smile, and crooks her finger as she lifts up onto her knees. "You know you're going to have to let me do most of the work, right?"

I push my pants down to the floor and carefully step out of them. "I'm okay with that if you are."

She nods.

"As long as you remember that the second I can, I'll be returning the favour. Tenfold."

"Promises, promises," she teases, her eyes dancing with lust.

I move to lunge across the bed to her, stopping at the last second when my knee reminds me there's not a chance in hell of doing that. Lily interprets my grunt correctly and the lust fades to concern.

"Jude, careful."

Moving more carefully, I stretch out on my back, grab her, and pull her over me. "I'm fine. Better than fine. And that's the last we're gonna talk about my leg until I've made you come at least twice. Got it?"

Just like that, the lust is back in her eyes. I sit up — thank God for core strength — and capture her in a dizzying kiss. With nothing but my boxers and her thong separating us, she starts to grind down on my cock. My hands find her tits and I start to tease her nipples, pinching them lightly, then rolling the pebbled tips.

"Need to taste these," I rumble, ducking my head down to pull one into my mouth. Lily's answering moan is a bolt of lightning straight to my dick.

My tongue flicks across the stiff nub, circling around the tip as my hands knead the fleshy mounds. She's the perfect size. Round and plump and delicious.

"Oh God, Jude," Lily gasps, her fingers tugging at my hair. I scratch my beard across her sensitized skin, relishing how it pinks up underneath.

"Fucking beautiful."

Lily grabs my face and tugs me up, her teeth sinking into my lower lip as we crash together in a kiss. I knew she'd be wild in bed, but this desperate need is more than I expected. She's giving herself over to me and that power is heady.

She releases my mouth and gives me a wicked smile. "My turn." For a second, I'm confused, but her intent is clear as she pushes me gently so that I recline back slightly, then folds her body down and starts to trail open, wet kisses down my bare chest. One hand snakes down between us and starts to stroke my dick. Even over my underwear, it feels fucking amazing.

But nothing compares to the moment Lily slides my boxers down and my cock bounces free. She licks her lips like I'm her favourite fucking lollipop and I almost come right there just from the desire painted across her face.

I lift up just enough to gather her long hair in one hand. "That's it, sunshine. Take me." She lets me guide her head down and I swear my entire body ignites at the first swipe of her tongue over my tip. I don't force anything, letting her lead her movements. But when she fills her mouth with my entire length all at once, my fingers tighten their hold on her hair. I feel her moan around my dick, and I tug gently on the silky strands. "Fuck, yeah. Oh God, you're good at that."

Lily's head lifts off my length, her eyes glassy with pleasure. "Tug my hair, smack my ass, I like it Jude. I like it all." God fucking damn that's hot, hearing her talk like a dirty girl.

"Shit, baby," I groan. The fact that Lily likes it a little rough doesn't surprise me. But the fact that I like that with her *does* surprise me. After all, she's Lily. The woman I want to protect from all the bad things she has to face. Apparently, she's also the woman I want to fuck hard and fast.

"I'm gonna come, sunshine," I growl when I feel lightning shoot down my spine and my dick starts to swell. I don't care if she swallows or not, but it's her choice. She pops off me, but her hand keeps working up and down, creating an intense friction that is doing nothing to slow down my impending orgasm.

Those stormy grey eyes meet mine again. "Good," she says saucily. I raise my eyebrows, but she just winks and drops her head down, sucking me in deep until I hit the back of her throat.

That's all it takes and I come with a roar, shooting into her mouth.

Chapter Twenty

Lily

I lift my thumb up to wipe away a drop of Jude's come from the corner of my lip, then suck it off. I love giving guys blowjobs; it's a total power trip for me to witness them lose control from nothing more than my mouth and my hand.

But this was something else. Watching Jude lose it and detonate under me was powerful, intense, and humbling.

He could have any woman he wanted. And he wants me. He's here with me.

The look he gave me when he wrapped my hair in his fist was one of reverent surprise. We might have a history of knowing each other for years, but this is the first time we've been anything more than friendly — not counting that magical morning after the wedding.

Even our kisses and touches since deciding to fake date have felt grounded in friendship and nothing more. At least, for me they have. He's doing me a favour by going along with this lie, helping me save face with my horrible family, and making my nana's wish come true. It's a messy situation, and probably not the smartest of plans, but you can't stop a runaway train. And that's what this feels like.

"That was incredible." His voice is hoarse, and I grin like a Cheshire cat.

"You're welcome." I'm still sitting to the side of him, my hand resting on his leg. He grabs it and brings it to his lips to kiss my knuckles. It's so sweet, my heart swoons a little. This romantic, affectionate side of him is so unexpected, and like nothing I've ever had from a man before. And it's intensified by knowing he'll be like that even when we aren't in bed. He'll make a great boyfriend to some lucky woman. In just a few weeks of pretending to be with him, I've felt more cared for and cherished than ever.

That thought is a little scary. Because this is just pretend, but it feels more real than anything. Will I ever find this with someone who actually wants a true relationship?

"Where did you just go?"

I glance up at Jude. He doesn't look annoyed, just concerned. How is he so in tune with me and my messed-up head?

"Nowhere. I'm here." I crawl up beside him so I can kiss his lips. But Jude has other plans. Showing off his athletic prowess and insane strength, out of nowhere, he grabs my legs and lifts me over him so I'm basically sitting on his chest. My hands fall to the pillow on either side of his head as I bend in half so I can keep kissing him.

"Those aren't the lips I want, sunshine." Jude's hands land on my ass, and he pushes me up toward his head.

I grab the headboard, heart pounding. Despite my experience, I've never once had a guy want to do this. And Jude isn't asking. He's telling. God, that's hot.

He grips the edges of my thong and stares up at me. "Hope you aren't attached to these."

I'm still shaking my head as he tears them off. Mark that down as another first for me. Holy. Hell. Then his beard is nuzzling between my thighs, the scratchy feeling a delicious tease.

My head falls forward, my hair cascading around like a curtain as I stare down at his head buried between my legs. And when his tongue swipes up my slit the first time, I'm transported to another freaking planet.

"Ohmygod. Yes." I hold myself perfectly still, letting Jude grip my ass, and pull me down to meet his mouth. His tongue dives into my pussy, swirling and licking every fold, nibbling, and sucking. I'm so used to guys heading straight for my clit to get me off as quickly as possible, but not Jude. He takes his time. The anticipation, the build, it's almost too much. "Jude, please. Please, I need to come." I'm begging and I don't care. Apparently, neither does he. I feel him shake his head, the brush of his whiskers making me moan.

Finally, after what feels like forever with him tormenting me using light flicks of his tongue, his lips latch onto my clit, and I feel him slide two thick fingers inside. Slowly, he thrusts them in and out. I need him to curl them over and find my G-spot, but he doesn't. For someone who normally comes quite easily, the way he's playing my body and stretching it out is the most exquisite form of torture.

"Fuck!" I cry out, my hips rocking into his touch. I reach down and grip his hair, needing to anchor myself to him. "Oh God. Right there. Don't stop. Please, don't stop." My body starts to writhe over him, the movements completely out of my control. I'm chasing an orgasm that promises to be like nothing I've ever experienced, but he's holding me back, right at the edge.

"Jude, please, I'm so close." My voice takes on a keening sound, pure desperation lacing my words.

"Now."

One word and I explode, feeling my body release a flood of wetness all over his face. His tongue flattens as he laps it up, his rumbling moans telling me just how much he's enjoying it. When I finally stop quivering from the aftershocks, I lift one shaky leg over and collapse down beside him. My chest is heaving; I'm both exhausted and energized. I sense him roll over, but my eyes refuse to open, in case this was all just a really, really sexy dream. But then the bed dips, and I look over to see Jude's deliciously naked ass slowly walking into the bathroom, his limp barely noticeable. Then again, I'm a little distracted.

Hockey butts are a thing of perfection.

A tap turns on for a few minutes, then he returns. "Never had to clean my beard after eating pussy."

I cover my face with my hands. "I don't know if I should be proud or mortified."

The mattress sinks again as he stretches out beside me and a warm hand lands on my stomach. I can smell the soap on his skin as he leans in and bites my earlobe gently. "Proud. It was fucking hot."

Rolling onto my side, I kiss him deeply. There's a faint hint of a musky smell that's probably from me. And he's right. It's freaking hot.

His hand goes to my leg, and he lifts it again, this time to drape it over his. "Wait, that's your bad leg." I stop him, holding myself still. But Jude pushes my leg down to rest on his hip.

"Keep it up high, around my waist."

I scoot in until we're pressed together. It's taking naked cuddling to a whole other level. His cock is hardening again; I can feel it sliding between my open hips. We stay like this, just kissing and letting our hands travel all over each other. It's an incredibly erotic position to make out. But my body is craving his. I don't even know if I'll be able to climax again so soon, but I don't really care. I need him inside of me.

"Condom?" I whisper against his lips.

Jude freezes. Not the reaction I expected. "Shit."

My mouth turns up as I watch his brows pull together. "Don't worry, big guy. A girl should always be prepared." Carefully, I untangle myself from him, climb off the bed, and go to the living room to grab my purse. When I return to the bedroom, he's on his back, propped up on his elbows. I take a second just to drink him in. His hair's a mess and his beautiful eyes are hooded with pleasure. Muscles ripple across his torso. He made no effort to cover himself up and thank God for that. Because Jude's body is a work of art. A light dusting of hair on his chest trails down to his semihard cock. Strong legs, surgical scars and all, heck, even his feet are sexy, somehow.

"You're so hot," I blurt out. "Like, really freaking hot. Ten chili peppers. It's not fair."

To my utter shock, hell freezes over and pigs fly.

Okay, no. But Jude's head falls back and he laughs. Like a deep, true laugh.

My mouth falls open and my purse drops to the floor. When he lifts his head and looks at me, I get another surprise.

He's smiling.

And it's the most beautiful sight to see. His face lights up, the skin around his eyes crinkling. It's almost blinding, it's so amazing.

I approach him slowly after pulling out the two condoms I keep stashed in my bag. My hand reaches out and traces the lines of lips, still upturned in a grin.

"Miracles do happen," I whisper, and his smile grows even wider. "Why now? What did I say?"

Jude tugs me until I'm up on the bed beside him. He doesn't answer until we're back in the sideways cuddle position, my hips splayed open with one leg draped over his. Even then, he says nothing, but his face grows serious — not grumpy, just serious, and he pulls me in to kiss me softly.

"You make me happy."

Those four words make my heart stutter. But for once, I'm at a loss for what to say. Letting my body do the talking, I reach for one of the condoms, rip it open, and back away just enough so I can roll it down his length, stroking a few times to make him even harder.

Lining our bodies up, I tilt my hips so that he dips inside. Just that makes me gasp, feeling him run through my sensitized folds. He grabs my ass and starts to move me back and forth, keeping it teasingly shallow. It's an exquisite torment, too much and not enough at the same time.

"Oh my God," I pant as I curl myself up, making his dick hit the place I'm desperate to feel him. "Deeper. I need you deeper."

Jude pulls back, his strong hands pushing my hips away at the same time, then he slams us together, making me shriek from the overwhelming sensation of fullness. Taking him in at this angle is lighting up places inside of me I never knew existed. He does it again, and again, and every time, I cry out his name as his length fills me perfectly. My body starts to writhe, twisting and undulating, needing to feel him everywhere. But Jude's hands squeeze my ass tightly. "Don't. Move," he grinds out. My eyes blink open, *huh, I hadn't realized they were closed,* and I see wildfire in his eyes. He's breathing heavily, staring so deeply at me, I just know he sees everything. All of me.

"You feel like heaven."

"Jude," I whisper, cupping his cheek with one hand. His grip loosens just enough to let me move and I slowly start to rock my hips back and forth. His hand grips my ass tightly, then suddenly, there's a crack as he smacks me lightly. "Oh God! Do that again!" He does, and every time his hand lands on my flesh, it sends a pulse of wetness to my pussy.

Moving my hips in this position is difficult, especially with my leg so high up. But the ecstasy on his face is enthralling to see. When his eyes flutter closed, I lean down and kiss his open mouth, plunging my tongue in at the exact same time as I push onto his cock.

"Fucking hell, you're amazing, baby. So goddamn hot, sunshine, what you do to me is insane." I hear the raw vulnerability and utter wonder in those words. It all feels so real, but I know it's just the heat of the moment. Passion makes people say crazy things. I can't let myself get caught up in what he says, no matter how much it makes my heart hurt with wishing it wasn't pretend.

I didn't think I'd find myself falling for Jude. Call me a fool, but I truly thought I could save myself from heartache and just keep things friendly while we pretended otherwise. After all, Jude needs someone who will be with him forever. Someone who will love him and show him how much he has to offer. And I'm not that girl. I've never been that girl. And even if, by some crazy chance, he wanted more from me than just a fuck buddy and a fake girlfriend, he'd realize soon enough that I'm not who he truly wants, and I'd be cast aside. And any promise we've made that our agreement won't mess up my friendship with his family would be out the window.

I fight back my intrusive thoughts before I completely ruin the mood. Right now, Jude's amazing dick is doing things to me that I really, really like. And that's what I need to focus on.

This moment. Not the future.

I pull back, lift my leg even higher, then push myself back onto his dick with as much force as I can from this position. Jude's eyes flare wide, but he doesn't comment on the change. He meets me thrust for thrust, his hands gripping my ass and helping me to rock into him, our groans filling the air.

"Damn. Lily. Fuck, I'm gonna..." His voice trails off as we both let go, my orgasm hurtling through me stronger and faster than a freight train.

"Jude!" I gasp as my pussy clenches tightly around him. Wave after wave of sensation rolls across me, making me breathless.

Eventually, I come back to earth, Jude's hands rhythmically stroking up and down my back.

"Holy shit," he says quietly, his hands coming to rest on my damp skin.

"Mm-hmm." I can't muster any more of a response than that.

"C'mon, sunshine, let's clean up, then get some sleep." His voice is gravelly, laden with satisfaction and something sweeter. Something I don't let myself think about too hard.

Instead, I carefully untangle my legs from his, and watch out of sleepy eyes as he ties off the condom before dropping it into the waste basket conveniently located beside the bed. Then Jude gathers me back in his arms, tucking my body against his. I reach down and tug the blanket up to cover us both.

And the last thing I remember before falling asleep is Jude's lips pressing a sweet kiss to my head.

Chapter Twenty-One

Jude

This is the second morning in a row I've woken up actually feeling rested. Not only that, but I don't remember being awake all night. Even pre-injury, mornings sucked, mostly because insomnia robbed me of any possibility at restful sleep. It didn't matter if I was waking up on game day or a day off, I hated mornings.

Until now, I guess. Well, until the first time I woke up with Lily in my arms. That fateful morning after the wedding, I thought it was just a weird, crazy fluke. But now? I'm wondering if she's what I've been missing all along.

Because two nights ago, she slept in my arms, and it was the best night of my life. And even though I was alone last night, I still slept. The whole damn night.

Walking into the shower, even my leg isn't hurting as badly as it was just yesterday. My gait feels smoother, and I feel overall stronger and steadier.

Sex with Lily is a goddamn miracle cure.

See, jackass, you just needed to get laid to stop being a grouch.

I chuckle to myself at that thought, and the memory of joking with Lily about which grumpy character I was most like. And the excited hug she gave me simply because I cracked the tiniest of smiles. She has no clue that I've been fighting them back when I'm around her for a while. I've been resisting the fact that she makes me happy — happier than I have been in a long fucking time.

In the shower, I lean my hands against the wall and flex my quads, feeling them fire. Sure, the right side isn't as strong, but it's getting there. Thanks to her.

It always comes back to her.

For just a second, I let myself think about what it would be like if things were different. If Lily's feelings for me were as real as mine are becoming for her. If we had a future together.

One hand travels down and grips my cock. Because just thinking about her like I have been has me sporting a semi. And seeing as I have to go to a session with her this morning, it's probably best I deal with this now instead of showing up and popping a boner the second she lays her hands on me.

I pull and tug on my dick, letting the hot water provide a little bit of lubrication. It's not as good as her hot mouth, or her even hotter pussy, but if I close my eyes, I can envision her dropping to her knees in the shower and sucking me in between her lips. I groan as my dick immediately swells in my hands. Fuck, if just the *thought* of her can get me hard... It's witchcraft.

An embarrassingly short period of time later, I'm spraying the shower walls with my orgasm, shouting her name loud enough that it echoes back at me. Panting, I lower my head and close my eyes. I want more. I want her. I want her back in my bed, and I want to tie her up there so she can never leave.

And with that surprisingly sexy image in my head, I quickly finish my shower, eager to get to the clinic and see her for real.

With the weather clear outside, I decide to walk to the clinic, which I realize too late was a bad idea. Because now, I'm standing in the reception area with her in front of me, both hands on her hips, looking adorable and alluring all at once, with long white feathers dangling from her ears. And my fucking leg is visibly shaking.

"Why do I not see one of your brothers' vehicles out front?" she demands, and I give her a small sheepish grin.

"I was feeling good. So I walked."

Lily walks up and smacks my arm. Not the greeting I was expecting or at least hoping for, that's for fucking sure.

"Jude, that was not smart. You know I work you hard on therapy days, so you're meant to save the longer walks for in-between. Now we'll have to back off on our exercises, so you don't over do it. And you better text your brothers to ask for a ride home when we're done. Am I clear?"

I'm biting my tongue, trying not to say anything about the *work you hard* part of what she just said, even as a mental image of bending her over the damn massage table in that private room and driving into her from behind fills my head.

"Sorry," I mumble. But she can sense the lack of sincerity in my voice, judging by the huff and eye roll I get in return. God, she's so fucking cute, I just want to reach out and pull her into my arms to fill myself with her light.

Instead, I trail after her into the room we always start in. Once the door is closed, however, all bets are off. I don't know who reaches for who first, but we're grabbing for each other, lips landing wherever they can within seconds.

"Fuck, Lily," I groan quietly when her hands dig into my ass. I press forward, and I know she feels the hard imprint of my dick straining behind my joggers.

"Jude. We can't do this here."

Her words say one thing but the frantic kisses she gives me say another. Still, she's right. This isn't the time or place.

I force myself back from her and find her eyes blazing with need. "I slept again last night." Those beautiful eyes widen at my seemingly random statement. Because she alone knows why that's important. "I told you, sunshine, you're working miracles on more than just my knee."

Lily drops her gaze from me to the floor before turning and busying herself with lining up the bottles of massage oil on the shelf. "We should get started."

I can take a hint, even if I don't want to — or even understand why she's pulling back. When she eventually turns back around, I reach out and finger the feather hanging from her ear. "At the risk of sounding like a cliché poster found in a school counsellor's office, don't let anyone dull your sparkle. I can guess you're not used to receiving compliments, but that's not going to stop me from telling you how much I respect you, and how much I enjoy spending time with you."

Her mouth flaps open and shut like a fish, and with one finger and a gentle smile I push her chin up to close it. Then I pull down my joggers, revealing the shorts underneath, turn and climb up on the table, and stretch out. We need to move things back to normal, and I'm willing to do that — for now.

After just a brief pause, Lily snaps out of whatever hesitation she's got going on. She grabs the bottle of oil, pours some into her hands, and rubs them together. Of course, despite my earlier shower session, the second her hands land on my thigh, my dick jumps.

"Ignore that. Can't help it around you," I mutter, lacing my hands and putting them behind my head.

Lily makes a strange noise, and I cast my gaze down from the ceiling to see her fighting back a smirk.

"What?"

Her eyes fly to mine and that smirk breaks free, into a mischievous smile. "Oh, nothing." But her hand drifts up, higher than she normally goes and definitely higher than would be considered appropriate. The back of her hand grazes my dick and I let out a low rumble.

"You're playing dirty, sunshine."

Immediately, her hand travels down toward my knee, and I have to convince myself not to grab it and place it right back where I want it.

But Lily's all business now. She gets to work with her usual torture, digging into my muscles and breaking down the tension and scar tissue. It's nowhere near as painful as it was in the beginning, but it's uncomfortable enough to kill any desire I was feeling earlier.

After a few minutes of her working in silence, her hands slow. "Should we be doing this?" she asks, the words barely above a whisper.

I know what she's referring to. But I'll be damned if I want to be the one to answer. Because I would say resoundingly *yes, we should be*, but that's selfish. I don't want to lose how good she makes me feel.

"Can we truly add sex into an already weird situation and not have it get even more complicated?"

I lift up on my elbows to see her gnawing on her lip with worry. Running my thumb over it to free it, I tug her down to meet me for a kiss.

The instant our lips touch, she melts. And that's all the answer I need.

"It might complicate things, but I don't give a fuck. Because now that I've had a taste, there's no chance I'll be able to resist coming back for more. The only thing that will make me back off is if you tell me right here, right now, that you don't want this."

I hold my breath, waiting to see what she'll do. It would be a complete lie if I said there's no feelings involved and no chance of getting hurt if she refuses me. There's no avoiding the truth for me. I like Lily, a lot. And I would be more than a little upset if she wanted to walk away. Even if she never wants anything real with me, I'm not ready to lose what we have going on.

"I want this."

Three words. Said so softly, I almost miss them. But there's no mistaking the smile breaking free on her face. I go to kiss her again, but I'm stopped by her hand on my chest.

"But not here. There will be no happy endings to your massage today, mister. Now lie back down and let me finish."

I grumble, but it's good-natured. And inside, I'm smiling like a fool.

She wants it. She wants *me*.

Later in the afternoon, I finally respond to the voicemail left by the Westport Ravens team. They're not annoyed by me taking a few days to get back to them and briefly outline their offer. It's more than generous.

But first, they invite me to come to the arena and check it out, and to meet with some people from management, as well as the goalie coach. When they mention the name Igor Louka, my interest skyrockets. The man is a legend in the hockey world. He's coached multiple championship teams. Rumour was he moved to the West Coast, but I lost track of things with the chaos of a new season starting, and then my injury. The idea of working alongside him makes it slightly easier to accept reality.

I've been holding onto the faint hope that I might be able to return to the team, but despite the work I'm putting in — that Lily's putting in — I have to face facts. My knee is not going to magically be better in time to skate this season, if ever.

Which means, it's time to grow the fuck up. Getting to my age and still being an active player is a rarity. But my love of the game and my commitment to my team kept me going and made me turn a blind eye to any hint of conversation about retirement.

Joke's on me, I guess.

I text my dad to ask if he wants to come with me to check out the arena. Partly because I need the ride, and partly because I value his opinion above almost anyone else.

What awaits us in Westport somehow causes the decisions I need to make both easier and harder. The arena is a thing of beauty. State of the art, top of the line everything. From the multiple rinks to the gym, to treatment areas, locker rooms, offices — all of it is amazing. It's clear LaRoy and management spared no expense. Meeting with him, and with Brody Olsen the GM, I start to actually get excited about the idea of coaching.

But on the drive home, my dad is silent. Even more than normal. And that silence opens the door for doubts to creep into my head.

"I don't know what to do."

Dad's head moves up and down thoughtfully, but he says nothing.

"I don't want to stop playing. I don't want to sign the fucking paperwork that ends my career. How do I walk away from so many years with the team? I know I'm the fucking idiot who stuck his head in the sand and didn't think about retirement, but I did. And now I feel like I'm being forced to make a decision I'm not ready for." Now that the words of self-doubt and grief and anger have started, I can't stop them. They flow out of me like a river of lava, burning me from the inside as they pour out. "And what if I'm not cut out to be a coach? What if I take the job, and in a few months, they realize I'm a total hack and they let me go? Then what? Then I'm not only a washed-up player, but I'm also a failed coach. I've got nothing to fall back on. Jesus Christ, I'm an idiot. I have nothing to offer except hockey, and now I can't even do that right."

One hot tear tracks down my cheek and I brush it away angrily. *No. More. Tears.* I shed enough in the early days after my injury. I'll be damned if I'm gonna start wallowing again.

Dad swings his car into the parking lot for some diner along the highway between Westport and Dogwood Cove. "Let's get a cup of coffee."

He climbs out without leaving any room for discussion. After taking a couple of deep breaths, I follow him into the diner. It smells like greasy food and cheap coffee. The vinyl booths are cracked and worn, and there's only one other guy sitting at the counter.

We slide into a booth and I pick up a menu just for something to do. I'm not hungry, however. When a waitress comes over, Dad orders a cup of coffee for each of us. She leaves and then his hand pushes the menu down away from my face.

"No hiding, son. Not from me, not from your future, not from your emotions."

The waitress drops off the cups of coffee and I busy myself with stirring in some creamer. I take a sip and grimace. "This is nasty."

Dad lifts his cup to his mouth and his reaction mimics mine. "We aren't here for the coffee."

A sigh escapes me. "I don't know what you expect me to say, Dad. I'm not hiding. *I can't.* Because every goddamn morning when I wake up and see the scars on my leg, I get a dose of reality. Every day that I don't lace up a pair of skates and hit the ice, I have to face facts. I just don't have a fucking clue what to do with those facts."

"You just keep moving. Doesn't matter if it's forward, backward, or sideways. You keep on moving. And every step will eventually lead you to a place where you know what to do. Where the choice becomes clear, and then when you're ready, you step into your new future."

I exhale loudly. "Okay, so what do I do *now*?"

"You need to figure out how to get your heart to accept what your brain already knows. It's time to move on and figure out a life after the NHL. Think about where you want to be, who you want to be with, what you want to be doing. And none of those answers have to include being here, with your family, and taking this job if that doesn't feel right. But no matter what, you need to take a step."

A vision fills my head, well, more like fragments of a vision. Different moments in time, flashing through my mind at lightning speed. Some of them feel right, some of them don't.

My apartment in Montana, empty and cold.

My parents' house, filled with my family for family dinners.

Poker nights with my brothers. Going for drinks and watching the game at Hastings.

Max and Heidi's inevitable wedding, or Kat and Hunter's, if they get there first.

Events that have happened or will happen, that I'll actually have a chance of attending if I'm not tied to the NHL schedule. The chance to get to know my siblings' loved ones. To reconnect with my cousin and his family. The chance to build a team from the ground up and to watch that team succeed.

And Lily.

She's in every moment, every vision. Because I want her there. I want her with me, for real. No more pretending when my feelings are very fucking real.

But are hers? Is it even possible for her to have true feelings for me when the only thing women ever wanted from me is no longer available?

Logically, I know Lily doesn't care if I'm a player or not. But old wounds still fester. And if I stay stuck, with no direction or plan for my future, then what right do I have to even consider asking Lily to try a relationship for real.

It might be foolish to hinge my actions and choices on a woman. A chance at a woman, at best.

But if anyone's worth fighting for, it's Lily.

"Don't suppose you know a good real estate agent in Dogwood Cove?"

Dad's answering smile is all the evidence I need that this is exactly what I should be doing.

CHAPTER TWENTY-TWO

Lily

"Breathe deeply into your belly and exhale slowly. Feel the calm."

I try to do as Summer instructs, breathing and filling myself with calm. But I fail. *Because I'd rather be full of something else...*

Yoga class is normally my happy place. I love connecting with my body, feeling the strength and flexibility I've worked hard to achieve. I can either push myself, build up a sweat, or I can take it slow and use the poses and breathing techniques to relax and de-stress.

But lately, I've been a little...distracted, shall we say.

I can't stop thinking about Jude. Naked Jude, fully clothed Jude, grumpy Jude, smiling Jude, growly protective Jude, sweet and romantic Jude. All Jude, all the time.

He's consumed every inch of my body and every thought in my head.

And as I fall out of my dancing warrior pose for the third time, I guess my frustrated exhale is a little too loud. Serena turns to me from her mat.

"Everything okay?"

I nod, averting my eyes. She owns the studio where the class is being held, and she's engaged to Jude's cousin. She's the last person I want knowing I'm too preoccupied with thoughts of Jude to focus.

Then again, Serena's like me — completely open and free about sex, not shy in the slightest. Kat and I even went to a sex toy party she hosted a few months back. So, maybe out of anyone, she'd understand my obsession with the man who's giving me more orgasms than I thought possible.

Summer's serene voice is still leading the rest of the class through a flow, but I call it quits. Quietly rolling up my mat, I flash an apologetic smile to Serena before sneaking out the door. Guess it's a good thing I was late today and had to find a spot near the back.

Once I'm in my car, my head falls against my steering wheel with a thunk. "Get. It. Together. Chapman," I say in time with knocking my head against the wheel over and over. A sharp rap on my window makes me shriek and sit upright, mortified that someone caught my mini meltdown.

That mortification grows into dread when I see my mother's disapproving frown. With her hair pulled back in a severe bun, the crow's feet around her eyes, and the boring grey pant suit she's wearing, she looks like she belongs in a boardroom, not standing outside a dance studio.

When it comes to my mother, she might as well be a Borg from *Star Trek*. *Resistance is futile.* It's no good harnessing my inner calm, because as the yoga class I just abandoned proved, I have none right now. Instead, I simply open the door and climb out.

Her eyes rake over me and I know she's not pleased.

Is it my lime green yoga shorts? Or the tank top with a cat wearing sunglasses. Maybe it's my hair, I'm pretty sure the purple is showing. Or maybe it's my car. Let's be real, it's all of the above. And I brace myself for the attack. It'll be sneaky, full of passive-aggressive barbs couched in "good" intentions, but it's coming.

Then she speaks and it's so much worse than I could have ever expected.

"How long were you planning on avoiding me, Lilian? I've tried to contact you several times since your cousin's wedding to speak to you about your conduct."

Oh boy. Here we go.

"My time is valuable, and when I have to waste it leaving you voicemails that go unanswered, it displeases me."

Right, because talking to your daughter is never *a valuable use of time.*

"Don't think it went unnoticed that you and that man you were with disappeared long before it was appropriate to leave.

Your poor cousin was mortified when she had to field questions about your disappearance."

Now she's gone too far with this self-absorbed victimization. "Mom, be real. No one at that wedding gave a shit if I was there or not, except for Nana."

I regret the sharp words the instant I say them. My mother's lips thin with anger and her fingers start to drum on her arm.

"When are you going to grow up, Lilian, and stop assuming the world revolves around you and your childish ways. The wedding was a very important day for your cousin and our family, and your lack of maturity and inability to put your own feelings aside for once cast a dark shadow on it all."

I bite back the snort of derision. There's so much wrong with what she's saying. So many lies. And yet, the little girl inside of me, the tiny part of me that is still desperate to feel something other than contempt from my parents, wilts even further.

"Your grandmother must be getting senile with her inability to see what a disappointment you are. Why can't you be more like Marnie and live up to your potential? Or at the very least, contribute to this family in a meaningful way. It's no wonder Clay moved on to your cousin. What could he possibly want from you? You're a disgrace."

Turning on her heel, the woman who gave birth to me, who by all rights should love me unconditionally above all else, walks away. If she saw the tears that I couldn't stop from streaming down my face, she certainly didn't show it.

I brush them away angrily before getting back in my car. Thank fuck no one walked past us and witnessed my humiliation. There's been other occasions when I haven't been so lucky.

"Fuck you!" I sob, smacking my hand on the steering wheel. "Fuck all of you."

I sniff back any more tears. Because I realized a long time ago that my family doesn't deserve the energy it takes for me to feel like this.

If I wasn't so attached to this town, to my friends and my work, I would leave. I would move to the opposite end of the earth to get away from the people I fervently wish I was not related to.

Rolling my neck from side to side, I turn on my car and drive home. It's taken a lot of years of therapy to get to a point where I can convincingly tell myself that my mother is wrong. That I am not a failure, that I do provide value to the world. My energy, and refusal to conform, is not a bad thing.

I repeat that mantra over and over until I pull into my driveway. When my phone chimes with a calendar alert, my gut instinct is to say *fuck it* to whatever I had planned and just curl up on the couch with a pint of ice cream and a cheesy movie. But then I remember what it is.

Nana invited Jude and me over to her apartment for afternoon tea. Somehow, when I decided to go to yoga, I forgot entirely about this. Which means I now have less than five minutes to change and get back in my car to pick up Jude.

Inside, I toss my yoga wear on the floor and grab a sweater dress. A pair of socks and ankle booties and some gold earrings that are a bit tame for my taste, but were a gift from Nana, complete the look. I'm out the door again in four minutes.

By the time I get to Jude's house, I've mostly moved on from the conversation with my mother — if you can call a mostly one-sided criticism a conversation. Okay, maybe *moved on* is the wrong sentiment. I've compartmentalized. Buried it in the box in the back of my head with the thousand other sharp knives she digs into my heart any time she sees me.

Jude's waiting outside, and just the sight of him makes me sigh with...well, with a lot of things.

Need. Want. Desire. Affection. Sadness.

Most of those make sense. After all, the man is a god in bed, even with one leg out of action. Who knows how many orgasms he'd give me at full capacity. I shiver just thinking about it.

But the sadness is the one that has me squirming in my seat as he walks to the car. I'm getting hot sex from a guy with no expectations or strings. Why am I sad?

Oh. Right. Because a foolish part of me wishes there was a chance of him having real feelings for me beyond friendship and mutual sexual satisfaction.

But my dating history has made it abundantly clear that's not even remotely possible.

He slowly lowers himself into my car and the therapist in me sees the slight grimace cross his features. "What did you do?"

Jude's lips tighten at my question. "Nothing."

"Liar." I pick up my phone and wave it at him. "Do I need to text your brothers and ask what stupidity you all got up to?"

"No," he grumbles under his breath before running his hands over his short beard. "I might have been trying out the gym facilities at the new arena in Westport."

I gasp in only partly mock outrage. "Jude! Are you trying to ruin all the progress we've made? What did I tell you about working out?" I slap at his bicep, but it's hard as a rock, so my hand just bounces off.

The sheepish look I get in return tells me he knows he screwed up. "I know. But I was there for another meeting, and the assistant coach and I were talking, and then I just..." His voice trails off, leaving me to fill in the blanks.

"Then you just ignored your physical therapist and did something dumb."

"In my defense, you did say I could *start* doing some weight training."

I lean my body against the window of my car and fold my arms across my chest. "Yeah. Start *slowly*. And judging by your face when you had to squat down to get in the car, I'm guessing you did not hear that last word."

"I'll be fine." His gruff reply stings slightly. It feels like a rebuff. Which is probably just an echo of the dismissal I'm still feeling from my mom, but it hurts, nonetheless.

Turning forward, I start the car and pull out onto the street. The next few minutes are tense and I hate it. I hate that my sour mood from earlier isn't gone. Then Jude's big hand lands on the back of my neck.

"I'm sorry, Lily."

Pulling to a stop at a red light, I look over at him. "Sorry for..."

"For not listening to you or respecting your opinion, for pushing myself too far, and potentially undoing all the amazing progress you've helped me to gain." Sincerity rings in his voice and that alone is enough to make me shift from annoyed physical therapist to concerned friend.

"Thank you. And I'm sorry you're hurting today. We'll go easy tomorrow, and I'll spend some time mapping out a strengthening plan so that you know next time what you can and cannot do."

His hand squeezes my shoulder gently. "Thanks, sunshine."

A short while later, we reach Nana's place, and soon after, we're sitting on her floral couches that are far more comfortable than they look, sipping tea. Jude has his arm over my shoulder, forcing me to lean into him, while Nana watches us with a suspiciously smug expression.

"Jude. I'd just love it if you could tell me again what made you fall for our darling Lily. It makes me so happy to see her with someone who truly cherishes her for the wonderful woman she is."

"Nana," I mumble under my breath, more than a little embarrassed at how she's putting him on the spot. Taking a sip of tea, I chance a quick look over at him, only to find his eyes squarely on me, a soft smile on his face.

"Where do I begin," he murmurs. "Lily has this light about her. It's infectious. Doesn't matter how dark it is around you, she brightens everything, just by being who she is. Her heart, her strength, her loyalty, she's a better woman than almost anyone else I know. I came home a broken man, and I don't just mean my leg. Somehow, almost immediately after we reconnected, I found my jagged edges softening, the wounds knitting back together, inside and out. She makes me have hope again." He takes in a deep breath, and only then do his eyes flick to my grandmother, and then back to me. This time, the smile is bigger. "And she's the most beautiful woman in the world. I consider it an absolute honour that she puts up with me, and I never take it for granted that she could do a lot better than a grumpy injured hockey player, yet she chooses to be with me, anyway."

Oh God. I don't know if I can do this. I don't know if I can sit here, listening to him say all of this, pretending that it's real, when on the inside, I'm dying because I know it's not. This hurts even more than what my mother said to me earlier, and she flayed me alive.

Because when I remind myself that her words are not true, it makes me feel better. When I remind myself that Jude's words are not true, it makes me feel empty.

"Excuse me." I stand up abruptly and bolt to the bathroom. I turn the lock on the door and sink down to the floor, leaning against the wall.

What am I doing?

I didn't mean to fall for Jude. I might have been naive, but I honestly thought my attraction to him was purely physical and that I could maintain a platonic relationship — even once sex was added in. We had mutual objectives in placating our family, and faking a romantic relationship seemed a logical option.

God, I was so wrong. Because I have fallen for him. Everything I feel is so freaking real, and it's harder and harder to keep pretending it isn't. Hearing him say all those amazing things about me was a slap in the face. A reminder that the only time I'll ever hear a guy say those things is when he's faking it.

I draw in a ragged breath. No way am I crying twice in one day.

Several deep breaths later and I've got myself reasonably controlled. Enough, I hope, to make it through the next hour or so with Jude and Nana before I can escape home and make good on the ice cream and movie I wished for earlier.

Sure enough, my fake smile seems to satisfy the two of them for the rest of our visit. And the drive back to Jude's apartment starts out just fine. I ramble on about the hockey game from last night while he contributes the occasional grunt.

But halfway to his place, as we're passing by the turnoff for the public beach, Jude puts his hand on my arm.

"Turn here."

"What? Why?" I ask, even as I'm flicking on my indicator and making the turn. I follow the road down a short way until it opens out into the parking lot for the day-use area. The lot is empty, so I pull up right in the front, the waves of the ocean a stunning vista in front of us.

When I shut off the engine and turn to Jude, he's facing me head-on. "You're not going for a beach walk, mister. You already overdid it on that knee." The teasing tone I was going for falls flat when he just gets out of the car and walks slowly around to open my door.

"Come on. We aren't going far, but I always think better when I'm outside."

I want to ask him what he's thinking about, but I also don't know if I want to hear his answer. Instead, I follow until he sits down on a bench overlooking the ocean.

"After I said those things to your grandmother about what I like about you, you bolted," he starts, casual and relaxed. Meanwhile, I feel anything but. "Care to tell me why?"

My hand starts to play with my earrings. I don't want to tell him. I seriously don't. But I also feel as if I owe him my honesty. If for no other reason than to give him a chance to back out now before I get too crazy and fall in love with him or something stupid.

As if I'm not already halfway there...

"I'm sorry I disappeared. I just... It was —" I huff out a sad laugh. "Hearing you say that stuff meant something to me. It meant a lot, actually. You've met my family; compliments are not their forte, especially not toward me. And guys have never thought of me as a long-term option. I'm the perfect fuck buddy, but when it comes time for something more, they move on to someone more suitable."

"Just like Clay did."

I nod at his muttered curse. "Yeah. So when you suddenly started telling Nana all that stuff about me, about your supposed feelings, it was like rubbing salt on a wound. Except you had no idea it would hurt me." I hurry to clarify as I take in the horrified look on his face. God, this man, the very thought of causing me pain is making him upset. "I'm not mad at you. Not at all. I'm mad at myself for not being able to remember it's all fake and those beautiful words were part of the act. I'm mad at myself for falling for you when I know better. When I know you don't want me that way, that this isn't real for you."

"Lily," he starts, then stops, his head falling forward as he exhales. When he looks back up at me, the raw emotion in his eyes makes me gasp.

"Lily, it was real. What I said, that was the truth. Every word. I'm not pretending, hell, I haven't been for a long time. Actually, no. I never was. It's been real for me since the beginning. Since that god-awful wedding when I saw your spark being dulled by those people, and I knew I wanted to protect you from it all."

I'm frozen in place as he turns to face me, his hands lift to cup my face, tipping it up to meet his. "My feelings for you are absolutely not fake. They're very deep and very real, and I'm hoping like hell yours are, too."

His lips brush against mine, and the electric current that runs through me at that light contact wakes up every nerve ending, every cell of my body. Cautiously, my hands lift to land on his chest. I'm still terrified I'm going to wake up and find this was all a dream. But the second I touch him, his chest vibrates with a deep, satisfied growl.

When his lips land on me again, there's nothing light about it. This kiss is a claiming one, possessive and strong, full of promise and hope — and truth.

CHAPTER TWENTY-THREE

Jude

The second we fall through the door to Lily's house, clothes start flying off. We stumble our way down the hall to her bedroom. Then I pick her up and carry her the last two steps before dropping her down on the bed, kneeling on the mattress on my good leg so I can hover over her.

"If you bust your knee trying to fuck me, I'm not going to treat you anymore," she says, slapping at my bare chest. I just smirk down at her, ducking my head to kiss her collarbone before burying my head in the crook of her shoulder, just breathing her in. The feel of her soft skin under me, her hands trailing up and down my spine, and the damp heat between her legs fills me with such a primal satisfaction.

Mine. She's mine.

The insatiable need I have to touch her everywhere, to feel her everywhere, supersedes everything else. She makes me lose control like nothing else ever has.

I stand up and push my boxers down to my ankles to step out of them. As soon as my cock bobs free, Lily's tongue darts out to lick the seam of her lips, and that's all I can take.

I grab her hips and yank her toward me, then reach for her panties and pull them down her legs slowly. When she's finally naked, I run my hands along her silky skin, bending forward at the waist so my lips can trail up her legs, kissing my way up to her glistening pussy.

"Jesus, Jude," she gasps when I pull her clit into my mouth and suck hard. Her hips lift off the bed, and I anchor myself by gripping her ass and lifting her sweet pussy up to meet my tongue. It takes no time at all before she's bucking and writhing in my arms, and I'm covered in her essence.

"Your pussy is the best damn thing I've ever tasted, sunshine. I want you to come all over my face."

Her hands grip the sheets beside her as she cries out, my tongue unrelenting in its assault. I lick and suck and nibble at her lips until I feel her body tense up. She explodes with a hoarse scream of my name. I lap up every bit of her release, stroking her through her orgasm with gentle licks until her thighs are quivering.

When I lower her hips down to the mattress, my leg is aching but it's dull and distant, the pain mostly overshadowed by pure pleasure from watching Lily come undone.

I climb up on the bed and pull her up so she's lying beside me, still a boneless mess. When she blinks open her eyes and gives me a dreamy smile, I'm a goner. I kiss her, deeply, fusing our lips together.

When my cock is so hard it hurts, I pull back from her and roll over. "Condoms in the bedside drawer?"

"Yes, but wait —"

Her hand reaches out to stop me, but it's too late. Shifting up to sit, I lift two of the items I just discovered out of the drawer and face her with a smirk.

"These seem intriguing." I pretend to inspect the turquoise vibrator and black... Well, to be honest, I don't know what that one is, but I sure as shit want to. "Does my sunshine like to play?"

Lily blushes, but the fire in her eyes tells me she's more aroused than embarrassed. "I like to take care of myself. Orgasms are good for your health."

"I know." I grin lasciviously at her as I push the button to turn the vibrator on. It's powerful, and from the way her pupils dilate, she's familiar with what it feels like. Slowly, I start to circle the tip of it around her nipples.

"Oh my fucking God," she gasps, arching her back.

"Mmm. You're so sensitive. I love watching your body pink up under my touch. If I put my hand between your legs right now, how wet would you be?"

"Drenched."

Contorting my body, I manage to nuzzle her pubic bone, and I can smell the musk of her arousal. "Fuck, Lily. I could eat your pussy for hours."

"Then why don't you?" comes her saucy reply, making me lift my head and grin at her.

"Your choice. Come on my face or come on my cock."

I move the vibrator down her stomach and drag it across from one hip to the other and back again, dipping down, but not down far enough.

"Stop teasing," she groans, trying to push my hand down to where she wants the toy. But I'm stronger and I happen to like teasing.

"If it helps your decision-making, I can use the toy while you ride my dick, but probably not while you ride my tongue."

Lily immediately pushes at my chest and I get the point, rolling onto my back with a deep-throated chuckle. Once she's straddling me, she leans over and grabs the condoms I was looking for earlier. I keep drawing patterns over her skin with the vibrator, now focusing on her upper thighs.

"How are you making me even wetter by touching my freaking leg," Lily whines as she tears open the condom packet. She makes quick work of rolling it down, and I have to fight back the urge to thrust into her hand, it feels so fucking good to have her wrapped around me. But patience is a virtue. And I know something even better is coming.

Lining up her pelvis, Lily lifts up so she's hovering over me. One hand lands on my chest as she bends forward to kiss me, the other grasps my cock and lines it up with her entrance. Agonizingly slow, she lowers herself, and it yet again takes all my restraint not to push my hips up and inside her.

Apparently, I'm not the only one out to tease tonight. She keeps her movements small, lowering onto me just barely before lifting off again.

"If you want the toy, you better get your pussy on my cock in the next three seconds, sunshine," I growl. And thank fuck, she listens, dropping herself down my length with one long moan.

Immediately, I zero in on her clit with the turquoise bullet. Her entire body convulses and she falls forward, grabbing her headboard.

My mouth falls open on a silent moan, as speech escapes me. There's never been anything more beautiful than Lily losing herself to passion. Her tits jiggle as she rocks herself up and down my cock and I feel her inner walls flutter as the vibrator intensifies everything. Hell, I can even sense the vibrations, more so when she lifts herself off me, but even when she slams back down, it's there.

But then Lily leans back, and everything I crave is right there on display. I keep circling the toy around her wet clit as she grinds down on me. Then everything goes fuzzy when she drags a hand up my leg and cups my balls.

"Shit! Lily!" I shout, forgetting about the vibrator for a second. "How are you..." But any question about her flexibility disappears when she tugs on my sack and I feel the first pulse of my orgasm. Doubling down on my efforts with the toy, I can tell she's close. Hot waves of pleasure run up and down my spine when I feel her walls clenching around me, holding my dick in a vice.

She lets go of my balls and leans forward, her movements becoming erratic and desperate.

"That's my good girl. Come for me. Now." I roar out that last word as my own release crashes over me, and my come spurts into the condom. It feels never-ending, like I might spend the rest of my life here, in the middle of an intense orgasm, surrounded by Lily.

There are worse ways to go.

Eventually, I return to myself and to Lily draped over me, my dick still inside of her. We're both sticky with sweat, out of breath, and that perfect kind of exhausted that only comes from really fucking good sex.

As I run my hand up and down her back, she nuzzles into my shoulder.

"Mmm. I know it's not bedtime, but can we just stay here forever?"

I kiss the top of her head as her words sink beneath my skin and settle into my heart. A part of me still can't believe she wants to be with me for real. That her feelings are more than friendship, that she wants me for more than just a fake boyfriend to make her grandmother happy.

I never imagined I'd find this kind of happiness, with Lily or with anyone. But now I have it and I'll be damned if I'm letting her go.

An email I was expecting, but was still not prepared for, landed in my inbox this morning, probably while Lily and I were in the shower. Yesterday, after messing around in bed for another hour or so, she dropped me off so I could feed the damn kitten. But one thing led to another, and then clothes were off, and yeah. She stayed the night in my bed.

Honestly, I could get used to waking up with her in my arms. Not only am I sleeping better than I ever have, but waking up happy is a novel concept. And it's all because of her.

When I opened my email after she left for work, I sat there staring at it for a long time. The key to my future is right there in black and white in the form of an official job offer from the Ravens, and a damn good one, at that. I know I'd be a fool not to take it. But in my reply, I ask for a week to decide. They should be willing to grant me that, seeing as their goal is to have the program up and running in time for spring training, which won't start for several more months.

After hitting send, I stand up, my body twitchy with a sudden need to move. Grabbing my shoes and my keys, I head out for a walk. I'm mindful of the fact that I have an appointment with Lily this afternoon, which brings a smile to my face, but I can't just sit in that apartment, waiting.

Somehow, my wandering brings me to the street that my sister lives on, and on a whim, I decide to see if she's home. Her car is in the driveway, which is promising, and sure enough, she answers my knock.

"Hey, what are you doing here?"

I pull her in for a hug, squeezing tightly. "Can't a brother come and visit his sister without needing a reason?"

She laughs as we pull apart. "I mean, of course, but it's not exactly something you've done before. Come on in."

We head inside, and I toe off my shoes before following her into the kitchen. Her cat, Gigi, struts over the way only cats do, rubbing against my ankle. I bend down to scratch her head.

"I was about to make some coffee. Want a cup?"

"Sure, thanks." I stand up and wander over to lean against the counter next to her. "You and Hunter are happy living together, right?"

She tilts her head to look at me. "Of course, we are. Besides, it was silly to keep living right next door to each other when we spent every single night together."

"I'm still not quite ready to hear about your nighttime activities, sis," I say, playfully ruffling her hair. Kat ducks away from me and crosses her arms across her chest.

"Who are you and what have you done with my brother?"

I hide my smile at her mock annoyance. "What are you talking about?"

Kat's hand flaps around as she gestures at me. "You. You're...you're happy. I see that smirk. Where's the grumpy silent guy, or the mopey guy who wanted to be left alone?"

"Would you prefer I go back to that?" I arch my brow at her.

"Of course not. I'm thrilled you seem to be doing so much better, it just takes some getting used to, I guess." Her eyes widen with a sudden understanding. "Oh my God, this is because of Lily, isn't it?" She clutches her hands together at her heart. "Your love for her is healing your broken heart. It's so romantic!"

The grin that stretches across my face cannot be contained because there's not a word she's saying that's wrong. "I'm not sure we're ready for the *L* word, but yeah, she is the reason I'm done moping."

Kat's high-pitched squeal makes me wince, but then she throws her arms around me, almost knocking me off-balance. Just as fast, she pulls back and the levity is gone.

"Jude, be careful with Lily. And with yourself. She's been hurt so many times, I don't know if she believes she'll ever fall in love. But I know she could. She has so much to give someone, but she needs a man who's going to give it right back to her tenfold. She'll probably try to run at some point because she's convinced she's not good enough to be anyone's happily ever after. Don't give up on her, okay?"

My hands wrap around the mug of coffee still sitting on the counter. Kat hasn't said anything I don't already know.

"As long as she doesn't give up on me." My own insecurity infuses that statement, and I know my intuitive sister hears it.

"You're also worth loving, Jude. Hockey or no hockey. You believe that, right?"

My shoulders lift and fall.

"Oh, big brother. You two need each other more than you know. Lily's not the type to care whether you're a famous player or just a regular guy. All she wants, all she needs, is a man who can make her feel loved, and important, and cherished. And you are that man. I know it."

Chapter Twenty-Four

Lily

"If you break my hand by squeezing it too hard, you're gonna have to fix it," Jude says drily as we walk up the sidewalk toward the restaurant in Westport where my torture awaits.

I let go immediately. "Sorry." But he picks up my hand again, lacing our fingers back together.

"Don't apologize. Just breathe for me. You're not facing them alone; it's just lunch and then we leave."

"Yeah. Just lunch," I mutter. Honestly, if it weren't for the fact that this family lunch is to celebrate Nana's birthday, I wouldn't be here. But when she called me to make sure I was bringing Jude, I had no choice but to agree. Thank God he was willing to suffer alongside me. I know he has a million things on his mind, with the coaching job offer from the new feeder team being the biggest. When he mentioned it to me the other day, I had to hide my very mixed reaction. Excitement for him, and for us, that he could have an amazing opportunity right here on the island, mixed with fear that it wouldn't be enough for him and he'd wind up resenting the job, resenting Dogwood Cove, and resenting me.

I tried to excuse him from coming to the lunch, but the possessive expression in his eyes when he said there wasn't a chance in hell he was letting me face my family alone was loud and clear.

"Besides, the restaurant serves alcohol, and someone cleared me for short drives. So feel free to get drunk." His quick grin does the trick in lightening my mood slightly. But then I see my cousin and Clay arriving at the same time as us, from the opposite direction, and my heart sinks. Of course, they don't do more than glance my way. There's no greeting, it's as if we are invisible.

When we get inside, my parents, aunt and uncle, and Nana are already there, along with some other people I recognize from various events over the years. I know for a fact that none of them are Nana's friends. They're here because it benefits my mom and aunt. It benefits the Chapman name, somehow.

My father is at the bar with my uncle and a couple other men and judging by the half empty glass in front of him, he's on his way to drunk. I used to wonder how he tolerates my mother, but as soon as I was old enough to understand, I knew. He just detaches from reality with alcohol. Staying just sober enough to do his part at Chapman Consulting, and that's it.

I lead Jude straight over to Nana, who, thankfully, is only chatting with one other person, someone I don't even recognize.

"There are my darlings!" she says excitedly, grabbing first me and then Jude in her strong embrace. "Thank you both for coming, I'm so pleased to see you."

"Happy birthday, Nana," I say, handing over the small box I wrapped earlier. It's an early edition of *The Great Gatsby*, one of her favourite classics.

"Thank you for extending the invitation, Margaret," Jude says warmly, producing the bouquet of flowers he had when I picked him up earlier. I was so touched that he thought to get her something, we were almost late for lunch as I showed him just how much it meant to me.

"Well, aren't you quite the charmer. Thank you, Jude." Nana pats him on the arm. "The two of you make such a lovely couple."

We stay and chat with Nana for another minute before Aunt Dora walks over, giving me the barest nod and ignoring Jude completely. She leans in toward Nana and speaks far too loudly, as if Nana's going deaf, which she, of course, is not.

"Mother, you need to come and spend some time with your other guests."

Nana gives me an apologetic smile and lets herself be led away. I exhale loudly as Jude wraps his arm around me. "Your aunt is such a lovely person."

A pained laugh escapes me at his obvious sarcasm. "Yeah, well, you knew what you were in for, coming here."

His lips land on my forehead. "I did. And I told you, you do *not* need to face the firing squad alone."

"Thank you." I smile up at him.

"How about I go get you a drink. Beer? Or stronger?"

This time my laugh isn't quite so harsh. "Better stick to beer. My dad's probably going to be drunk enough for everyone."

Jude's wince is a sympathetic one. "Got it. Beer, coming up. Don't run away without me, okay?"

"Promise."

I move over to the corner of the private room my family rented out and lean against the wall.

My eyes linger on him to the point that I don't notice my mother's approach.

"That's what you chose to wear to your elderly grandmother's birthday luncheon? Really, Lilian."

A knot immediately forms in my stomach as I stand up straight. "Hello, Mother."

Her eyes rake up and down my body, and I hate how it makes me want to cover up. I love my dress. It's one of my favourites, with swirls of maroon and navy mixed with white flowers. Okay, so it shows some cleavage and lands above my knees. So what? My arms are covered, my hair is up in a subtle twist, and I even kept my earrings relatively subdued — or at least, I thought I did. I guess the teardrop cascade of gemstones is too much for her.

Everything I do, or say, or wear is too much, and yet, not enough at the same time.

But when Jude saw me in the flowy wrap dress I chose, his reaction made me feel beautiful.

"That's all you have to say for yourself?" She grabs my arm and yanks me around the corner so we're just outside the room. "You look like a trollop. A slight gust of wind and you'll be showing the world your underwear. Honestly, Lilian, are you so desperate for attention you feel the need to dress provocatively, even to a family event? It's disgraceful, Lilian, an absolute embarrassment."

"If you ask me, you're the embarrassment." Jude's hard voice comes from behind me. His arm wraps around my waist, and when I chance a quick look, the rage I sense emanating from him almost knocks me back. "You try to hide how horrible a person you are, but guess what? I see it, I hear it."

His voice is loud enough to carry into the other room, and soon, my family and other guests have migrated close enough to hear.

"I don't know how you sleep at night, knowing that you call your own daughter a slut, simply because you don't like her clothes. You've criticized every decision she's made, belittled her very successful career, and made her feel worthless her entire life. For God's sake, you turned a blind eye when her own cousin stole her boyfriend from her, then repeatedly made Lily feel like *she* was the problem. You don't deserve the title of mother. Because a mother is meant to love their child, defend them, *protect* them from abusers like you."

Someone gasps when he says the word *abuser*, but Jude doesn't even flinch. My mother, on the other hand, is turning beet red. I expect her to explode at him any moment, but Jude isn't finished.

"Your family is the disgrace. You all think you're above reproach, but from the little I've seen, you're nothing but arrogant, narcissistic assholes. You don't deserve to breathe the same air as Lily, much less be near her or speak to her. And I'm going to make damn sure you don't have the chance to hurt her, ever again."

"Alice, is what he claims true?"

I whirl around, my eyes zeroing in on Nana. The shocked look on her face says everything, and I feel a momentary stab of sorrow that she's having to learn the truth about how my mother talks to me at her own birthday party.

"Did you honestly call Lily a...slut?" she whispers the last word, as if she's too horrified to utter it out loud.

"A trollop, but it's the same damn thing, pardon my language, Margaret," Jude says in a gruff, firm voice that leaves no room for debate.

Nana slowly walks over to me and takes my hand before narrowing her gaze at my mother. That silent show of support, along with Jude's steady strength, is what keeps me upright. The eyes of everyone in this room are on me, and I can't help but feel the weight of their curious scrutiny. Are they seeing what my mother sees? A woman who dresses too provocatively and deserves those harsh words. Or are they seeing my mother for what she truly is, a horrible woman bent on destroying her own daughter.

I fervently hope it's the second option.

"I'm ashamed to call you my daughter. No, I take that back. I'm ashamed to share a last name with all of you. Every single one of you, with the exception of Lily. You call yourself family but treat her like she's less than you? That girl is the best thing this family ever produced. She has the biggest heart out of anyone here and deserves a hell of a lot more than what she's ever received from her so-called family. I am ashamed. This party is over." Nana shakes her head, glaring at my mother, and then my father, aunt, and cousin in turn. "Jude, be a dear and give me a ride home, won't you? I don't think I want to be around these people any longer."

Unbidden, my eyes dart from my grandmother over to my mother, just in time to see the faintest flash of pain mar her face. It's gone before I can even register the fact that my mother might feel a shred of remorse over her actions. Then again, it's far more likely she's just embarrassed at being called out in public, by her own mother, no less.

I wonder how she likes the taste of her own medicine.

Jude nods at Nana, and keeping one arm firmly around my shoulders, he offers his other to her. We leave the restaurant and my family behind as he guides us to where I parked the car not so long ago. On the short drive back to Nana's place, she fills the silence with mindless gossip about some of her neighbours. I'm grateful for the space to process what just happened. I've never told Nana just how awful my mother can be, not wanting to cause any harm to their relationship. But now she knows, and not only that, she stood up to all of them.

And Jude. My grumpy knight in shining armour. I've never had anyone defend me like that. And while it wasn't fun having the spotlight on us as he called my mother to task for her cruel words, listening to him put all of them in their place was... Well, it was amazing.

He spoke as if he loves me. As if I am the most precious thing in the world to him. As if he would protect me at all costs.

We pull up in front of Nana's building, and Jude opens her door and then mine before stepping back to give us some privacy. Nana opens her arms and beckons me closer. I fold into her embrace, letting her love seep into me and soothe the damage done earlier.

"I'm so sorry, my love. We'll talk later about why you never told me how bad things were with your mother. For now, just know that none of it is true. I can't pretend to know what possessed my daughter to speak to you that way, but now that I'm aware of it, I'll be setting them straight. No one deserves that cruelty, Lily, no one. Least of all, you. And I'll be making it very clear that I won't tolerate it."

The hard edge in her voice surprises me. I don't think I would want to be on the receiving end of whatever she's going to dish out to my family.

"I'm sorry, Nana. I didn't want to come between you and Mom."

"Darling girl. *You* did not. Any problem between your mother and me is of her own doing. She's been a jealous girl since she was young. I thought the closeness she shares with your aunt was a good thing, that their drive would give them strength. But it hasn't. It has clearly made her cold and heartless. That is not on you at all."

She pulls me in for another hug before releasing me. "Now, promise me you'll go and let your wonderful man comfort you and cherish you and forget all about what happened earlier."

I muster up a small smile. "I'll try. I love you, Nana."

"I love you, too, darling."

After I get back in the car, I'm expecting Jude to drive us home, to his place or mine, but instead, he goes back to the parking lot at the beach where he confessed to me that his feelings are real.

"Is this our spot now?" I try to say teasingly, but the rawness that I feel in my soul bleeds into the words.

"I think so."

Jude turns in his seat and strokes back my hair, his fingers landing on the earrings my mother despised earlier.

"I know you're smart enough to realize that everything your mom said is wrong. That your family is toxic, horrible, and cruel, and none of what they said should be taken seriously. But I also know your heart is sensitive enough to be breaking right now."

Tears form behind my eyes, and when the first one spills over, Jude's there with his thumb, gently wiping it away.

"They're my only family," I whisper brokenly.

"No, they're not. Your grandmother was correct when she said those people don't get to call themselves your family if that's how they treat you. You don't need to ever have anything to do with them again, Lily. They don't deserve you." He leans in and kisses my cheek softly. Then he tips my chin up so I'm looking into his eyes. "You have my family. You have for a long time, and you know it."

Chapter Twenty-Five

Jude

Ever since the luncheon when the shit hit the fan with Lily's family, she's been different. Quieter, but not necessarily in a bad way. More like I can sense she's rearranging her entire understanding of herself and her life.

It's been over a week and she hasn't mentioned anyone from her family or anything about that day with the exception of her grandmother. She didn't invite me to their weekly tea date, which was hard to accept, but I told myself it was just because they needed the opportunity to debrief it all in private.

It doesn't mean I scared her away when I told her my family was hers as well.

At the time, I didn't realize what that declaration implied. But it stuck with me, and throughout the last few days, I've started to feel it as a state of being.

She's mine.

The deadline to sign the paperwork for my job with the Ravens is approaching, and at this point, I can't see a reason not to. Sure, there will be travel involved, there always is with even semi-professional hockey. But the idea of having my home base here is appealing in more ways than one.

Lily's at work when I get a phone call from someone I truly never expected to hear from again. The general manager for the Montana Blaze is a busy man and usually never contacts players except around contract time. I don't have the first clue why he's calling me, unless it's to demand I sign the damn papers for them to buy me out.

"Hi, Trevor," I say, with no shortage of confusion.

"Jude, good to hear your voice." His words boom down the phone line and I have to actually pull it away from my ear slightly. I forgot how loud he is.

"What can I do for you? I know you're probably waiting on the paperwork; I'll get to it soon. I've just been busy with my rehab."

"No, no, that's not why I'm calling. Although, do tell — how's your progress?"

A genuine smile crosses my face. "Good. Really good. My physical therapist has me feeling stronger every day."

"Great news. Now, listen. I heard through the grapevine that Gilles LaRoy is trying to hook you into a coaching position with his new team. And it just so happens, we could use a new defensive line coach. You know your home is with the Blaze, so I'd like you to consider entertaining an offer from us."

I don't hear the rest of what he says over the roaring in my head as I try to process the news. My old team wants me to coach. In the NHL.

It's not that the offer is a surprise, a lot of retired players go on to coach. It's just not something I was expecting.

"We're in Vancouver for the next couple of days and it would be great to sit down and chat. Maybe see how you jive with the boys from the bench instead of on the ice."

I tune back in just in time for that last part. "The team's here?"

"Yes, son. We've got a game tomorrow night, then an off day before traveling down to Seattle. It's a strange schedule this week, but it does allow us some time to connect about this opportunity. So what do you say? Can I have my assistant organize a flight?"

When Lily gets home from work that evening, I'm sitting on her front porch, anxiously waiting for her.

"Jude? Is everything okay?" she calls out as she grabs her bag and hurries up to meet me. I grab her face in my hands and kiss her several times before letting her go, smirking at the breathless and dazed look she gives me.

"Yup. Just wanted to see my girlfriend."

My use of that title is not accidental. But it's also the first time and I watch her closely to see her reaction. Her throat moves as she swallows and her pupils dilate. But then she looks down at the ground before moving past me to open the door.

"How was your day?"

Wow. Okay. I wasn't expecting fanfare or anything, but it stings for her to not even acknowledge it. And it makes me all the more nervous to share my news with her. I follow her into the house and drop down on her couch. "Fine. Good, I guess. How was yours?"

She gives me a soft smile. "Well, aside from not getting to see my favourite patient, it was okay. Let me just change out of my work clothes."

Normally, I'd follow her into the bedroom and we'd probably end up naked. But something's still off. And her lack of reaction to me calling her my girlfriend only confirms it. Instead, I wait for her, staring at the email in my inbox with flight details. I have to head to Vancouver first thing tomorrow morning.

Lily returns, wearing my old Blaze jersey. The irony of seeing her wearing it after the call I got today isn't lost on me. But it is secondary to the bolt of desire that hits me. I want to fuck her wearing that and nothing else.

"Christ, sunshine, you look good wearing my name," I say hoarsely. She gives me a sultry smile and sits down right on my lap, cuddling in, and pressing a kiss to the side of my neck. "I missed you today."

I lean back slightly and turn my head so I can kiss her lips. "I missed you, too." I run my hands up her legs, covered in thin leggings. My jersey is way too big, but it looks so goddamn right on her. I want nothing more than to give in to temptation and show her exactly how I feel seeing her in it, but I know we have to talk. And I'm nervous as fuck about it.

"Did you want to order something for dinner or cook?"

"Pizza sounds good, if that works?"

I nod and open up the app on my phone, placing an order, and feeling a little ashamed of my feeble attempt to delay the inevitable.

"What you said earlier," Lily starts, her hand coming to rest on my chest. "What you...called me." She turns her face up and I see a mixture of hope and fear. "Did you mean it?"

Even now, after finding out exactly how broken and dysfunctional her family is, and how her sunshine exterior hides a wounded interior, it still surprises me when Lily's vulnerability shows. The girl I remember as a child was full of energy and bold, brash confidence. Even later on, as an adult, I never thought of her as anything but outgoing and happy. Now I know better. Now I know that, yes, she is happy and confident and outgoing, but she's also got more than her fair share of inner demons. And sometimes, that outer confidence is a mask for the anxious self-doubt she hides.

This is one of those moments.

"Yeah, sunshine, I meant it. I never say words I don't mean. You're my girl. Mine." I tuck her hair behind her ears, running my fingers over the purple strands. "I'm crazy about you. Your wild side and this quieter side that I'm lucky enough to see. I'm here and I'm yours for as long as you'll have me."   .

"You're my boyfriend." There's a sense of wonder to her voice and it makes me smile.

"Yes."

I abandon my good intentions at keeping my hands off her until after I tell her about the call from the Blaze. Instead, I wrap my hand around the front of her throat, possessing her, claiming her, and making it really fucking clear I mean what I say. "Mine," I growl before crashing my lips to hers again. I shift us so that she's stretched out on the couch under me, praying my fucking knee lets me do this.

I trail my lips down, tugging the neck of the jersey lower as I go, so that her tits pop free. "No bra. Good call."

Lily's body shakes with laughter. "I need to do laundry."

"Nope," I say, releasing one nipple with a pop. "That's not necessary at all. This is just fine with me."

I continue to lavish attention on her tits until she's squirming under me, her hands roaming my back, pulling my own shirt up in a feeble attempt to get it off. But a knock at the door has her growling in frustration.

"Pizza's here," I say, standing up with a wicked grin. "I'll save what I was doing for dessert."

I pay for the pizza and carry the steaming hot box back to set it on the table between us. Sitting down again, I grab her feet and swing them up into my lap, open the box, and hand her a slice. After taking a bite of my own, I turn to her, only to find Lily staring at me, her untouched pizza in hand. "What?" I mumble around my mouthful of food.

"How can you... You just... Ugh!" Lily shrieks, smacking my shoulder with her free hand. She tries to pull her feet away but I'm holding them tightly.

"Feeling frustrated, sunshine?" I tease. The truth is, I'm halfway to rock hard myself. But the light is back in her eyes. She needed me to reassure her that we were good, that my feelings were real. And I don't care if I have to do that a thousand different ways every fucking day, I will. Because seeing her smile is worth it.

I finish off my slice as my mind drifts back to the news I really need to tell her. I might be almost certain what my decision is, but I also know I'd be a fool not to consider the offer from the Blaze. Even if my priorities have changed.

"You know, I'm not the best at the whole girlfriend thing, but I'm pretty sure part of it is getting you to talk when I sense there's something going on."

My hand stills from moving to pick up another slice before I shift my gaze and give her a sheepish grin. "Is it that obvious?"

Her gentle smile gives me the push I need.

"I got a call from my former GM today. He wants me to fly to Vancouver tomorrow and spend some time with the team, not because he wants me back as a player, but he wants me back as a coach."

She doesn't say anything right away, just looks at me thoughtfully with those big eyes. It's hard not to rush in and try to reassure her that this doesn't change how I feel, but I have to trust she knows that. Especially after what we just talked through earlier.

"The NHL was a huge part of your life for a long time. If you've got a chance at that again, you have to explore it."

I exhale. I don't know what I wanted her to say, but I'm definitely not loving the fact that she's pushing me to go. Still, she has a point.

"I could be happy here, coaching the Ravens. There's potential to build something amazing with them, and it lets me be close to my family and close to you."

Lily nods and moves so that she's closer to me. She picks up my hand and laces our fingers together. "You've got two great opportunities. And I don't want to influence your decision at all. I also don't want you to regret not exploring something that could make you really happy."

You make me really happy. I should say that out loud. I should tell her that staying here, being with her, that's what would make me happy.

But she's right. I have to satisfy my curiosity and see if being back around my teammates in a different capacity is something I want to consider.

"I have to fly out tomorrow. I'll be gone a couple of days."

"Then I had better not waste any more time." Lily lifts up and swings her legs over mine, straddling my lap and circling her core down on my dick, which instantly jumps to attention. "After all, I don't want you forgetting about your *girlfriend* while you're being wined and dined by the NHL."

I hear the vulnerability behind those words that I'm sure she hoped she was hiding. As my hands grip her juicy ass, I make sure she's looking at me, *seeing me*, when I reply.

"Not a chance, sunshine."

Chapter Twenty-Six

Lily

"Care to tell me why we just got a text from my brother saying he wouldn't be at dinner this week because he was on a plane to Vancouver to meet up with his old GM about a job?" My front door slams shut behind Kat as she storms into my house.

"Nice to see you, too," I say drily as I walk out of my kitchen with a cup of coffee. It's my second of the day and it's only ten in the morning, but who's counting.

"Seriously, Lil, what's he doing?" Kat's features are creased with worry, and I beckon her back into the kitchen.

"You need caffeine."

After we both have mugs of coffee and are curled up on my couch, I give Kat the bare bones version of what Jude and I talked about last night. But as soon as I see the flash of pity in her eyes, I frown. "Don't look at me like that."

"Like what?" she asks innocently, but I see the guilt.

"Like you think I made a mistake encouraging him to go, like you think he's not going to come back."

"No, oh my God, Lily, no." Kat sets her drink down and drops her hands onto my legs. "That's not it. I'm relieved you pushed him to go and meet with his old team, truly. You're right that he'd always wonder what if. He needs to decide whether that part of his life is over or not. Any worry you saw in me is simply because I know how much he loves hockey. I'm only hoping he's smart enough to realize he loves you more."

I spit my coffee back into my mug to avoid choking on it at her words. "Whoa, there. Slow down. Love? That's not... We're not..."

The sick feeling in my stomach is intense as wave after wave of realization hits me, knocking me off my feet.

I love him.

"I'm gonna be sick," I mumble, standing up and starting to pace. I hate this. I hate the idea Kat unknowingly just planted in my brain, that he might choose hockey over me. We haven't said anything about love, heck, we only just had the boyfriend-girlfriend talk last night. There's no way.

"Kat, I love him."

"I know, sweetie."

I sink back down and let her pull me in so that my head is on her shoulder. "He called me his girlfriend last night," I whisper. She hands me my coffee, and I take it, sipping slowly. The warmth feels good, but the liquid still sloshes around in my tied-up-in-knots stomach.

"He might not have said the words, but he loves you, Lily. I'm sure of it."

"So, what do I do if he chooses the NHL over me?"

Kat doesn't answer. She can't. Because we both know the possibility of that happening is a little too real.

After Kat eventually leaves, I do something I've never done. I fake a sick day and call in to the clinic. After Sukhi reassures me she'll contact my patients, I crawl under the covers and close my eyes. I can still smell Jude on the pillow I hug into my chest. When the tears build, I don't fight them back. I let them fall as I think about how quickly he changed everything I thought I knew about myself.

Jude saw parts of me I never showed anyone. He saw beneath the layer of positivity and he uncovered the wounds I tried to hide. The only person who's ever bothered to try and see all of me was Kat. Though even she didn't get it all. I might love being known as the happy one, the fun one, the crazy, wild, outgoing one, but Jude alone showed me that I could let go of all that and just be me. Sometimes quiet, lost in my head, feeling everything deeply *me*.

I must fall asleep hugging Jude's pillow — *when did I start thinking of it as his* — because the chime of my doorbell startles me awake. Light is streaming in through my open curtains, and when I groggily look at my clock, I see it's just past noon.

Pulling my hair into a messy bun as I go, I stagger to the front door, trying to blink back the dazed feeling I always get on the odd occasion I fall asleep during the day.

"Nana?" I blurt out when I see her standing on my doorstep holding her purse.

"Hello, my darling." She pushes past me without waiting for an invitation. Not that I would ever deny her, but her audacity makes me smile, ever so slightly. If anyone wonders where my bold side comes from, they'd only need to meet Margaret Chapman to figure it out.

Nana settles herself on the large wingback chair I keep by the window for reading and fixes me with her features schooled in an impassive expression.

I sit down on the edge of my couch and twist my fingers together. For some reason, I feel like a little girl caught doing something wrong, but for the life of me, I don't know what I did.

"I'm here to confess something."

My breath catches.

"I know you and Jude were playing along, pretending to be together to humour me."

Shame floods my cheeks with red. "Nana, I..."

"No, stop. Let me finish, child."

I close my mouth and nod quickly. Confusion mixes with relief inside of me. I hated lying to Nana.

"At the wedding, it was clear he was there as a friend only. And given his absence around town until now, it was evident there was no romantic history between the two of you. However, I sensed the peace and strength in him, and just as evident to me was the fact that he filled *you* with a similar strength. His very presence made you stand up tall at that circus of a wedding. I had a feeling he could be the man to help you realize how worthy you truly are of love and happiness, or at the very least, of friendship and affection." Nana drops her gaze for a second, and when she looks back up at me, I'm shocked to see moisture pooling in the corners of her eyes. "My child, I failed you. I should have seen just how awful things were for you, how ridiculous and cruel my daughters were becoming, and how it was all being taken out on you simply because of your beautiful, free spirit. They nearly crushed you and I'll never forgive myself for not realizing it sooner."

"Nana, it wasn't your fault," I murmur, standing and walking over to sink down to the floor in front of her. I take her hands in mine, feeling the papery skin, and the warmth, strength, and love that I always get from her. "I could have come to you and told you, but I didn't. That's on me."

"Because your pure heart wouldn't let you say a bad thing about your own mother. Darling girl, you are the victim in this. You are not to blame."

I nod because finally, I feel I'm at a place in my life where I believe those words. And it's largely because of Jude.

"I'm sorry we lied to you, Nana."

She pats my hand. "Don't apologize, my dear, I forced you into it. Just tell me you're happy. Because I can also surmise that things didn't stay pretend for very long."

I smile at her intuition. "You would be right on that." Laying my head down on her lap, I stare out the window as she starts to stroke my hair just as she would when I was a young girl and we would read together. "I fell in love with him, Nana. He's wonderful, just as you suspected. He's kind, and strong, and loyal, and he makes me feel so special. That sounds cliché, but it's true."

"Nothing wrong with a cliché, countless romance novels were written about them, and they all have happily ever afters."

I giggle at Nana's observation. "But he left. He's in Vancouver right now finding out more about a job with his old team. If he takes it, he'll leave."

"Ahh. That's what Kat was talking about."

I lift my head and look at her in confusion. "Kat?"

"Well, why else do you think I'm here? She called me and asked if I would come and check in on you. Said something about Jude being gone and how sad you were."

My heart fills with affection for my best friend and the fact that she knew Nana would be the best person to be with me while I sort out my feelings for Jude.

"Since we're dealing in clichés today, let's add another. If you love something, let it go. And if it comes back, then you know it's meant to be."

"Easy for you to say, you're not the one who has to wait and find out if that happens or not," I grumble.

Just then, my phone vibrates on the table. I look at it with some trepidation. The wistful part of me wants it to be Jude, telling me it was a mistake to go and he's on his way back. The realistic part of me knows that would never happen.

Reaching for it, I swipe to unlock and open the messages.

JUDE: Hey sunshine. It's so weird being back in an arena and not lacing up to play. But it feels good in a way. Wish you were here with me.

He sent a selfie standing in front of the ice, and as I stare at his handsome face with that small smile he doesn't show to a lot of people, I see the excitement in his expression. I wish I could match it with my own, but I can't. Because seeing the hope and happiness in his eyes fills me with dread that my worst fear might come true.

Jude could easily choose a future that doesn't include me, and I could be left alone again. Only, unlike every other time it's happened, this time my heart is fully invested and would be fully broken.

Tears blur my vision as another message comes through, and I have to wipe them away with a sniff before I can read.

JUDE: Could you do me a favour and go by my apartment to check on the kitten tonight? I'm not sure how long I'll be here and don't want her getting lonely.

A fresh wave of tears fall. He's such a softie, and he's so attached to that kitten. At least a cat can go with him when he moves away. He can find a cat sitter for his away games.

"Lily, darling, what's wrong?"

I startle slightly at Nana's gentle words. I'd almost forgotten she was here.

"Just a couple messages from Jude. He's having a really good time, I think." My voice breaks at the end, and I drop my head back into Nana's lap as the tears fall.

I finally fell in love with a good man, the very best man. And now, I'm going to lose him because I'm not enough for him.

Nana says nothing, just murmurs something as she strokes my hair and lets me cry. A small voice inside of me is telling me not to jump to conclusions, to wait and talk to him before giving up, but the broken part of me is louder. And it's reminding me of all the times someone or something else was chosen over me.

Why would this be any different?

Much later that evening, after moping around my house all day, I drag myself out to Jude's apartment. Steeling myself, I open the door using the key I picked up on the way from Sawyer. A wave of memories hits me as I step inside. This place might not be his permanent home, but it's where I fell for him.

The kitten comes bounding over, and I scoop her up and cuddle her into my chest.

Wandering into the kitchen, I see a collar sitting on the counter and pick it up with a watery smile. For a guy who swore he wasn't keeping the kitten, he certainly has invested a lot of care and attention into her.

A small metal charm runs through my fingers and I look at it. A name tag.

He named her.

My heart fills with love for the sentimental softy who hides his heart underneath a grumpy exterior. We're not so different, Jude and me. Two sides of the same coin.

I flip over the tag and read the inscription. And I blink a few times, certain I'm reading it wrong.

Lifting the kitten up in the air so I can stare at her, I shake my head in disbelief. "Are you fucking kidding me?" I pull her back into my chest and sink down to the floor, taking the collar with me. The kitten squirms and I let her run off as I stare down at the name tag again. There it is, plain as day. One word that has come to mean so very much to me. And apparently, enough to him that he chose it as a name for his damn cat.

Sunshine.

CHAPTER TWENTY-SEVEN

Jude

"Fuck, it's good to see your ugly face again." Kasey slaps me on the back as he steps off the ice after their warm-up. The game starts soon, and Trevor wants me behind the bench with the other coaches, observing and contributing, if I want.

I'm not sure what I want. It's only been a few hours since I left Dogwood Cove and I miss the town already. Okay, no, that's not entirely true.

I miss Lily.

"Yeah, well, I figured you guys might be missing me," I joke, accepting handshakes and greetings from some other team-mates.

I follow them down the tunnel that leads to the locker room, listening to the conversations that flow around me. It's very weird to be here in a suit instead of a jersey. Not necessarily bad, just different. A lot of things are different. The guys look at me differently, some of them with pity, some of them with confusion, like they can't figure out why I'm here. Who knows what they've heard. I only told Kasey why I was coming, no one else, figuring it was up to management what they decided to say.

There's a sharp disconnect between us all now. They're ribbing each other good-naturedly as we always used to do, but I'm not in there with them anymore. I don't know what scuffle they're referring to when they tease Sharpe about his black eye. I have no clue why someone slaps a sticky note with the number *16* on it onto Chen's cubby. I can guess it has to do with his puck bunny count this season, simply because I remember him being a horny motherfucker last year, but the fact remains — I'm on the outside looking in.

And if I take on a role coaching these guys, I'll still be on the outside. Doesn't matter how well we get along with our coaches, there's a separation between player and coach. There has to be.

It's one thing to have that separation with a bunch of young guys I don't have history with. It's another to have it with a team I used to lead.

I step out of the locker room and lean against the wall, opening my phone to see if Lily's sent me anything. She hasn't.

That troubles me, maybe more than it should. I want to trust that we're good, that she knows me being here doesn't change my feelings, but I'm also starting to have a better understanding of just how hard it is for Lily to trust. I consider it an honour that she *does* seem to trust me, that she has opened up to me, and I can't help but worry that me leaving like I did is going to damage that somehow.

I type out a quick message and hit send before I can second-guess it.

JUDE: I miss you sunshine.

Pathetic as it might be, I stare down at the screen for several minutes, willing those three dots to show up that would tell me she's responding. But they don't appear.

Switching to my email, I see one that came in earlier from Stefan. It's short and to the point, essentially saying a couple other teams heard that the Blaze had approached me about coaching, and they want to put forward an offer.

It's staggering, to be wanted by so many organizations for a job for which I have zero experience. But as I scan the email and see teams that are down in the states, or over on the East Coast, basically as far from Dogwood Cove as possible, nothing excites me.

Someone calls my name and I turn to see Trevor striding down the hall. "There you are. Come on up to the management suite for a while, let's talk shop."

I push off from the wall and try to keep up with his quick pace, but the damn dress shoes I'm wearing are making my knee ache. Thank fuck the elevator isn't too far, and I can hopefully hide my discomfort by sitting down when we get to wherever he's leading me.

I spend the next hour making small talk with some of the team's upper management. Guys who I didn't pay much attention to when I was a player, but who now hold my potential future in their hands — if coaching in the NHL is what I want.

At some point, I drift away from the conversations and find myself staring out over the arena that's quickly filling with fans.

"Still gives me chills looking out at it all," Trevor says, coming to stand beside me and handing me a glass tumbler. "Whiskey?"

I accept it with a nod, lifting the glass and taking a sip.

"So, Jude. I can tell your mind is not fully invested in the idea of coaching for the Blaze."

I freeze for a split second. But where I expected to feel fear or panic that I've killed the opportunity before I even had a chance at it, I only feel a soul deep acknowledgment that he's right.

"That would be correct, sir. It's not that I don't feel honoured by the offer, and it really is tempting, but I was starting to appreciate the idea of working a little closer to home, closer to my family."

Trevor makes a hum of understanding as he takes a drink. "I'm guessing the opportunity to work with Louka and who-ever else LaRoy pulls together doesn't hurt. He's dead set on having a dream team, and the fucker just might do it. Especially if he lands you."

I turn to face him fully. "With all due respect, why do you say that? I've got no coaching experience, I'm just a player."

"All great coaches were once great players," he replies mat-ter-of-factly. "You know the game inside and out, you know what it takes to win, and you're a strong leader. To be blunt, Jude, I suspect out of everyone in the professional hockey world, the only person who's surprised you're being sought after by multiple organizations is you."

I let that statement sink in. Trevor has never been the type to blow smoke up your ass, so if he's telling me I have value as a coach, I better believe it.

"Every time a player signs with us, or renews their contract, I ask them one question. Do you remember what that is?"

I think back to every meeting with Trevor over the years. "Something about picturing where we wanted to be in two years?"

"Right. Depending on the player, I'd say one year, two years, or even five. But the point is, I wanted to make damn sure I was taking on players that wanted to be with the Blaze long-term. We take the idea of our team being a family very seriously, you know that. Getting my guys to clarify their priorities and goals is crucial to creating that family." Trevor takes a sip of his drink, his penetrating stare still seeing right down to my soul. "Speaking frankly again because, well, you've earned that, Jude. Retirement was coming for you. Whether it happened when it did because of your knee or a few years down the road when something else gave out. You had a longer career than most, and I hope you know how much the team appreciated you each and every year of that career. But now that it's over, there's one question you have to ask yourself. What's important to you *now?*"

After the Blaze decimate their opponents in a 3-1 win, Kasey finds me. "Come and grab a drink with us for old times' sake." He drapes his arm over my shoulders and guides me to the player's exit, where black SUVs are waiting. We're taken to a bar that has a private room already full of half the team and a bunch of women.

Kasey bypasses all of them and we find a small table to sit at. After ordering a drink, he steeples his fingers in front of his face and stares me directly in the eye.

"You don't want to coach the Blaze." He makes it sound like a done deal. Which, I guess, it is. I plan on meeting with Trevor tomorrow and respectfully declining the offer and handing in my contract buyout paperwork at the same time.

But curiosity makes me ask, "Why do you think that?"

"I've known you a long time. You're a hell of a player and you'll make a hell of a coach, but not for this team. It would feel like a step backward for you, even though it isn't. You always used to say if you were ever traded, you'd never come back to the Blaze. Once you're done with something, you're done with it. And somehow, over the last couple of months, you made peace with being done with the Blaze."

"Yeah, I have," I say, the finality of that statement feeling right.

"If I were a betting man, which I'm not," Kasey starts conversationally, but there's a devious glint in his eyes. "I'd wager there's also a woman involved."

I narrow my gaze at him. "What makes you say that?"

"The fact that you've checked your phone three times since we left the arena, and every time you do, you frown. You're waitin' on a girl and she's not answering you."

I let out a rueful chuckle. "It's insane how well you can read me, man."

Kasey just shrugs. "Yeah, well, how many years have we played together? How many road trips? I know you. So, is she worth giving up the NHL?"

It's a rhetorical question in a lot of ways because she's not the *only* reason I'm declining the job offer from the Blaze. But she is a big part of why I'm not even entertaining any of the others.

"Yeah. She's worth it."

Kasey and I lift our glasses, and we clink them together before drinking deeply. Some of the guys decide to move the party elsewhere and try to convince us to go. But Kasey bows out, choosing to head back to the hotel, and I decline as well. It's not that I don't want to spend time with my former teammates, my friends, but this isn't my life anymore. And where the vibrant nightlife used to interest me, now I find it too loud and busy.

You can take the guy out of the small town, but you can't take the small town out of the guy. That thought amuses me as I dodge a group of people on the street clearly fresh from a bar, judging by their laughter and weaving gait. In doing so, I end up catching sight of a used bookstore. That, of course, makes me think of Lily. Pulling out my phone for what feels like the hundredth time today, I exhale when I see a message from her.

It's a photo of her and Sunny. Yeah, I named the cat after my sunshine girl. A wide grin covers my face as I take in Lily's arched brow and pouty lips that are clearly fighting back a smile.

LILY: Nice to see you finally gave her a name...

LILY: I miss you. Hope you're having a good time. I'm at the clinic all day tomorrow, but call me if you get a chance in the evening and tell me how it's going.

I check the time and curse. It's too late to call her, no matter how much I want to. If she's got a clinic day tomorrow, she'll be up early.

I pocket my phone and look in the bookstore window. A display of classics is stuck in the corner, making me lean in closer. When I spot several very old-looking covers, I make the decision to return tomorrow and see what I can find. I don't know the first thing about classic literature or early editions, but I do know that Lily would love this place, and someday I'll bring her so she can see it for herself. For now, I'll have to make do with hoping the staff in the shop can help me select something she'll enjoy.

Buying a book for the woman I love feels weird, like it's not enough, somehow. I'm so jaded by my past, by women who weren't happy with anything less than extravagance. But Lily's different. And I know that an early edition of one of her favourites will mean more than all the jewels and fancy dinners I could possibly shower her with.

That doesn't mean I don't want to spoil her with everything I possibly can, however. She deserves the world, and I want to be the man to give it to her.

Chapter Twenty-Eight

Lily

Two days is a long freaking time. Okay, it's not, but when you're waiting for the man you love to give you some sort of indication of whether he's coming home or moving back to Montana, it's a long time.

I paced his apartment, holding Sunshine to my chest, for an hour last night. After I stopped crying, that is. He named his cat after me. That has to count for something, right?

After texting him the photo of me and Sunny, I forced myself to put my phone down. Then he didn't call. I know it was late when I sent him the message and I did tell him I had an early morning, but still. Did I want him to call anyway? Of course I did. I'm fickle like that.

I definitely didn't mean to fall asleep in his bed with the kitten curled up, purring beside me, but it was comforting to be there, surrounded by his stuff, and his sheets smell like him.

They smell like happiness.

But falling asleep at his apartment means that this morning, I'm almost late for work because of needing to rush home to grab my work clothes and lunch. I'm cutting it so close to my first appointment when I finally arrive at the clinic that I rush past Sukhi with a brief wave, not even bothering to get my schedule for the day.

The next few hours, thankfully, fly by with appointments. I barely have time to take a drink of water, much less obsess over whether Jude is signing a contract with the Blaze or not. Finally, I get a short break between clients and decide to pop over to The Nutty Muffin to grab some coffee.

I regret my decision the instant I see my mother walking out of Pages bookstore.

"Lilian." Her tone is cold as ever. "I've been waiting for you to call and apologize for that mortifying scene your friend caused at lunch."

Something bubbles up inside of me as I stare at her, the woman who was meant to love me unconditionally, but instead, she has done nothing but belittle me my entire life. It's not anger or pain, not anymore. No, it's pity. For her. For all of my family, who are incapable of seeing the beauty and uniqueness we all hold inside.

In that moment, the invisible chains around my heart burst open. I'm free from all of the judgment and criticism. It cannot touch me any longer.

Giving her my most sunny smile, feeling lighter than I have ever felt, I finally respond, "Thank you for letting me know, but you will not be receiving that call any time soon. Or any call from me, ever. Your words can't hurt me any longer and will never make me change. So you can stop wasting your *valuable* time waiting on them. Now, if you'll excuse me, I'm on a quick coffee run before I go back to work."

I give myself a second to watch her mouth fall open in shock. She recovers quickly, her hand coming up to pat at her hair in a weirdly nervous gesture I've never seen from her. There's a teeny-tiny pang in my heart, but it's overshadowed by the overwhelming sense of release as I fully let go of a toxic relationship that has ruled my heart my entire life.

Yeah, Mom, I'm done laying down and taking your bullshit. Welcome to the new dynamic.

With a little wave of my fingers, I walk past her, a smile still etched on my face until I get inside the café, where I finally let out a giggle of relief.

Damn, that felt good.

I wish Kat were working, so I could share with her how amazing I feel, but she isn't. So, after I have my drink in hand, I head back to work, a bounce in my step that wasn't there before. Now, if I would just hear from Jude, everything would be perfect.

I see a couple more patients, then at lunchtime, I finally allow myself to check my phone for messages, only to find the battery completely dead.

"Damn it!" I curse softly, hunting through the desk in the break room for a charger. Holding one up triumphantly, I plug in my phone, then quickly scarf down my sandwich before checking it.

JUDE: Hope my two sunshines are having a good day

That's it? That's all he's going to say? I swear to God, this man is driving me insane. The time stamp of his message is from earlier this morning, and there's nothing else. No missed call, no voicemail, nothing.

I write out and delete a response what feels like a hundred times before dropping my phone on the desk, my head following to rest on the cool surface, feeling way too overwhelmed with pent-up energy to type anything. The combination of elation at being free of my family, and worry over where I stand with Jude, is making my stomach churn.

Sukhi chooses that moment to stick her head in the break room. She doesn't seem to react to my slumped posture, instead simply asking, "Hey Lily, your next patient is early. Do you want me to bring them back?"

I lift one hand into a thumbs-up gesture. Might as well drown myself in work and try to ignore the fact that my boyfriend is leaving me in the dark about our future. Sitting up in my chair, I keep my eyes closed and make myself take a few deep breaths. *Forget the boyfriend issues and focus on my next patient, then the next, then the next.* I'll go home and wallow in confusion later.

I make my way out to the main area of the clinic, but all the beds are empty. "Sukhi, where's my patient?" I ask, and she points toward the private room. Weird. I didn't realize I had another patient who needed that space. Anyone can request it if they want privacy, but normally, we save it for patients who need massage.

"The chart?" I ask when my eyes don't immediately see it in the usual place, the folder by the door.

"Oh, sorry, I put it inside with the patient."

I frown at that. We don't normally leave charts with the patients, mostly so we can do a quick review before a session. "Okay, next time can you leave it out here for me, please?"

Sukhi nods without looking at me. I don't really feel like digging into why she's acting so weird. I've got enough of that to do with Jude.

Knocking softly on the door, I open it slowly. "Hi there, it's Lily."

"Hey, sunshine."

I gape in disbelief at the handsome man sitting on the table in front of me. "Jude?" I whisper, moving into the room slowly. "What are you doing here?"

He gives me a gentle smile, but the passion burning in his eyes makes me shiver. The man certainly does have great bedroom eyes. "I'm here for physical therapy. I don't want to miss a session."

The door snicks shut behind me and I lean against it, still keeping some distance between us when what I want to do is run over and jump into his lap.

"Don't the Blaze have trainers that could have treated you?"

He pushes off the table and covers the short space between us in one large step. Then he's there, right in front of me, so close

I can smell his minty breath, layered with the earthy scent that is just Jude.

"They're not as good as you."

I suck in a breath, overwhelmed by his very presence.

"I know it was only a couple of days, but I missed you a hell of a lot." His gravelly voice, combined with his echoing how I've felt this entire time, makes my eyes flutter closed as warmth floods my body.

Lips land on my forehead just before hands, rough and strong, cup my face with all the gentle care and tenderness in the world. My eyes open as he kisses me lightly. But that touch is enough. My arms go around his neck and I jump, confident he'll catch me. With his arms holding me up, Jude walks us back over to the table where he sits down with me straddling his lap.

"Fuck," he growls against my lips as my hips automatically press into his. I can feel him hardening underneath me. Our kiss turns me into molten lava, every part of me melting into him. Vaguely, I'm aware that we're at my place of work, and this is completely inappropriate, but having him here in my arms is making all the uncertainty I've felt over the last forty-eight hours disappear. And that is euphoric.

But sounds from the clinic trickle in, voices walking past the closed — but not locked — door, and I pull back. "Damn. I... We..." I blow out a frustrated breath as I climb off his lap, straightening my shirt that went askew when he reached underneath to palm my breast. "Not here."

Jude gives me a rueful smirk. "Sorry, sunshine. You're irresistible."

Narrowing my eyes in a mock glower, I take another step back. "You're here for physical therapy. That's all."

He shakes his head. "That's definitely not all."

His statement is loaded with meaning. But I know if I start to unpack it, any chance of maintaining my sanity and professionalism will disappear. The high I was riding after confronting my mother has faded into the background, and while part of me desperately wants to know why Jude's here, and what his plans are, I also know I can't let myself go there now.

"Can we focus on therapy?" I ask quietly.

Jude studies me for a minute, his expression undefinable. "Yeah. For now."

I give a sharp nod. "Great. Okay. I hope you took some care in Vancouver and didn't push too hard."

He sits back on the table and bends his leg. "Nope, I was a good boy." The wink he gives me is adorable and makes my heart swoon. Grumpy Jude is sexy, but sweet, silly Jude? He's addictive.

Over the next hour, we somehow manage to keep the conversation focused on his knee. I put him through the full massage protocol and all of his exercises before finally walking him to the front of the clinic.

Sukhi looks at us with a knowing smirk that makes me stop. "Did you not let me know it was Jude on purpose?" I ask, popping my hand on my hip as my eyes dart from Sukhi to Jude.

"I asked her not to tell you," Jude replies easily. "I wanted to surprise you." My expression softens into a smile. How can it not?

He leans in and kisses my cheek before whispering loud enough only for me to hear, "I'll be waiting for you to finish work. We've got a lot to catch up on."

When he pulls back, I search his expression for a clue, but he's unreadable. Then the door opens and my next patient walks in, forcing me to give Jude a nod and a smile. "Okay. See you soon."

In comparison to the morning that raced by, the afternoon drags on at a snail's pace. When I finally say goodbye to my last patient, I fly through my chart notes and clean up, desperate to get to Jude's place. But as I push open the front door to the clinic, I get my second surprise of the day. The sexiest man alive is standing right there, leaning against a dark grey SUV, smiling at me. This time, I don't freeze. I drop my bag and run at him, once again trusting him to catch me in his open arms. He does, spinning us around as I giggle, my face pressed into his neck. When he sets me back down, I peer behind him at the giant car.

"Did you rent that beast?"

He looks over his shoulder, then back at me with a wry grin. "No, I bought it. Picked that up in Victoria this morning. I figured I needed to have my own car over here."

I try not to get too excited by what that might mean. "That's no car, that's a tank."

Jude's grin grows. "Well, can I give you a ride home in my tank?"

I point over to my much smaller — and brighter — car. "And what's wrong with my car?"

Jude just picks up my bag, then wraps his arm around my shoulder and guides me over to the passenger side of his giant vehicle. "Nothing. It's perfect for you. Small and cute. But I need something of my own to get to and from work."

My hand drops away from the handle. "Work?" I ask cautiously, turning around to face him.

"You're looking at the new head coach of the Westport Ravens." His smile is huge now, creasing across his entire face, lighting him up. It's obvious how happy he is.

"You're staying," I say, feeling my own lips turn up in return.

Jude leans down and kisses me deeply. "Damn right, I am. How could I not, when everything I want and everyone I love is here?"

My breath catches. "Wh-what?"

His one hand comes to rest on my hip, the other behind my neck, sliding just under my braid. He pulls me in flush against his body, using his grip to tilt my head up.

"I love you. And I'm here to stay, if that's okay with you."

Instead of answering with words, because I'm way too choked up to formulate anything meaningful, I lift up on my toes and kiss him over and over again, trying to infuse my lips with all the feelings bubbling inside of me. When I feel wetness on my cheeks and realize I'm crying, I pull back laughing, swiping at my cheeks.

"I love you, too, in case that wasn't clear," I manage to say right before Jude crashes his lips back into mine.

"I need to get you home and naked, immediately," he growls, opening the door behind me. "Get in."

I climb in and buckle up, and as soon as he slides into the driver's seat, we're kissing again, all the pent-up love and desire exploding around us. "Drive fast," I whisper, making myself back away. The lust-filled promise in his eyes takes my breath away as he backs out of the parking lot to leave the clinic.

When we get to his apartment, we race up the stairs as fast as his leg will allow, our hands constantly roaming over each other. Once inside, our clothes start to fly off until we're only in our underwear. But as we walk to the bedroom, kissing everywhere our lips can reach, I see something out of the corner of my eye.

"What's that?"

Jude's grumble of discontent doesn't phase me. I break away from his embrace and pick up the book. Turning it over, I gasp. "Oh my God. Where did you find this?"

Tears are forming as my eyes roam the cover. It's a very early edition of *Little Women*, and it's beautiful.

"The entire time I was away, all I could think of was you. I wanted you there, watching the game with me, going out after, and sleeping in my hotel bed. I found this little used bookstore and they had a huge section of the classics. I couldn't resist getting you one."

"I love it," I say, my eyes shining.

"And I love you."

I set the book down carefully and walk back into his open arms. Resting my head against his bare chest, I let the sound of his heartbeat fill me with all the happiness in the world. Then, tipping my head up, I wind my arms around his neck, letting my fingers toy with the hair at the nape of his neck.

The book is perfect. It's wonderful. But right now, I want something else from him even more.

"Make love to me, Jude."

Chapter Twenty-Nine

Jude

When I got up to make coffee, Lily was just starting to stir. By the time I make it back to the bedroom just a few minutes later, she's sitting up, reading the book I gave her.

Leaning against the doorway, I pause and just watch her. Wearing one of my jerseys, her hair a mess, she's perfection. A fucking goddess. And she's in my bed. She loves me.

Her eyes glance up from the pages with a quirk of her lips. "Like what you see?"

"Love it," I answer honestly, pushing away from the door and walking over to set the mugs of coffee down on the table next to her. Then I tilt her chin up and kiss her. As if there was a chance in hell of me resisting those lips when I'm so close to them.

Her eyes are closed and there's a dreamy smile on her face that makes me feel way too smug. I pick up my coffee and make my way around to the other side as her eyes trail after me.

"Hockey butts are truly a gift from God."

I snort. "Or they're the result of countless hours of hard work in the gym and brutal training sessions for years."

"I like my theory better."

"As long as it's my hockey butt in question, you can think whatever you want." I settle back under the blanket, on my side, and press another kiss, this time to her arm just below the sleeve of my jersey. She giggles and I look up at her with my eyebrows raised.

"It's a weird spot to kiss me, you have to admit."

My hand slides under the covers, lifting the hem of the over-sized jersey so I can lightly stroke across her bare stomach. "I happen to love kissing you any fucking place on your sweet body I can reach. But if your arm feels weird, perhaps you'd prefer here?" I circle her belly button, then slowly trail my hand up higher to thumb her nipple. "Or here?"

Her mouth falls open slightly as her pupils dilate. But just as I think I've got her, she shakes her head, and pushes my hands away. "Nope. No. Back away. I want to read my new book!"

"Hmm. You sure about that?" I resume my attack, lightly circling her skin. "Haven't you read that one a hundred times already? I think my idea is much better."

"Yes..." She shivers when my fingertip grazes her nipple again and her eyes blink shut. "Yes. I mean, no. No distracting me. Book now. Sex later."

"Sex should be *always*," I comment casually. "But that's fine. You read; I'll find something to amuse myself with."

Lily starts to lift her book, then drops it as my statement registers at the same time my fingers dip below the waistband of her panties.

"Jude," she whisper-moans as I stroke through the already damp curls.

"Tell me you want me to stop and I will. You know that." I lean in and kiss her jaw, then her cheek, then her lips. "But I'm pretty sure you want me to distract you." I dip one finger just inside, then pull it out and swirl around her clit. Repeating the action, I lift my eyes to see hers burning with fire.

"Never stop."

With my other hand, I lift the book out of her lap and put it on the table. Then, I slowly drag my jersey up and over her head before tossing it to the ground. I want my mouth on her tits. I want to feel them with my hands and my tongue. There's no end to the number of ways I want Lily, and a lifetime will never be long enough with her.

"I love you," I murmur, dipping my head down to suck her breast into my mouth. My tongue swirls around her nipple before I let my teeth graze the tip ever so lightly. Hands grip my hair, holding me in place.

As if I would want to be anywhere else.

"I love you," I repeat, moving my attention to the other soft peak. I go back and forth, teasing her with my fingers between her legs, and my mouth on her tits, and my words of love floating in the air.

This romantic side of me is unfamiliar, but it feels so fucking right with her. Everything does.

"I need you." Her needy gasp is the hottest thing I've ever heard and I feel pre-cum leak out of my cock.

I push down my boxers with one hand. It's not coordinated, but it gets the job done and it means I don't have to stop stroking her wet pussy with my other hand.

"Hold on, sunshine," I grit out, grabbing her panties at the seam and ripping them apart with a grunt.

"God, that's hot," Lily breathes with a smirk. "But you're going to have to buy me more if you keep ripping them."

I wink at her. "Happily." Then, holding her hips, I roll us so that she's on top. "I want you to ride me, sunshine, let me fill you up so you can feel how much I love you."

I grab Lily's ass, lifting her up. She doesn't waste any time, grabbing my rigid dick, and then slowly lowering herself down. Our groans echo one another. Lily's hands drop to my chest as her hips start to rock up and down my length. I lift my upper body to meet her, tangling my hands in her hair and holding her in place so I can kiss her senseless, swallowing down every whimper of pleasure.

A mini orgasm shudders through her almost immediately, and the effect of her pussy clenching around my cock has me seeing stars. She moves back and forth a few times, her face turning up in rapture. She's a goddess. The most beautiful woman I've ever seen. I could come, easily, just from looking at her lost to pleasure, but I hold off. There's not a chance I'm letting go until she's exploded at least once more.

"Give me another, sunshine. Wreck me."

I feel her pulse around me again, and I know she's close.

I grab her and flip us over, manhandling her while I'm still inside, to the edge of the bed so I can stand. Finally, I can get the position and power I need and crave. And if her screams of pleasure are any indication, Lily needed it, too. Pretty soon, I'm yelling out her name as we crash into oblivion together. I collapse onto her, trying to hold some of my weight off, but Lily wraps her arms around me tightly.

"No. Stay. I like having you here."

"I don't want to crush you," I murmur, pushing some hair back off her face.

"You would never hurt me."

The raw, honest trust in her statement floors me. All I can do is kiss her forehead and shift us up the bed so that I can lay down. We're still tangled up but I'm no longer worried about my much heavier body crushing her.

"I swear to you, I will always do whatever I can to keep you safe and protected. I love you. And I will never intentionally hurt you. But I've been told I can be a real grump sometimes, and I shut myself off from people. It's never been easy for me to trust women, but I do trust you. Just promise me you'll tell me when I'm being a dumbass and help me do better."

Lily moves until we're lying on our sides, our bodies a sticky mess. But neither one of us seems to care right now.

"I've seen your grumpy side and it's not that bad. If you can love me despite my family, I can love you despite the moody moments. We've both got baggage, but it'll be easier to carry together."

Her lips find mine and we share a kiss that seals our words into a promise.

Eventually, we drag ourselves out of bed and into the shower. But when Lily drops to her knees under the steaming water and takes me in her mouth, our plan to clean up quickly and go out to get breakfast is delayed.

An hour later, we're ambling down the sidewalk toward The Nutty Muffin. Lily's small hand is tucked into my much bigger one and I'm struck dumb by how perfect this moment feels. Every moment I spent wondering what to do, what retirement would look like for me, whether I could be happy away from the NHL, they all led me to right now. With this woman by my side and a future I can't wait to start living with her.

"Does your family know you're back this time?" Lily asks suddenly, turning to me with a sly grin creeping across her features. "Or did you sneak back under a cloak of secrecy again."

A chuckle bursts out of me. "That's a bit overdramatic, isn't it?" I wince as soon as the words leave my mouth and I realize how that might make her feel. "I'm sorry, sunshine, I didn't mean —"

Lily's lips press to my cheek. "It's fine, Jude. It doesn't hurt when you tease me like that because I know that you love me. All of me, the wild and crazy, and the soft and serious."

"And the sexy. I definitely love the sexy," I tease, dropping another kiss to her upturned lips. "But to answer your question, yes, they know. I needed someone to drive me to the car dealership when I got off the ferry."

"They must be happy you're staying." She swings our hands playfully as we continue walking down the sidewalk.

"I guess so. But their opinion wasn't the one I was most worried about."

Lily comes to an abrupt stop and steps around to face me. "Jude Donnelly, were you honestly worried I wouldn't be thrilled you were staying here instead of going back to Montana?"

I lift my shoulders in a slightly sheepish shrug. "I mean, I don't know?"

Lily places her hands on her hips and glares at me, except it comes out looking a lot less intimidating and a lot more adorable than she probably means it to, mostly because of the smile fighting to break free on her face.

"Listen, I'm only saying this once. I love you. I would *still* love you if you moved back to Montana, but I would also really, really miss you. Because I don't think I could do long-distance. Seeing you maybe once every couple of months and a little bit more during the off-season? No thanks. Our love might be strong enough, but I don't know if I am."

I don't like to interrupt her, but I do, pulling her into my arms. "Don't say that. You're the strongest woman I know."

Her huff is muffled by her face being pressed against my chest, so after kissing the top of her head, I let her step back.

"I'm happy you're here. More than happy. Relieved? Thrilled? Excited about all the hot sex we can have once your knee is fully healed?" Lily waggles her eyebrows and I let out a bark of laughter. "But seriously. I don't know how to put into words how I feel. It's just too big of a feeling. Too big of a love."

Speechless, all I can do is gently tug her back into my arms and lower my head to meet her lips in a deep, drugging kiss that I feel all the way to the depths of my soul.

This time, it's Lily who pulls back first, giving me that impish smirk I adore.

"But I sure hope you at least negotiated some good seats for when the Blaze play in Vancouver as part of your exit contract."

Once again, her light has me laughing. "Box seats, sunshine. Nothing but the best for my girl."

"Good boy." Her wicked grin has me stifling a groan.

I don't think I'll ever stop wanting her. And a lifetime of just that sounds pretty fucking good.

Chapter Thirty

Jude

The past two weeks have been nothing short of amazing. I found a more permanent home in Dogwood Cove in the form of an upgraded rental apartment. I prefer Lily's house, or to be more specific, Lily's bed, but it's too soon for that. And having some roots of my own feels good.

The Ravens had their first round of tryouts, and the talent we saw was nothing short of incredible. I've spent every spare minute poring over coaching material, texting the coaching staff at the Blaze incessantly, and coming up with more plans and strategies than I care to admit.

And today, thanks to my new life, I get to celebrate Kat and Hunter's engagement instead of missing it because of hockey. Best of all, I get to do it with the love of my life by my side. Mom and Dad got Mila to agree to rent out the entire café and bakery space for the night so everyone can celebrate with us.

"The two of them are so perfect together," Lily sighs, leaning her head down on my shoulder. I turn my head slightly so I can breathe in the scent of her shampoo and kiss her, of course. My lips have a built-in Lily magnet and always seem to find their way to some part of her.

"Not as perfect as you."

It's not just a line. When I saw Lily step out in the sky blue dress she's wearing, she stunned me with her beauty. But not just because of what she wore, or her makeup, or anything physical. The real beauty came from the joy radiating from her. A joy brought on by her freedom to fully be herself today, and every day, since she decided to close the door on her family forever.

It took a lot of tears, and even a couple of sessions with Hunter's therapist, but Lily came to me, eyes shining, last week and sat down on my lap with four simple words that brought a tear to my eye.

"You are my family."

I'd said something similar back on the beach after Nana's birthday lunch. But to hear her say it, to know she believes it and she's at peace with letting go of people who caused her nothing but pain makes me so proud, so awed by her strength and conviction in herself.

But today isn't about Lily or me. It's about my sister and her now fiancé, and the life they're building together.

It feels like the whole town turned out to celebrate, which makes sense. Everyone knows Kat from working at the café, and Hunter's not only a cop but just a fucking likable guy. My dad gave a toast to the couple, and then countless people followed with their well-wishes and congratulations. I've never seen Kat happier, or Hunter more embarrassed, but I know it's hard for him having all the attention centered on him. Still, it's clear there's nowhere else he'd rather be than wrapped up with Kat.

After the speeches are done, and Lily and I have made the rounds talking to more people than I realized I even knew in town, I leave her standing with Kat to go in search of a drink.

Digging two beers out of one of the large coolers sitting beside the table laden with food, I turn to go back to Lily, only to stop when I see Beckett standing off to the side, staring at his phone as if he's just seen a ghost. I make my way over to him, concerned about what's rattled my usually unflappable younger brother.

"Beck? You alright?"

He blinks up at me from behind his glasses. "I...I don't know. Cam just called; her grandfather died."

My eyebrows lift at the mention of his friend from college. "Shit, man, that sucks. What can we do to help?"

His shoulders lift in a helpless expression. "I need to get to Manitoba and be there for her."

I pull out my phone, open up my preferred travel app, and type out a few things. "I'm booking you on the next flight out."

Beckett lets out a grateful sigh. "Yeah. Thanks. I guess I should go tell Mom and Dad."

I hit confirm on the ticket purchase, quickly forward him the email, then pull him in for a hug. "I'm sorry, bro. Tell Cam we're thinking of her."

He nods brusquely before spinning around and going in search of our parents.

"He looks upset, is everything okay?" Lily's arms slide around my waist, and I turn to let her into my arms, kissing her hair.

"Just some bad news about an old college friend of his. He'll be okay."

Lily's smile falls. "Oh, shit. That sucks. I was just trying to figure out where you went with my beer."

I wince. "Oops. Sorry, sunshine. Got distracted by Beck's situation."

She squeezes me tightly. "That's fine, your brother is more important than my beer."

Together, we make our way back over to the table and get her a fresh drink. We find an empty chair and I sit down, tugging her into my lap.

"Someday, this'll be us," I whisper, nuzzling into her neck, kissing the warm skin. "I'm gonna marry you, sunshine. You're gonna be mine forever, okay?"

Her light giggle vibrates against my chest. "If that's your idea of a proposal, it needs some work."

I chuckle in agreement. "Don't worry, when it's for real, you'll know it. I'm just telling you that's my plan."

"I like it."

"I like you," I rumble. "Actually, I love you."

Lily tilts her head to give me more access, one arm lifting up to wrap around my neck.

"I love you, too. And just so you know, when it's for real, I'll say yes."

Her promise makes every fiber of my being light up. "You have no idea what it does to me, hearing you say that."

Lily subtly pushes her ass back into my pelvis, where she can obviously feel my cock starting to harden. "Oh, I think I have an idea. How soon can we get out of here, do you think?"

"Now. Right the fuck now."

Keeping her in front of me, we make our way over to my parents and hug them goodbye. Mom tries to get us to stay, but Dad gives me a knowing smirk. Then we search for Kat and Hunter in the crowd and get a similar reaction when we say we're leaving.

Not soon enough, we're back at my apartment.

"I can't wait to taste you, sunshine," I growl, dropping down to one knee and pushing her against the door. I lift the skirt of her dress up and slide down the lace panties that are the only thing standing in my way. "Hold this." I take her hand and make her hold her dress up because I want all access. As soon as she's got it, I dive in, wasting no time before plunging my tongue inside of her. She cries out and her free hand grips my hair so tightly, the sting of pain only adds to my own mounting desire.

Changing my motions, I slow down, keeping the touch of my lips and my tongue light and soft. Teasing, instead of devouring. I want to keep her on edge as long as possible to make her climax that much more powerful.

I drag my fingers through her folds, swirling around her clit. Then I lift them to my mouth and lick them off. "Fuck, you're sweet." I lean back in and bite gently on her inner thigh, sucking just enough to leave a mark.

"Are you marking me?" she asks, her voice teasing, yet breathless with arousal.

"Damn right I am." I do the same to the other side before finally going back to where I really want to be. This time, I'm not light with my touch. I suck her clit in between my teeth, letting them graze over the sensitive skin as my tongue plays with her outer folds. I can't control my own arousal, so with one hand, I open my jeans and rub my cock while I thrust my fingers into her heat. The pulse of her body around me is driving me fucking insane.

She consumes all of me.

"Oh my God, right there!" Lily's cries of ecstasy have me blind with pleasure as she clenches down, her pussy gripping my fingers as floods of moisture hit my tongue.

I lap up every goddamn drop. Only when she stops quivering do I slowly stand up, running my hands over her hips, up the side of her body until I can tangle them in her hair and kiss her. She doesn't shy away, even though her pussy made a fucking mess of my face, and for some reason, that's incredibly hot.

"Pretending to date you was a really good idea," she says with a tired giggle. "Falling in love with you was an even better one."

"Fucking right, sunshine." I drop my forehead to meet hers. "But it was never fake for me. That morning I woke up with you in my arms after the wedding, a part of me knew even then that the most important thing in my life was no longer hockey. It was you."

EPILOGUE

Lily

"Look at how packed it is in here." Pride fills my voice as I take in the rapidly filling arena. Tonight is the first game for the Westport Ravens and Jude's entire family is here with me.

My man is down in the locker room with his team, no doubt filling them with encouraging words and advice. He's an amazing coach, but I never doubted he would be. *He* did, however, until their first preseason game when his boys absolutely crushed their opponents.

Since then, his confidence has grown. But no matter how good he is behind the bench, nothing beats the pure joy I see on his face when he comes back from a practice when he got on the ice. The day I cleared him to start skating, he dragged me to the arena immediately after work and made me dizzy, skating circles around me.

But the orgasms he gave me after made up for any worry I felt that he might overdo it that day.

"This is incredible. I'm so proud of him," Jude's mom murmurs, linking her arm with mine. "I'll always be grateful to you for helping our Jude find his way after his injury. You saved him, Lily."

"He saved me, too," I reply quietly. Claire squeezes my arm in understanding as the lights dim and the music starts to swell, pumping up the crowd, who are ready to see their new team play.

The next two hours are a rush. The Ravens dominate the game from start to finish, coming away with a solid 3-1 win.

Everyone else takes off, heading back to Dogwood Cove, where they plan to meet up at Hastings to celebrate. Jude has to deal with some postgame business, but he asked me to meet him in his office and we'll head back to town together.

Letting myself into his office, I wander around the small room, trailing my fingers over the large wooden desk, pausing at the photo frame. He saved the picture I took the night I discovered Sunshine's name on her collar and printed it. Every time I see it, I smile, remembering the moment I realized just how deeply he loved me.

The door opens, then closes behind the most magnificent man I've ever laid eyes on. He slowly undoes his tie and the top two buttons of his shirt before taking off the tie and his jacket completely and setting them down on a chair. Walking past me without a word, he drops down into his chair, and beckons me with a crook of his finger. Anticipation shivers down my spine.

"Everyone's expecting us at the bar," I say, trying to hide my grin. Jude gives me a look that makes it clear what he thinks.

"I don't care. I need you now, and I'm gonna need you again later. Only when we get home, you're gonna wear my jersey and nothing else. Got it, sunshine?"

I shiver at the heated promise in those words. Nothing gets Jude hotter than me wearing his old Blaze jersey. The sex is always amazing with us, but there's an added layer when I have his name on my back. It makes him wild. "Got it."

"Good. Now get over here and sit on my cock." He leans back in his chair and opens his pants, pulling out his hard length and stroking it once or twice.

I slip off my leggings and lift off my Ravens hoodie, prowling over to him wearing nothing but a bra and panties. Straddling his lap, I lean in and kiss him. "I'm proud of you, Coach."

Jude's only response is a growl as he pulls my panties to the side and impales me with his dick. We make love, but it's hard and fast. When our orgasms hit, we smother each other's cries with our lips so that no one hears exactly what's going on in the coach's office.

"Fuck, I love you," he pants when we finally come down from the high of our release. "Do we have to go and meet up with everyone?" His half pout makes me giggle.

"Yes, we do. They want to celebrate your success."

"The only person I want to celebrate with is you."

I cup his face and kiss the tip of his nose. "Jude, your grumpy side is showing."

His huff of frustration is laced with amusement. "Fine. One drink. Then I'm taking you home."

"Home..." I murmur, still loving the sound of that word. It means so much more now that we live together. I'm no longer alone. I'm loved by this man and his entire family.

Jude reaches into a desk drawer and hands me some tissues before we stand up. I clean up as best I can, then give him a mock glower. "Everyone is going to know exactly what we did."

His indifferent shrug is kind of adorable but still makes me roll my eyes. He takes my hand and lifts it to his lips. "Good. You're mine and I'm yours. I'm fine with the world knowing that."

I lean my head against his arm, letting his romantic words seep into my soul. "I love you, but maybe they could know that I'm yours in a way that doesn't involve me having wet panties?"

Jude's throaty chuckle is one of my favourite sounds. The only sound that's better is when he utters the four little words he never lets a day go by without saying.

"I love you, sunshine."

Curious about how Jude will balance life as a coach with his relationship with Lily? You can read their extended epilogue to find out by signing up for my newsletter: https://bit.ly/JuliaJ arrett_PTLY_bonus.

Acknowledgments

This book was an absolute joy to write. Jude and Lily were voices in my head, telling me exactly what they wanted me to say, and the words flowed. But it was not always easy. And if it weren't for a few select people, there's no way this story would have been as amazing as it is.

Thank you Chelle, for being a sports guru, even when I'm not writing sports romance.

Theresa, your advice and encouragement helped me take this story to the next level.

Alex, Georgia, Mae, Claire, Amy, Molly, you kept me moving forward, with your encouragement, advice and friendship.

And as always, Mr Jarrett and the boys, thank you for your patience and unending love.

XOXO Julia

ALSO BY JULIA JARRETT

<u>Dogwood Cove</u>

Always and Forever

Rumours and Romance

Work and Play

Truth and Temptation

Then and Now

<u>The Donnellys of Dogwood Cove</u>

Dare To Kiss You

Hate To Want You

Pretend To Love You

Promise To Marry You

One Night To Win You

<u>Standalone</u>

Seductive Swimmer - A standalone novel set in the Cocky Hero World, inspired by Vi Keeland and Penelope Ward's Cocky Bastard series

About Julia Jarrett

Julia Jarrett is a busy mother of two boys, a happy wife to her real-life book boyfriend and the owner of two rescue dogs, one from Guatemala and another one from Taiwan. She lives on the West Coast of Canada and when she isn't writing contemporary romance novels full of relatable heroines and swoon-worthy heroes, she's probably drinking tea (or wine) and reading.

For a complete listing of Julia Jarrett books please visit
www.authorjuliajarrett.com/books

Follow Julia:
Instagram @juliajarrettauthor
Facebook Reader Group: Julia Jarrett's Nutty Muffins
TikTok @julia.jarrett.author

Made in United States
Troutdale, OR
09/16/2024

22832860R00184